This is Not America

by Georgios Andritsos

© Copyright 2023 Georgios Andritos

ISBN 979-8-88824-047-2

Editing: Julian Hussey

Re-editing & Proofreading: Sofia Vergini

Published by

köehlerbooks™

3705 Shore Drive
Virginia Beach, VA 23455

800-435-4811

This Is Not America

(or . . . Is It?)

SHORT STORIES BY

GEORGIOS ANDRITSOS

VIRGINIA BEACH
CAPE CHARLES

I dedicate this book
to my daughter, Matina Kirsten Andritsou,
and to my friend Konstantinos Valkanos, or Varonos.
In memory of Konstantinos Ioannidis, or Ahoy.

Introduction

This deeply human collection of short stories explores the institutions of family and friendship and the shaken sexual relationships of people in Greece. The characters in these stories fight back against a tough reality as they are pushed to the very brink. Each story carves a sincere, dynamic path ending with a sense of harmony, justice, and optimism.

In Greece, nothing reminds us of America. Here, there is no Hollywood, Las Vegas, or Route 66 with motels built in the middle of nowhere. Here, everything seems different. Well, this is not America (or . . . is it?).

Contents

A Good Day on the River

THE SUN IS HIGH in the blue sky with strokes of white here and there. A yellow Ford speeds on the ring road. Listening to the wind rushing past his window, Alexander pushes his Ray-Ban sunglasses up on his nose and runs a hand through his short hair. He glances at his brother, Phaidon, who sits deep in the passenger seat, his long hair hanging around a tired face. Alex strokes his goatee and lets out a silent breath.

The two men are on their way to see their aging mother without her knowing it. They haven't seen her for twenty-five years. They heard she had recently lost her second husband to a heart attack. Their aunt broke the news to them up in the village in the mountains while they were drinking coffee in the shade of a chestnut tree.

"Her fat husband went over in his chair and breathed his last in front of her eyes." She made her cross. "I was waiting for it, though. Your mother's paying for her sins."

They drive past cars for sale parked in lots, buildings, and empty ground-floor spaces with For Sale signs stuck on their tarnished windows. In the scorching sun stand half-built houses, and spades protrude from dunes of sand beside rusted concrete mixers.

"Greece is falling apart," Phaidon says, rubbing his face as if to wipe the crusted fatigue from his eyes, and from the pocket of his trousers, he pulls out his smoking paraphernalia. "I don't recognize Thessaloniki anymore." He rolls a cigarette and brings a Zippo lighter to life.

The car eases to a stop at the traffic light. Alex watches a few dogs cross the street. They look like they have come back from a battle.

Two of them have clipped tails, and Alex sees every rib in one of them, its spine pushing against blotched skin.

Alex moved back to Greece a couple of months ago, and his brother came from London to visit their father. More recently, when the brothers were sitting at a tavern in the shadow of a plane tree, partaking of appetizers and white wine, Alex suggested they visit their mother.

"What the hell," he said. "She's our mother."

Phaidon didn't say anything. He smoked and watched the people go by. The last time they'd talked with their mother was years ago, when they were both living in London and had called her from their coffee bar. She was glad to hear they were doing well.

"Keep in touch," she said but didn't ask for their numbers.

When the light turns green, a man in a van right behind them leans persistently on his horn. Phaidon turns and glares over his shoulder. "What's your problem, you idiot?" He waves his hand at the driver angrily.

"Calm down," Alex says as the car lurches forth with a roar.

"Fucking Greek drivers!" Smoke shoots out of Phaidon's mouth.

Alex gives a silent sigh. "Can you roll me a cigarette?"

Phaidon thrusts his hand at his brother. "Here! Take this one. Do you want it or not?"

Alex puts the cigarette in his mouth with a grin.

They reach the outskirts of Peraia, a good thirty kilometers from the city of Thessaloniki. The air here smells of pine and the sea.

"I'm doing this for you," Phaidon says.

"What you mean?"

"You know what I mean."

Alex smokes idly as the car passes through a tunnel of tall trees. "You're doing this for both of us," he says and glances sidelong at his brother.

Phaidon sighs and lets his brown-eyed gaze drift with a few clouds traveling east. The car drives past rusty swings, vertical roads lined with houses, cafés, restaurants, and shops. When he sees the sea and a ship near the horizon, he wishes he were on it. He sits up in his seat. "How far is the house?"

"About an hour's drive."

"I need a coffee."

"Coffee again?" Alex draws on his cigarette and shifts the car into fourth gear. A long, straight stretch of road unfurls before them. On either side sprawl tawny fields and scattered summerhouses with fences covered in ivy, jasmine, and bougainvillea, then lines of olive trees, their fully bloomed, light-green leaves shimmering like silver beads.

His eyes straining, Alex tucks his sunglasses into the pocket of his denim shirt and squints in the sunlight. "I need a coffee too. And the car needs gas." As if to punctuate the decision, his steering suddenly feels out of whack, pulling hard to one side. "I hope that's not what I think it is," he gripes and sees his brother screwing up his face. Half a mile down, he pulls onto a narrow shoulder.

Phaidon lights another cigarette and watches his brother walk to the front left fender and study the flat tire. A car drives past with its horn blaring.

Under the scorching sun, Alex says, "Don't just sit there like a brick! Give me a hand!"

Phaidon clenches his teeth and squeezes his eyes tight. He pushes the door open with a snappy movement as his brother rolls the spare tire over the hot asphalt. The air is warm and thickened by the sound of crickets.

Alex jacks the car up and puts the lug wrench on the rusty bolt. After several attempts, he stops and takes a few deep breaths. He can't unscrew the bolt. He goes at it again, but nothing gives. The veins on his arms and his temples bulge, and sweat beads on his forehead.

With the cigarette wedged between his lips, Phaidon says,

"Give it to me," and yanks the wrench from Alex's hand. After a few unsuccessful attempts of his own, he makes a face and throws the lug wrench on the ground. It bounces and lands in a ditch. "Why the fuck do you want to see her now?" His anger moves to his gaze, and he glares at his brother, who moves to collect the lug wrench. "Why now?" He balls his hand into a fist. "You think she cares? You think she'll be happy to see us after all these fucking years! Hey! Look at me when I talk to you!" He bangs the top of the car with his fist.

Ignoring Phaidon's jabbering, Alex tries to turn the lug wrench again. Once more, nothing. He curses silently for not having bought a newer car, but he wasn't sure at the time whether he would stay in the economically broken Greece. "After the summer, I'll know the score," he said over the phone to his friend. This friend owned a cocktail bar in New York and wanted Alex to become his business partner.

He stands, bends into the car, and picks up a canteen. As he takes a sip of water, he glances at Phaidon, who stands at the shoulder of the road, hands tucked in his pockets, and tells him that he's going to walk to a gas station.

"Why don't you call roadside assistance?"

"Because by the time they get here, I'll have come back from the gas station, which is two kilometers away. I saw a sign."

"You think she gives a shit about us?"

"For Christ's sake, can you please fucking drop it!"

Alex slings the knapsack over his shoulder and slaps on a baseball hat with the initials NY, then sets off along the shoulder of the road. Phaidon watches until his brother's image disappears behind a bend. Rage burns in his heart. As he turns his angry gaze toward a slice of the sea behind the hills, he lets out a frustrated scream.

At one point, a truck comes to a stop alongside the shoulder. A fully-grown pig encrusted with mud lies in the bed of the truck, and an old man with a sunburned and wrinkled face sits at the wheel and adjusts his weathered straw hat.

"You okay, friend?"

"I'm fine."

"Need any help?"

"I'm good."

"You sure?"

"Thanks for stopping."

"As you wish, young man." The old man drives off.

When their parents broke up, Alex was nine years old and Phaidon was seven. Their mother said that she couldn't go another step. She was an artist who wanted to paint the world. She left their father for a poet, but the new relationship didn't last long. Right before Christmas, she asked her husband for forgiveness, but he turned her away. For years, she drifted in and out of relationships with artists, but in the end, she found a good man who owned a fish restaurant and moved into his house on a knoll facing the sea.

After the breakup, their father sent the boys to live with their grandmother in Siatista, a town two hours by car from Thessaloniki. He went to see them every chance he got. They went swimming and fishing in the river, and in the summer, they went to the sea. He taught them how to play poker and backgammon and, most importantly, how to hold their heads high. As teenagers, they went to live with him in an apartment in Thessaloniki. Their father had a lorry and transported wine throughout the Balkan region. He was a simple man, spoke little, and minded his own business. After becoming a pensioner, he moved to Siatista and now keeps busy by growing a vegetable garden, a few cherry and chestnut trees, and a vine field, always in the company of his best friend, Max, a German shepherd.

The door of the car stands open. Phaidon smokes and listens to James Brown sing "This Is a Man's World" on the radio, growing more impatient.

Finally, a van slows to a stop alongside the shoulder, and Alex climbs down from it.

"What took you so long?" Phaidon says. "I called you three times."

Alex tosses his knapsack in the back seat of the car. "The lady who drove me here was busy with other customers."

"What the fuck you got?"

"It's a spray."

"What does it do?"

"It fixes flat tires."

After Alex fills the tire, they roll down the road toward the gas station to change the flat and get coffee. Seeing Phaidon close his eyes, Alex knows that the fight between them isn't over. A feeling of dull doubt creeps into his heart. Perhaps my brother's right, he thinks. What's the point of this trip?

If Phaidon ever found out what Alex said to their mother over the phone when he was a teenager, he might never forgive him. Alex told her to neither call nor visit them again. He told her she had made her choice and had to face the consequences. On that day, Alex was very angry. And he stayed angry for many years.

The car pulls into the gas station. The warm air smells of oil and gasoline and, under that, pine trees. In the shadow of the gas station's shed, a one-legged man sits in a chair by a table. He wears dungarees and a white T-shirt. His slightly wrinkled face is tanned, and his hair and beard are gray. With a pair of pliers, he works on the knee clasp of a worn-out wooden leg. A pair of crutches is propped against the wall.

Alex emerges from the car, stretches, and hears his joints crack as a young lady in dungarees, her black hair tied in a ponytail, moves toward him. She is tall and athletic. "I'll change the flat tire first," she says and opens her palm to catch the keys as Alex tosses them to her.

Alex looks over at his brother, who is shambling toward the shed, then lets his gaze drift over a wrecked car-wash machine, the old man putting a match to his pipe, and a dog stretching. At the far end of the lot, he spots a house with its rusty gate open. One side of the house is in the sun and the other stands in the shadow. Behind the house are olive trees, and further away, tawny fields.

The air in the restroom smells of chlorine. Alex runs the tap. The cold water feels good on his face and nape. In the cracked mirror, he notices wrinkles near his green eyes. His brother's words come to his mind. *Do you think she cares?*

Alex exits the restroom and finds his brother sitting with the old man at the table under the shed, legs crossed at the ankles. He sits in the chair across from him.

"I ordered Greek coffees," Phaidon says with a smirk. "The man's daughter's brilliant at reading the cup. She may tell us what to do, right? Maybe the flat was meant to be. Maybe she'll tell us that I'll go back to the city and you'll continue your journey."

"Brohim, drop it."

The old man draws on his pipe, and through plumes of smoke, he studies the brothers. Rubbing his chin, he says in a husky voice, "I'm Dimitris."

The brothers introduce themselves in turn.

Alex lights a cigarette, enjoying the coolness of the shade. The men smoke and look at one another as if waiting to hear some news from afar. When Alex sees the young woman approaching the table, wiping her hands on the oily cloth, he stands.

"I changed the tire and filled the tank. It's forty-five euros."

Alex puts a fifty-euro bill in her hand. "Keep the change."

"Thanks." She smiles.

"You're my seventh customer today," Dimitris says. "And it's almost six o'clock. Five years ago, at least thirty to forty cars would've pulled in by now. I don't know what the hell we're keeping this gas station open for. Nowadays people don't even have money to put bread on the table. Even though in this part of Greece the sea water is crystal clear, people go to places closer to the city instead. If I were your age, I might've moved out of Greece."

A gust of wind blows and rattles the sports section of the newspaper lying on the table next to a skipper's hat.

Alex says, "For many years, I lived in London, but I moved back a few months ago. Our father's getting old. But my brother still lives over there. He's here on a holiday."

Dimitris regards Phaidon with curiosity in his young eyes. "What line of work are you in?"

"I have a café bar."

"How's it working out for you?"

"I can't complain. But I'm weary of the weather. It rains a lot."

"I feel you, young man. I was in England forty years ago, when the Beatles were hot—you know, singing the famous 'Let It Be.' I was working on a tanker. We'd docked in Liverpool. What a place, huh?" He thinks and smiles. "I had the weekend to myself, and I rode the train to London. I remember the fog and the rain. I can still feel the damp cold in my bones. But I had good fun. I saw Big Ben, the Thames, and the Greek marbles, drank in a few pubs, and ate fish and chips. I was as strong as a Spanish bull. Back then, I had both my legs."

The brothers smoke and watch Dimitris fiddle with the clasp of the wooden leg. The young lady sets a tray at the corner of the table and serves them coffee and cold water. Alex smells suntan lotion on her skin.

Phaidon says, "I hear you read the cup."

"Who told you that?"

"Your father."

She puts her hand on her hip and says with humor, "Father? I'm not a cup reader." Her black eyes seem to be smiling.

"Eirini, I said it to keep the men here," he says in a playful voice, and with the pair of pliers, he returns his attention to the wooden leg.

She turns gracefully and leaves them back to their coffee.

Eventually, Dimitris puts the wooden leg back on, stands, and stamps it on the ground a couple of times. "Good as new," he says with a hearty laugh. He pulls the pant leg down, and the wooden leg disappears.

In the coming hours, they drink coffee and beers and talk about the Greek economic crisis, the roughneck politicians, lobbies, and the World Bank. Dimitris learns how it feels to live and work in a foreign country for so many years and how life in England compares to the Greek reality and tells the brothers interesting stories of his travels around the world.

While the men talk, Eirini fills the tanks of a few cars, makes coffees, sweeps and mops the shop, then listens to the news on the radio.

When Dimitris comes back with more beers, Phaidon rubs his hands on his knees and stands up. "Gentlemen, I enjoyed your company, but it's time for me to go back to the city."

Alex smirks. "To the city, brohim?"

"Dimitris, could you call for a taxi, please?"

The old man sets the beers down on the table. "You sure you don't want to have one for the road?"

"Thanks. But I've got to go."

"Hey!" Alex sits up in his chair. "I thought we were going someplace."

"Look, I don't want to meet her now, not ever. Can't you get this into your thick head?" He stares at his brother, his gaze determined, hard.

Dimitris watches the scene with mounting curiosity.

Phaidon paces to the edge of a gravel road leading to the fields behind the gas station and watches the heavy, red sun sink into the horizon. A car zips past the gas station at high speed, and Greek music streams from its open windows, reaching Phaidon's ears in a burst of distorted sounds.

Alex gets to his feet and, with bravado in his strides, follows his brother to grab hold of his shoulder and yank him around. "Why are you so difficult?"

"You're the fucking difficult one." Phaidon glares at him.

"You're acting like a brat! I've had enough of you!" The veins in his neck and temples bulge out.

"I've had enough of you, too! Leave me the fuck alone!" Phaidon pushes his brother in his chest, hard. Alex trips back, and before he has time to regain his composure, Phaidon pushes him again, harder this time, and watches him fall over, scraping his elbow. "Get the fuck up!" he shouts, and spit comes out of his mouth.

Dimitris hurries toward them. "Hey, give it up!"

The commotion takes shape. His eyes filled with rage, Alex punches Phaidon in his chin. Eirini dashes out of the shop with an expression of worry and wonder. As Phaidon makes a headlong dash toward Alex, she shouts, "Stop it!" and rushes over.

The brothers throw amateur punches at each other. Some connect, others don't. Alex feels a strong pull. It's Eirini. "Take it easy, man."

When Dimitris grabs hold of Phaidon's arm, he tries to jerk it free, but the old man's grip is too strong. Blood trickles from Phaidon's nose, and some of it has stained his shirt.

"Settle down. What the hell is wrong with you two, huh?" His eyes dart between the brothers. "Settle down!"

Phaidon takes a step forward and jabs a finger at his brother. "Look, she never cared for us! Never! She's selfish! Don't you get it?" His eyes are filled with intense judgment.

"Settle down." Holding his elbow, Dimitris steers Phaidon to a spigot beside the gas station to wash his face. Eirini sets a roll of paper towels on the table, and her father draws up a chair. "Sit down. Please. Sit down."

Alex's hands tremble, his chest heaving with emotions, and his face burns as he sits. He can't believe he punched his brother. The last time they came to blows was when they were kids. *Fuck me,* he thinks as he wipes his face with the paper. *Pull yourself together.* He tastes blood in his mouth.

There is silence. Alex and Phaidon face each other across the table. In the middle sits Dimitris, who pushes tobacco into his pipe. Eirini tucks her hands in the front pockets of her dungarees and studies the brothers as they wipe their faces and shoot regretful glances at each other.

Dimitris says, "Eirini, could you please bring us the bottle of ouzo and clean glasses?" He puts a match to his pipe and lets the smoke dribble from his mouth.

A gust of wind blows, and dogs bark in the distance.

In a moment, the men watch Eirini fill the glasses with ice cubes and ouzo.

Dimitris says, "Drink. It'll calm you down. It always does."

They pick up their glasses and drink.

Once Eirini places salty fish, black olives, feta cheese, tomatoes, and a bit of bread on the table, she draws up a chair and sits as well. For what seems a long time, they all drink and eat in silence as if the evening wind blowing in their faces has taken their voices.

Phaidon regards his brother. "Look," he says, "If our mother cared, she would've tried to get us to live with her when we were kids. But she didn't. She could've turned to the law. But she didn't do that either. Did you forget, man?"

His regret waging a war inside him, Alex sips his ouzo and listens to his brother. "In the eight years we lived with our grandmother, how many times did she come to see us? I'll tell you how many times. She came to see us three times—just three fucking times." He draws in a breath. "She betrayed us. She's a stranger to me. I have more feelings for these people right here." He raps the table with his knuckles. "If you still want to go and see her, be my guest. But I'm not going with you."

Alex feels lost for words. In all these years, this is the first time he has heard his brother talk about their mother in this way. Whenever he tried to bring up the subject before, Phaidon would either fall silent or start talking about something else.

Little by little, his brother's words make Alex realize that he never really missed his mother. Even before she left them, save for a few times, he couldn't remember any of her embraces or her kisses, nor any of her motherly words. The closest person to a mother in his life was their grandmother. Before their parents broke up, the boys went to the village to see her almost every other weekend, Christmas and Easter, and spent every summer with her.

It was their grandmother who showered them and tended their scraped knees and elbows. It was their grandmother who rubbed their chests down and put a wet towel on their foreheads when they ran a fever. It was she who sat at the kitchen table and helped them with their homework, the one who read bedtime stories and watched their favorite cartoons and films with them. It was their grandmother who got angry with them when they went into the coop and scared the chickens, or the day they rode the neighbor's donkey to the river and almost drowned the poor animal.

The sun hides behind the horizon, splashing the sky with streaks of orange and hues of red and purple. The evening air moves in the pine trees next to the house across the lot, brushes over Eirini's bed of flowers, and ripples the leaves of her vegetable garden.

Rubbing his beard, Dimitris studies the brothers. "Is your mother's name Anna?"

The brothers look at each other in wonder.

"Yes, her name's Anna," Alex says.

Dimitris wrinkles his forehead. "She's a painter, and her second husband, who owned a fish restaurant not far from here, died of a heart attack, right?"

"That's right," Phaidon says and leans forward with a curious expression.

Alex feels a rush in his blood. "How come you know our mother?"

With excitement in her voice, Eirini says, "I didn't know Anna was your mother. I thought she had no children. At least, that has been the assumption around here. We know that woman, don't we, Father? She and her husband, Manolis, lived in a house half an hour's drive from here, a house that sits on a knoll facing the sea. Rumors had it that he couldn't have children. For years, they filled their car with petrol in this very gas station. When my mother was alive, we went to eat fish at their restaurant. Manolis was a good cook and a generous man. I remember that their place was always busy."

Eirini takes a sip from the ouzo and tells them that Anna never spoke much. "She usually sat behind the register, smoked roll-ups, and drank white wine. In her low voice, she would ask me about one thing or another. I loved the way she sat and talked, the way she drank wine and smoked cigarettes from a red, leather cigarette case. Her movements were soft, effortless—I would say . . . hypnotic."

The brothers listen to Eirini's words with reverent concentration.

"I don't know why, but a couple of years ago, she stopped coming here. About a year ago, I drove by the restaurant, but it was up for rent. And six months ago, her husband died in the kitchen right in front of her. That's what people say. And imagine her living in that huge house all by herself."

Her bewildered eyes shift from the brothers to her father, who rubs his beard again, and after he fills his glass with more ouzo and passes the bottle around, he looks at the brothers and says, "About two years ago, when my daughter had gone to the city, Anna knocks on our door. It's past ten at night, and it's pouring rain. She stands under an umbrella and asks if I can fill her car with gas because she must go someplace. She says she's sorry for bothering me at such an hour. I smell alcohol on her breath, and her eyes are red and worried. I ask her in. She stands in the hallway as I go to turn off a burner. When I get back, she has her face in her hands and sobs."

With a pensive gaze, Dimitris takes a hit from his ouzo, runs a thump over his lips, and goes on. "We sit at the kitchen table, drink tea, and listen to the rain pattering against the window. Through her tears, she tells me she needs to talk. She tells me about her two boys and that she wanted them to live with her, but their father told her that she didn't deserve to be their mother and that they'd be better off without her. And she agreed to that madness. She agreed because she was young and immature. She tells me that her head was in the clouds."

He clears his throat. "Manolis didn't know about you guys. Save for her family and a few close friends, nobody else knew. She didn't tell him because she was afraid she might lose him. As the years wear on, she found it more difficult to come clean. She says it's way too late for that now. The news would surely shock the family, friends, and the village community. They would think of her as a whore. It's impossible to tell him the truth. Your mother tells me she's just happy to hear your voices on the phone. She tells me that she can't find it in her heart to forgive herself for what she did. She also says she wouldn't be able to look you in the eye."

The brothers sit silently, shell shocked.

Eirini's eyes are filled with subtle delight. "What a coincidence you hear all this because of a flat tire."

Dimitris picks up his skipper's hat from the table and runs his fingers along its brim. "After she wipes her eyes, your mother takes a photograph out of her wallet. She puts it on the table under the light and pushes it toward me, gently. The edges of the photograph are worn out, but the rest looks just fine. In the photograph, two lean boys in swimming pants stand on the bank of a river, holding fishing rods. Next to their feet sits a tin bucket. The river is calm and shines in the sun. Behind the boys, you can see rocks, and further away on a hill, you can see oak trees. 'They're my boys,' your mother says to me."

Alex's face brightens. "I remember that day. She drove us in that Deux Che Vaux of hers with its roof rolled back. We both sat in the front seat. We loved sitting up front. Didn't we, Phaidon?" He sees a faint smile playing on his brother's lips as Phaidon leans back in his chair, his gaze faraway as though watching a movie scene. Alex goes on, "We were wearing blue shorts and straw hats. She had a flowery dress on, and her dark hair shone in the sun. She told us how good we looked in those hats. She said that we looked like Bolek and Lolek, those Polish cartoon characters we loved to watch on TV. She laughed at that. We laughed, too."

Phaidon breaks in and says excitedly, "We put our gear down in the shadow of a willow tree, we ate cheese-and-ham sandwiches and drank cold apple juice. Later, we went fishing again and caught three trout. One of them was quite big," he says, spreading his hands and looking at the space between them, and Alex adds, "Our mother helped us to pull the fish out. It twisted and turned and thrust about in the air, water trickling from its tail and shining in the sun."

Phaidon looks at his brother with smiling eyes. "And then we put the fish in the bucket, and we all jumped in the river. We swam and splashed at each other with our laughter echoing around the rocks and boulders and the trees. And then she pushed our heads under the water, and after that, we lay down on the riverbank and caught the sun. We were over the moon. It was our mother who took the picture." His voice trails off.

A car drives by with its headlights on. The man behind the wheel talks with a woman, who drinks from a beer bottle, nodding. When Alex sees the man turn his head toward them and then back to the road, he wonders, *How did we seem to the man? What kind of emotions rose in him, seeing four people sitting around a table? Would the man care if he knew what we are talking about? And does any of it matter?*

From the dark fields behind the gas station, a dog emerges, sniffs the air, and sits next to Dimitri's feet. "Hey, Jack," he says and pats his head. "Where you been all day?"

The dog looks at Dimitris, whines, rests his muzzle on his paws, and closes his eyes.

The sky has grown darker, and the wind colder. The lights on the lampposts along the road come on. Two crows sit on the wires between the poles and watch the two brothers, who have just lit cigarettes and smoke quietly.

Alex feels as though something inside him has started to slip. For a moment, he contemplates the sensation, and then he shifts his eyes out and over the road to bales of wheat sitting heavy on the field. At the far end, he sees a house with a lighted window. Behind the house rise tall trees, and further down, past a stretch of land, lies the sea. But he can't see it now. It's too dark. All he sees is a line of flickering lights along the coast at the far end of the horizon.

Dimitris relights his pipe. "It was a good day."

Phaidon brings his glass to his lips. "It sure was." He drinks slowly and looks at his brother, who rubs his goatee and says in a meditative voice, "A good day on the river. That's what it all was. A good day on the river."

Do the Right Thing

I͟T'S DARK OUTSIDE, and the spring rain has stopped. A tall man steps into the elevator and presses the button marked *2*. He has short gray hair and a three-day stubble. *I've hit rock bottom*, George thinks as he shakes the keys inside the pocket of his coat. *Thirteen thousand euros.* It is the most money he has ever lost on the stock market, and in just a few hours. The stocks are still spread across various companies, but they are not worth much.

A few days ago, he was planning to sell some of them so he could pay off his maxed-out credit cards. But as things stand now—unless, of course, in a week, the stocks rise (a far-fetched scenario in the Greek stock market, and especially now with a broken economy)—he will have to ask his mother for money again.

His rage feels like two hands tightening around his throat. He wants to scream. In the mirror, the man who looks back at him is an exhausted, bitter person. *You idiot!* He punches the aluminum wall, leaving a small dent in it.

In the hallway of his apartment, he smells cigarette smoke and sees layers of it hanging in the space. Petra, his Swedish wife, is sitting on the sofa, but from where he stands, he can't see her. After contemplation and talking to her parents, Petra has decided to move back to Sweden with their thirteen-year-old daughter. She is breaking the news to him tonight.

"Petra," he says, but he doesn't get an answer. His gaze falls on the table, where a crystal vase with fifteen red roses stands under the light of a lamp—one rose for each year of their marriage. They celebrated their anniversary a couple of days ago.

George pictures himself in his dark-blue suit and Petra in her sexy, black, knee-length dress and high heels. They came back from a restaurant in Ladadika, a downtown district, and stayed up drinking more wine. Their daughter, Zoe, had gone to a sleepover at her best friend's house. The couple was relaxed and in a good mood, and the atmosphere was filled with eroticism. Later that night, they made love on the carpet in the living room. Over the past year, they had gone through some rough patches, and they hoped that their anniversary would put the balance right between them.

Rubbing his tense neck, George moves into the living room and sees his wife crossing the dining space, glancing at him. She is wearing a crimson silk robe that shows off her long legs and has her blond hair tied in an elastic band. In the air, beneath the scent of smoke, he smells the perfume he bought for her. She takes a bottle of wine out of the fridge. He tosses the raincoat on the back of an armchair and the keys on the living room table. They land next to a large porcelain ashtray full of cigarette butts. He counts them and makes a face. The only thing he wants to do now is soak in the steaming tub with a glass of bourbon in his hand.

Petra says with a slight accent, "I can feel your stare." She throws him a playful green-eyed glance. "Why are you looking at me like that?"

"How am I looking at you?"

"You know how—as if I've done something wrong."

"Haven't you?"

Petra sits on the sofa and pours a generous glass of wine. Holding his eyes, she fires up a cigarette. "Yes, George. I'm smoking."

George and Petra met on the Greek island of Skiathos, in June, eighteen years ago. They were both in their early twenties. At that time, she was living and studying to become a social worker in Malmø, Sweden, and was vacationing in Greece. The last night on the island, she went to eat at a restaurant where he worked as a waiter. George was studying to become a doctor, but in the autumn of that same year, he dropped out. "Look," he said to his parents. "I don't see myself becoming a doctor. I don't have the emotional detachment."

In the summer months, he enjoyed swapping Thessaloniki for Skiathos. He had free room and board, swam in the sea every day, and worked at a friend's taverna. That night, Petra waited for him to get off work, and with a bottle of wine in hand, they went to the beach, where they stayed until the sun rose on the horizon. Petra returned to Sweden, but after a month she came back to the island and stayed with George until the end of August. Back in Sweden, she said to her friends, "Those summer months were as sweet as a blueberry pie. Scents and colors everywhere. Turquoise sea and tall blue skies."

In the kitchen, George pours a glass of bourbon. He crosses over to where his wife sits and kisses her on the mouth. She doesn't resist, but she doesn't return his kiss. He plops down on the sofa across from her and holds back a sigh. They drink from their glasses and look at each other. The smoky taste of bourbon feels good in his mouth, and a warm sensation spreads in his chest.

George says, "I thought we'd made ourselves a promise."

"Promises are made to be broken. Of all people, you ought to know that by now."

He smirks. "Baby, who stole your cookie today?"

"I wish I still had a cookie."

"Look, honey," he says, squeezing his fingers around his drink, "I'm not in the mood to talk about serious matters right now. I'm dog tired."

"But I'm in exactly that mood." Her Baltic gaze is decisive.

George feels a sweet numbness from the bourbon—he had a few drinks at the office—but his mind is still on the money he lost today.

"I can't take this life anymore. In this country, my work as an English teacher is over. This country is going to the dogs. Are you listening to me, George?"

"For Christ's sake, Petra. I'm listening. Of course I'm . . . you were saying the country's going to the dogs."

She takes a sip of her wine. "The past year, I tried my best with us and with trying to get a job. You know that, don't you? From seven students, I'm down to two. And to be honest, I don't want to teach English any longer. I really don't."

"And what do you want me to do about it?"

"Just listen to me. That's all I want from you." She draws on her cigarette and blows smoke toward the ceiling. "I want to work as a social worker. That's what I was taught to do and trained for in Sweden. I want to come home from work and feel good about myself. I don't want to feel like I do now."

"And how do you feel now?"

"I feel like shit. That's how I feel. Like shit."

"Look, I hear you, but we've talked about this before." He studies her. "Haven't we?" He holds her gaze, and it dawns on him that his daughter is not home. "Where's Zoe?"

"I told you on the phone, didn't I?"

He thinks. "Yes, you did. She went to sleep over at Olga's house." He nods.

"Now," Petra says, "can you listen to me?"

"I'm all ears," he says with a tinge of irony in his voice.

Petra puts her glass on the table and crosses her legs at the knees. "I'm tired of the Greeks. I'm tired of their hypocrisy and their dishonesty. They speak and behave as if they are the best and the most morally correct people on the planet. They're pathetic losers, especially the politicians. They don't love this place. They're dragging the country deeper into the gutter. Your ancestors were different; they created a superior culture. And I'm left wondering, what have the modern Greeks accomplished?"

When she forms a zero with her thumb and her forefinger, he says, "And the rest of the world has things figured out, right? They know the score. Petra, what are you trying to tell me here?"

She drags on her cigarette again and carries on speaking as if she hasn't heard his words. "You modern Greeks are masters at sitting at cafés and taverns and bragging about one thing and another, bragging about the golden age of Pericles, bragging about Socrates and the writings of Plato and Aristotle. But only a small number of you have read their work and done what's right for this country. You talk about values and the knowledge and wisdom the ancients passed on to the rest of the world. But I can't see any of this in Greece," she says and points at the television.

She continues, "Today, you can't even watch a decent program on Greek TV. Greek TV is for birdbrains. The health and education system is semi-functioning, and the welfare system is nonexistent. And so is the Greeks' environmental collective consciousness. The whole system is rotten. Greek people are conservative and suffer from complexes and taboos. But I love this country and its people. When they unite, they work miracles. But my patience has dried up." She sighs and sips her wine.

George shakes his head, then knocks back his drink. Going to the kitchen and pouring another one, he says in one breath, "And the Swedish people are taboo-free and open, and they have all the qualities we modern Greeks lack, right? Go on, explain it to me because I don't know things. Isn't that it?" With his palm, he slams the cork back in the bottle and moves toward the living room table.

"I'm not saying that Swedish people are better, but our system works. We obey the laws we pass, and we have the best social system and the highest standard of living in the world."

George thinks, *If the system works so well and the standards of living are so high, then why do so many Swedes get completely wasted on booze and end up behaving worse than kindergarten kids every weekend?*

He drinks a mouthful. "You sure do. But please tell me, Petra, what about the people? You can live your whole life in an apartment, and you might never get to know your neighbors." He sits back down on the sofa. "Save for a head nod and a polite, plastic smile, that's all you'll ever get."

Petra looks at him as if he knows nothing. "How do you know, huh?"

"How do I know?" He smirks. "For Christ's sake, Petra. If you add up all the time I came with you to Sweden, and the winters we lived in Malmø when you were a student, it'd amount to a few years, wouldn't it?"

"Not everybody behaves the way you do. No, we're not as passionate and impulsive as you are, but I like it that way. I have family and friends who love me. And that's what matters to me. What do I have here?"

He rubs his forehead, feeling her slightly regretful eyes on him.

There is silence.

"Petra, what the hell do you want me to do about all this?"

"I don't want to raise our daughter in this country."

"And where the fuck do you want to raise our daughter? In Sweden?"

The word *Sweden* puts a cold shiver along his spine because he hates the cold, the gray weather, and the darkness. About a year ago, Petra wanted them to move to Sweden. But he held his ground. "They're too quiet for me, and I'm not for them." Those were his words. "And who's going to look after my mother, Santa Claus?" His mother suffers from arthritis, and since his father died two years ago, she hardly speaks anymore. "I don't trust home help. I hear appalling stories. Forget about it."

After a few days of silence, Petra asked him to drive her and Zoe to the airport. Minutes before she checked in, she embraced her husband and said that she would give things another try. George still remembers the feelings of loss and grief he felt that week.

"Look, Petra," he says softly and holds her green, wine-laced gaze, "Zoe has a good life in Greece. She has friends, enjoys school, and loves spending time with her grandmother and my sister's kids. She loves going to the house near the sea. They love her, and she loves them back."

He studies his wife. The way she smokes and drinks her wine irritates him. Feeling like he is choking, he stands and opens the balcony door. He closes his eyes and enjoys the spring wind blowing in his face and the freshness of the air in his lungs, the smell of wet leaves and the grass.

Petra's eyes cloud over. "Did you know I've been having nightmares? I wake in the dead of the night and try to catch my breath. Sometimes, I spend an hour at the kitchen table, drinking tea and looking out the window. And you spend your days in that office, looking at numbers on that stupid screen all day long, and go to dinners and drinks with your loser friends."

He turns his eyes toward her. "Look, my friends aren't losers, all right? They're just down on their luck. And can we not talk about my friends, please?" He looks out the balcony door and sees two crows sitting on an electric wire.

"Your friends—"

"Petra, stop it, for Christ's sake. Do I ever talk about your friends? Do I talk about that little bitch that always tries to talk you into moving back to Sweden because she has a boring life?"

She rolls her eyes and sighs. "Sandra never tried to convince me of anything. It's all in your imagination. And she has a good life. Her husband loves her; they love each other. God, George!"

"And we don't?"

"I didn't say that. Of course we do. But that kind of love isn't enough to keep me in this apartment, let alone in this country."

"What do you mean, Petra?" he says, frowning. "Are you saying I'm not a good husband?"

"George, I'm not saying that. I'm . . . never mind. It doesn't matter." She turns her eyes away.

"Hey, what do you mean 'It doesn't matter'?"

"Investing in the stock market, it's like playing on the roulette table in a casino. The house always wins."

George smirks. "To me, what I do is work. Every day, I sit behind a desk and spend hours looking at that screen, trying to figure out my next moves. And you should know the score."

"What score?" She chuckles. "George, I wonder how much money you'll have to lose before you understand that you'll never win." She tilts her head to the side playfully and narrows her eyes. "By the way, how much money did you lose today?"

"I didn't lose any money. Why?"

She looks doubtful.

Silence moves between them. George has had enough of this talk show. He feels like a bug trapped in a spider's web. She has upset him, and he feels a sudden desire to hurt her. Irritated, he snaps, "Look, I don't mind you moving back to bloody Sweden. I don't really care. I'll be glad to drive you to the airport. You hear me?"

"Look me in the eyes and tell me that what you just said is true. George. Is it true you don't care?"

Her voice soaks the space through with sadness.

Holding her beautiful eyes, George softens. "I don't know why I said that." He moves closer to her. "Listen, baby, I haven't lost any money yet. I'll get it all back. Pretty soon, I'll get it all back. You'll see. The stocks are still there."

"Of course you've lost money. You've turned two apartments into numbers that run on that stupid screen you keep your eyes glued to all day long. You've become blind, and you don't know it yet. I'm dying a small death here. Do you understand what I'm telling you?" She crushes her smoke in the ashtray and goes on. "Please, come to your senses. It'll take twenty years for the Greek economy to get back on its feet. You're bound to lose more money—and your family as well!" Her hands shake, and tears come to her eyes.

He steps forward. "Petra?"

She puts her hand up. "Don't. Please, don't," she says in a trembling voice and hurries off to the bathroom.

After Petra became pregnant, George shook hands with a constructor to build an apartment building in the Kalamaria quarter on a spot he had inherited from his grandfather. In exchange, he got three apartments, sold two, and moved into the third one. With the money he got from the sale, he opened a café bar near Navarinou Square in the heart of Thessaloniki and put the rest in the stock market, which had reached an all-time high. This was in 1999 when the socialist government was sitting on a soft cushion.

In a few months, he doubled the worth of his stocks, but soon afterward, when the full-bellied sharks swam away, most of his stocks hit rock bottom, wounding his morale and his finances. Thousands of Greeks lost the ground under their feet, and with panic fogging their minds, they made the terrible mistake of selling their stocks. But George waited for better days to come.

Since then, twelve years have come and gone, and not only has he not gotten his money back, but he has also lost a lot more.

In the meantime, the café bar chugged along like a locomotive. It made enough money to pay the bills and leave him a small profit for their holidays abroad. But coming home late at night with alcohol on his breath escalated the arguments with Petra. At that time, their daughter was six years old. To hold the family together, George sold the business, and even though Petra didn't approve, he turned his eyes entirely to the stock market.

George pours another drink, swallows a mouthful, and, listening to the running water in the bathroom, he starts to pace in the dining room like a caged animal. *I'm a fucking jerk,* he tells himself. The pack of cigarettes on the table is calling his name. A few moments later, Petra moves into the living room with her robe open. His eyes skip from her face to her breasts to her knees and back to her breasts, then climb up to her face again. He still has the hots for her. *She can have any man she wants*, he thinks and feels breathless. The words *I don't really care . . . I'll be glad to drive you to the airport* collide in his head like billiard balls. *Idiot, you should have kept your mouth closed.* He moves toward her. "Baby?"

"Don't *baby* me. We're moving to Sweden. A job and a nice apartment are waiting for me in Lund. I—"

"Don't talk crazy. Baby? Look at me. We can weather it. Can't we?" His heart sinks. Then he begins to think of all the money he has lost in the stock market over the years and feels like jumping out the window. He clenches his hand around the glass, hard. The glass breaks. Seeing the blood dripping on the floor, Petra dashes toward him.

In the bathroom, with a pained expression, he watches his wife in the large mirror as she applies iodine to the cut and wraps gauze around it. He loves the touch of her fingers on his skin, loves their tenderness.

"There," she says softly.

"Thank you."

They stand in front of the mirror and look into each other's eyes. Right at that moment, they come to realize that after all these years, they still feel a strong attraction for each other. They begin to touch each other and kiss passionately, and on the warm floor, they become one.

Now Petra sits Buddha style on the sofa, a blanket draped over her shoulders while he pours bourbon into glasses. He sits next to her; they touch glasses and drink.

"George, if we don't leave, I'm going to have a nervous breakdown. I can't ask my family for more money. I hope that soon you'll come to live with us as well. My family has fixed my grandparents' house."

"The one near Lund?"

"Yes, the one near Lund. It's going to be great for our daughter to live next to pine hills, fields, lakes, and stables. A month ago, at a local home care for mentally ill kids, a slot opened. I was offered the job, and I accepted. I start in ten days." Petra leans her head on his shoulder.

The news gives him a jolt inside, but he doesn't show it. He just swirls the drink, and in his mind, he sees the main square in Lund, where on Saturdays they went to buy food from people standing under canopies, their breath thick in the cold air. He remembers the smoke of all the chimneys rising in a steady climb, and he remembers the bicycles chained on a long railing covered with snow and glittering under a lamppost. But a few weeks later, the same snow would turn into brown slush and then into slippery ice, turning his walks into a nightmare. It was so cold that it made his fingers and temples ache.

"Are you sure you wanna move back?"

"No doubt about it," she says, and in her voice he hears no trace of hesitation to alleviate his growing sadness.

"How does Zoe feel about your decision?"

"When I told her, she cried, of course. But she feels better now. She knows that she can come to Greece whenever she wants."

He sighs quietly, and sadness spills into his eyes. He tells her that he loves them both, but he is not sure if he can live in Sweden. He tells her that for the past year, he has been turning that thought over and over in his head and trying to picture himself there.

Many years ago, he felt in his heart that one day she would miss her country, would miss her family and friends, and get to thinking of moving back. Being madly in love with her, he denied that thought with all his heart and convinced himself that this thing was never going to happen to him.

Petra looks into his eyes. "I still love you, you fool. But I need a start-over, and Sweden is my winning card." She snuggles next to him. George puts his arm around her and softly pulls her toward him. He feels her breath on his neck, he smells her skin and her hair, and sadness overtakes him.

They stay up listening to Chet Baker, drinking, and soul-searching. He asks her to reconsider her decision, but she is adamant. She says she told their daughter that they are not breaking up and that they will try to work things out.

George believes his wife because she has never used any gimmicks or tricks.

On the sofa, they make love again. Petra then sleeps in his arms, but he stays awake, feeling her warmth against his body. There and then, he decides not to break the news to the rest of his family and friends yet. He will tell them his wife and daughter went to Sweden for a few months because of matters concerning her parents. If he tells his sister the truth, he knows that she will take Petra's side and begin to school him about the stock market. And he knows his mother will become sadder than she already is. With these thoughts running in his head, and with the early-morning light breaking on the horizon, he drifts off to sleep.

A few days later, he watches Petra and Zoe pass the airport's check-in desk. They turn and wave goodbye. He waves back and forces a smile. Seeing Petra wipe tears from under her eyes, a sense of urgency blows through him.

Nostrils filled with the smell of airplane fuel, he gets in his car, tightens his hands around the steering wheel, and feels his eyes welling with tears.

He releases a long, drawn-out scream and wants to jump out of his skin.

In the weeks that follow, the sofa becomes his best friend. The first few days, he drinks himself to sleep and wakes early in the afternoon with a splitting headache and the television set still going. Over the weeks, the sadness turns into disappointment, a disappointment so sore that his heart aches. He feels betrayed. If Petra loves him as she said she does, how could she move back to Sweden? Shouldn't the vows they took on their wedding day keep their knot tight? Shouldn't they stay together through thick and thin and support each other? Isn't love supposed to be long-suffering, everlasting, and unconditional?

Every other day, he speaks with Zoe on the phone, but he doesn't speak with his wife. He spoke with her a few days after they left, and she told him that her parents could help him set up a café in Lund. He said he didn't think it was a good idea and that he needed more time to figure things out.

Two months have come and gone, and he hasn't made up his mind yet.

Every morning, he goes to see his mother in an apartment twenty minutes' walk from his place. She is a small-boned woman with gray hair and kind brown eyes and is usually dressed in black. From a neighborhood bakery, George buys bread, spinach, and cheese pies. He makes tea, and they sit at the kitchen table, eating and making small talk about family matters, the weather, and household chores. He still hasn't told her anything, but her eyes tell him that she knows the truth.

After breakfast, unless she must be someplace, she likes to read. On warm days, she reads on her balcony under an awning, and on cold days she sits in an armchair by the window in the living room, next to a wall of books. Her favorite writers are Alkioni Papadaki, Evgenia Fakinou, Toni Morrison, and Anton Chekov.

Every other day, her daughter, who lives in a flat on the first floor of the same building, brings dinner. She has a full-time job at the town hall, a demanding husband, and two teenage kids.

It is early afternoon. George crosses Mitropoleos Street between idling cars. He wears blue jeans, a black shirt, and a black blazer. He walks into his office building, nods at the janitor, and stands in front of the elevator next to a woman dressed in a gray suit and a black coat. Her perfume reminds him of his wife.

Since last night, he hasn't stopped thinking about his daughter and his wife. He hardly slept and feels out of sorts. He has a nagging urge to talk to Petra, but he doesn't feel ready yet. He wishes that someone could point him in the right direction, but he knows that the only person who can do that is himself.

On the fourth floor, he steps out of the elevator and smells detergent in the air. He pushes a glass door open and walks down the hallway past glass-sided cubicles occupied by men sitting at desks, looking at screens, and talking on telephones. In his office, the sun streams in through the gray window blinds, and smoke hangs along the ceiling. A woman sets a glass of ouzo and a small plate with black olives and salty fish on a table in front of a man with gray hair and a thick mustache. George hopes that he will not start talking about his bitchy wife (the man's words), who left him for a younger man, and how she managed to have him sign over a furnished two-story house, a nice car, and some cash.

"Hello, Gerasimos," George says, then realizes that the man clearly isn't in the mood to talk today. *Good.*

George moves over to a desk where his best friend, Elias, is staring at the numbers on the screen. He has dark hair, wears a white polo shirt, and chews the corner of his lower lip.

"Any luck?"

Keeping his eyes on the screen, Elias says, "Nothing much so far. I don't think it's a good day to trade."

George pats Elias on his shoulder. "Keep up the good work. We'll beat those sons of bitches."

At his desk, he drops his blazer on the shoulder of his chair, waving to a short man at an oval desk at the end of the room who has his arms crossed across his chest and his eyes fixed on the screen. No one really likes this man. "Shorty" made lots of money from a tip-off George ignored. Whenever this happens, he struts about like a four-star general, rubbing his hands and, with pure satisfaction in his little, black, button-like eyes, advises everyone, "I been telling you 'bout it, haven't I? But nobody listens to Shorty. You kittens got plenty to learn yet." But when he loses, he pulls down the blinds of his glass wall and doesn't speak to anyone.

George's heart sinks as he studies the general index of the Greek stock market. It stands at 1,341.24. In 1999, the same index stood at 6,355.26, and in the fourteen years since the crash, the general index has never risen above 2,500.25. Petra's words come back to him in full force: *"Come to your senses. It'll take twenty years for the Greek economy to get back on its feet. You're bound to lose more money—and your family as well!"*

If he sold his shares today, he would get enough money to pay off all of the bills and end up with a few thousand euros in his pocket. *What are you waiting for?* a voice demands. *Do it, and get the hell out of here before it's too late.* He clenches his fist.

On his screen, he reads the headlines: TROIKA CALLS FOR MORE

TRANSPARENCY IN GREEK POLITICS. PROPERTIES COST ONE-THIRD LESS THAN IN 2008 ON THE ISLANDS. GREEK UNEMPLOYMENT STANDS AT 27%. He draws in a breath and starts turning thoughts in his head.

That afternoon, in the shadow of drifting clouds, George and Elias walk across Aristotelous Square. George listens to his friend talk about his new girlfriend.

"She's driving me nuts," he says. "My knees are about to buckle. Brother, she's the devil in disguise." Elias is divorced and has a daughter almost the same age as Zoe.

As George listens to his friend talk, he notices an old man standing with his hand in a small plastic bag. Pigeons come flapping and fluttering their wings, landing around the old man's feet and working their beaks into seeds and breadcrumbs. George's gaze moves toward where the square ends and Nikis Avenue begins, over moving cars and couples walking and holding hands on the waterfront. Now his gaze skims over the port, over cranes and tankers, and all the way to the horizon, where Mount Olympus stands tall and snowcapped.

The tavern smells of fried fish and grilled meat. The two friends sit at a table and look at the menu. A woman in a black apron with red hair and freckles on her face smiles and puts a basket of bread on the table, two empty glasses, and a pitcher of water. She tells them about the dishes of the day and jots down their order on her notepad: one liter of white wine, two pork steaks, and lettuce salad, grilled feta cheese, and homemade fries.

They eat, drink, and talk about various things, but mainly about George's dilemma. Elias knows the score. They go a long way back, all the way back to when they were little brats playing pranks on each other and on other kids and skipping school. Elias listens to his friend and, after a long pause, speaks in a soothing voice.

"If I were you, I'd move to Sweden. Petra is a great woman, and Zoe needs you. You can spend the summers in Greece and the winters in Sweden."

George drinks his wine and regards his friend. He knows that Elias still likes Petra. The summer all three met on the island, both men wanted her, but they flipped a coin in the kitchen, and the matter was decided. George feels strange thinking about it. He looks into his friend's eyes and says, "And what about my mother?"

"Your mother will be fine. She has your sister, and she has the money to take on home help."

George sighs and lights a cigarette. "I don't know. I'm not sure if this thing will work."

"I think you make things more difficult than they really are. If I were you, I would move to Sweden—"

"But you aren't me," George says in an irritated voice.

"I know I'm not you. But what I know for sure is that you'll never find another Petra. You will never find another Zoe. You'd better be quick, brother, because the ship will leave the port without you."

Outside, it's dark. Elias offers to give George a lift, but he decides to walk back home along the seafront. On the way, he tries not to think about anything, but it's hard. He buys a bottle of bourbon from a woman in a late-night store in his neighborhood, and when she asks him about his family, he tells her that they are spending the summer in Sweden.

He unbuttons his shirt, sits on the sofa, drinks bourbon, and smokes a cigarette with the TV muted. As he drinks and watches the screen, a nice feeling rises in him; he is glad he has friends like Elias by his side.

The days drag by. George learns from Zoe that everything is going well in Sweden. Petra works, and Zoe has made new friends and is looking forward to riding her new bike to school in August. Every time he hangs up, his desire to be with his family grows stronger. But he is not certain whether he can live in Sweden—yet.

One week later, after dinner with his mother, he is doing the dishes when she tells him that she spoke with Petra on the phone. He turns off the water and grips the edge of the sink. He waits a minute.

Then he turns and sees his mother rolling a breadcrumb on the table with her index finger, deep in thought.

"It takes courage to do what your wife did." She speaks slowly, softly. "From the first moment I laid my eyes on her, I liked her. She's like a daughter to me. What are you trying to prove to yourself?"

Drying his hands on the towel, he sits across from her, holds her eyes, and tells her that he doesn't know yet, that he is confused, and that he needs more time to think things through. "Let's imagine for a moment that I went to Sweden. Who would look after you?"

She smiles and tells him that she has found a woman who will look after her. "She is in her late fifties and comes from the fishing village near our summerhouse. She knows people I know. Next week, she is moving in with me. I do not want you to look after me any longer." She touches his hand as he fumbles with the towel. "You have done enough for me all these years. I am proud of you. Now I want you to do something for yourself. I want you to put an end to the stock market business and look in a new direction. You hear me, son?"

She strokes his hand and goes on. "You ought to do the right thing, and the right thing is to be with your family." She tells him that when she was young, she didn't want to leave her house near the sea and move to the city and to this apartment. But it was her husband's decision. "The first months were hard, but step by step, I started to enjoy my new life in the city. I made a few friends, got a teaching post, and got pregnant with you." She smiles. "Do the right thing, and only then you will walk on a sunny path. Good things will come to you as if by magic. You will see. There is plenty of love between you and your family, and that is what matters. Family is a sacred thing. You hear me, son?"

The same night, he lies awake on the sofa, and his mind takes him back many years to the time when he stayed with Petra in Malmö, in a large room that overlooked Davidshall Square in the heart of the city. Her best friend, Sandra, lived with her as well. Every other weekend, they went out to see her family, who lived on a farm in a place called

Skåne. George got on well with her parents. They were part-time farmers who kept cows and cultivated barley fields. Her father worked as a manager at a hardware store, and her mother was a nurse. Out there, George and Petra took long walks in the woods, ate good food, sat by the fireplace, read books, watched movies, and lay in bed until late, talking about everything.

Now and again, he remembers wearing rubber boots, denim overalls, and a pair of gloves and helping her father muck out the shed where the cows stayed in the winter. He can still smell the manure and the dry hay they put on the ground for the animals to lie on. At other times, he would split firewood and stack the wood right under the window in the old pigsty. The next day, his arms and shoulders would ache, and his fingers would feel sore, but he didn't mind.

Now his mind drifts to days when he and Petra slept in Petra's room on the farm. The house was surrounded by a lawn that stretched a good twenty meters before it met with hedges and tall poplar trees. At night, lying under the heavy down comforter, they would hear the wind moving through the trees and bask in each other's warmth. They were rich in plans, he remembers. And he pictures the curvy fields behind the poplars and sees the cows grazing under a large sky, bending their heavy heads into brooks, and drinking the cold, clear water. His sleep was deep, and his dreams were vivid and colorful. And he pictures Petra and Zoe sleeping in her grandparents' house in Lund, and as he begins to feel the tyranny of the empty house, he thinks of the words his mother spoke at the kitchen table today. *"Do the right thing, and only then you will walk on a sunny path. Good things will come to you as if by magic."*

He draws back the curtain to the balcony and stands there, smoking and looking outside. After a moment, he sees a man and a woman sauntering past a lamppost casting its light on parked cars. The man has his arms around her waist, and she tosses her head back and laughs at something he says. The man laughs too and kisses the woman on her lips. George's eyes follow the couple as they amble down the road and out of his view.

At the sink, he washes his face and drinks a glass of water. He sighs. Then he lies back down on the sofa and tries to block out any thoughts that come to his mind. *I'm strong,* he thinks. *I'm strong.* Before he falls asleep, and with the picture of his wife and of his daughter clear as day in his mind, a feeling as if someone or something has woken him from a deep slumber begins to wash through him, as soft and gentle as a summer's night breeze.

A Few Words of Grace

IT WAS LATE on a Saturday afternoon. The snow had stopped falling, and the twins were making a snowman under the light of a lamppost. That is what their mother, Eleftheria, had told them to do. "Boys, stay in the light."

In the living room, the fire crackled in the stove, and lit candles cast shadows here and there. The apartment was warm and smelled of burning wood and of the chicken with potatoes in the oven. Eleftheria, dressed in jean dungarees, a black T-shirt, and a gray cardigan, checked the food and glanced at her watch. It was past seven. Her husband, Ioannis, was an hour late.

Eleftheria lit a candle and whispered a small prayer before a picture of the Virgin Mary holding baby Jesus. She felt the urge to call her husband but thought better of it.

They had talked on the phone earlier today, and in a happy voice he told her that the magazine was selling well. "I found a new spot in the city. I've sold almost fifty magazines so far. Can you believe this?"

Half a year ago, Ioannis had started to sell a magazine called *Raft*, which came out once a month and was sold by homeless and unemployed people. For many years, her husband and his partner ran a real estate office. The business was going so well that Ioannis managed to build a three-story house. From their balcony they could see Mount Parnitha. The family lived on the first floor. The apartments on the second and third floors were half built. The family had intended to rent them out once they were completed, until their kids grew older. But a year into the economic crisis, his partner, owning the larger part of the company, forced him to sell his share for less money than he had invested. By the time Ioannis took him to court, his partner had bankrupted the business, sold everything in his name, and moved abroad.

For the past two years, the family had been living on their savings, on the meager allowances for having several children, and on the help they received from Eleftheria's parents, who were farmers in a village up north. Every month, a box filled with olive oil, olives, feta cheese, honey, and flour arrived at their doorstep.

Looking at the clock again, Eleftheria thought, *Woman, stop thinking bad thoughts.* But her dream from last night gave her worries a stubborn staying power.

In the dream, she found herself in a wheat field. Along its edges, cypresses moved in the wind. Eleftheria at first felt at a loss, and worry and fear worked over her. But the white clouds in the blue sky, the warmth of the sun on her face, and the rustling of the wheat field put her at ease. She walked and wondered, *Why am I here?* By the time she realized that she was naked, smoke and flames had surrounded her. In a moment of panic, she felt like she was on fire: her eyes started to stream with tears, and she couldn't breathe. She woke up sweating and gasping for air, with a premonition telling her, *Something bad is bound to happen.*

In the living room, the guitar of Panagiotis Margaris wafted out of the radio. Eleftheria whispered this time, "Woman, stop thinking bad thoughts."

"Mother, did you say anything?" asked her daughter, Philio, who sat at the living room table, sketching the two boys making a snowman. She was good at sketching. When her mother didn't answer, Philio glanced at her with a puzzled expression. "Mother, what's wrong?"

"Nothing, honey. I was just talking to myself." She gave her daughter a thin smile. Philio smiled back and went back to sketching.

A few moments later, Eleftheria stepped out onto the balcony, held her gray, wool cardigan to her throat, and in the cold wind she smelled Christmas. Two crows perched on a wire between poles, regarding her curiously as she watched her boys form the head of a snowman. She didn't want to ask them in yet, because it rarely snowed in Athens, but she had to. She waited until they had put the last touches to the snowman and called out in a good-humored voice, "Boys!" She pushed a strand of windblown black hair behind her ear. "Time for a bath!"

One of them said, "Can't it wait?"

"Chop, chop. Your father will be home soon." She peered out to where the street curved to the left and saw a man in a coat and hat smoking a cigarette in the light of another lamppost.

Carrying in an armload of firewood from the balcony, she put it in a bronze basin next to the stove and brushed the wood dust off her clothes. "Philio, can you give me a hand, please? I need to bathe the boys. After I'm done, it's your turn to take a shower."

Philio set her pencil on the pad and stood up. She was only fourteen years old, but she was tall for her age, and thin. Were it not for her long eyelashes and full lips, one might think she was a boy. She wore jeans and a red hoodie and kept her hair short. She and her brothers took after their father; her mother was her height but fuller in body.

Eleftheria opened the door at the sound of the boys' laughter. Poking fun at each other and smelling of fresh snow and wind, they took off their boots, rushed to the balcony door to draw back the curtain, and gazed at the snowman with pride and joy in their eyes.

"Mother?" the boys said in unison. "Do you like our snowman?" Their cheeks were flushed, and their eyes sparkled.

Touching their heads, she told them that it was the most handsome snowman she'd ever seen and asked one of the boys to get ready for a shower.

Her seven-year-old peeled off his clothes and sat in the bathtub. "Mother, when can I bathe by myself?"

His mother smiled. "Here," she said, and the boy took the showerhead and sprayed water over his thick hair. "That's my boy."

She washed his hair with the bar of soap made of olive oil. She loved the soap's smell and its light-green color. It brought back memories of her childhood, of growing up in the village. She washed the boy's face and rinsed it thoroughly. She asked him to stand and mused that if not for the birthmark on the back of his neck, she could hardly tell the twins apart by looking at them.

She ran her soft hands over the boy's body, firmly, as though she were working on a piece of clay. When she was done soaping, she let her son rinse his body. "Now you're clean," she said, drying his hair with a fresh towel.

She picked up the warm clothes from the radiator, dressed the boy, brushed his hair back, kissed him on the forehead, and told him to go and sit by the stove and ask his brother to come to the bathroom.

She sighed, hoping that nothing bad had happened to her husband.

Over the past few years, Athens had become a war zone. Areas that were once humane and peaceful had become dangerous. Even the police had trouble venturing into them. On the news, something bad was always happening to people out in the streets. Two weeks ago, a man on his way to the hospital to see his newborn baby girl was stabbed to death for his video camera.

By the time Philio had taken a shower and came out into the living room, the time was eight thirty. Her mother had put the main course on the table, along with veggies, olives, feta cheese, and baked bread, ears pricked for the smallest sound of her husband coming home. The family usually ate at eight. Eleftheria's last call to Ioannis had gone straight to the answering machine. *His phone is old, and the battery is weak*, she told herself. But there was worry in her eyes and nervousness in her movements. She regarded her children, who sat on the floor by the stove, reading the Lucky Luke, Captain Mark, Spider-Man, and Superman comics their father had given them, and asked them over.

"Where is father?" Philio asked as they gathered around the table.

The boys' eyes skipped to their mother, who said softly, "At work. Where else could he be?"

"Shouldn't we wait for him?" Philio said.

"The boys are hungry." Eleftheria looked at them. "Aren't you guys?"

The twins nodded yes. Eleftheria asked Philio to say a few words of grace, knotted her fingers atop the table, and closed her eyes as her daughter started, "Dear God, thank you for . . ."

When she finished, they made the sign of the cross and began to eat. As Eleftheria's sense of urgency grew stronger, she hid it as best she could. She made small talk with her children, smiled, and tried to be cheerful. At the end of the dinner, the boys had eaten the chicken and the potatoes but left the vegetables untouched.

"Eat your veggies, please," Eleftheria said. "Some families can't afford that much.

The boys sighed and spoke in unison: "We aren't hungry."

"Look at your sister. She cleared her plate. If you want to grow strong and healthy, you must eat your veggies. Just eat a bit of carrot and broccoli," she heard herself say in a slightly irritated voice.

The boys lowered their eyes to their plates and resumed eating.

If their father were home, the dinner would have lasted longer. In a humorous tone, he would tell his family stories of people he had talked to and strange things he had observed on the way to work and back. The boys would listen with the concentration of scientists, and at times, they would sit so still—wide eyed, open mouthed, and holding their spoons in midair—that one might think that they had turned into stone.

A week ago, their father had told them about a clown who rode on a single wheel while two parrots sat on his shoulders and performed tricks at the command of a third parrot sitting atop the clown's high hat. This one was larger than the other two parrots, had green, yellow, and red feathers, and his name was Bravo. Two days ago, their father told them about a young man who talked to a forest cat until it winked at him and smiled.

"That's right, boys. The cat winked its green eye at the young man, just like that"—he winked at the boys—"and then the cat smiled, just like that. Isn't this a smile, or am I making a mistake?"

The boys said that it was a smile all right, then looked at each other and snickered. A while ago, they said, a cat standing on the top of a rubbish bin had smiled at them, too.

Outside, the snow had stopped. Philio helped her mother clear the table and do the dishes, then went back to her drawing while the boys played on the floor with their toys. Eleftheria stuck a piece of firewood into the stove and fished a bar of chocolate out of the pocket of her apron, giving it to the twins. The boys kissed her on her cheek.

"Share it evenly," she said and poked at their noses. She put another bar of chocolate on the living room table and, seeing her daughter smile as she drew, sat in an armchair, then picked up a book from a low table and began to read *Small England* by Ioanna Karystiani. But her mind was attuned to every little sound from outside, and every five minutes or so, she glanced at the clock. It was ten o'clock now. Ioannis was alarmingly late, and time pushed at her from all sides. She decided that if her husband didn't show up within an hour, she would call the police.

She turned her eyes from the book to the boys and told them to stop bickering over Legos. Then she rose from her chair, stepped out onto the balcony, put her hands on the cold railing, and peered down along the street, feeling the stiffness of the wind in her face. "Please, God, bring my husband back home safe. Please."

But Eleftheria now felt in her bones that something bad had happened to him. In their twenty years together, he had never been this late. He always made sure to let her know his whereabouts. *If his battery had run down,* she told herself, *he would've found a way to get in touch with me.*

"Mother, what is it?" Philio said.

"Honey, go back inside. You'll catch a cold out here." She nudged her back into the living room, closed the balcony door, and turned to face her daughter.

"Where is Father?"

Eleftheria stroked the side of her face. "He's on his way, honey."

Her mobile rang. Eleftheria's heart lifted, but when she saw that it was her best friend, Despina, she became disappointed. "Call me back later—or better yet, tomorrow. No, nothing's wrong. Just busy with the kids."

She hung up and turned her attention to the boys again. "Boys, put your toys away and get ready for bed."

"Mother, we don't want to go to bed yet," the boys pleaded.

"Put your toys away. Now."

"Please, Mommy."

"Do as I say," she said in a firm voice. There was no more room for protest. "Your sister will read you a story." Her daughter sighed. "Please, Philio, don't give me a hard time. I need to go out for a while."

"Now?"

"Yes, now. I won't be late."

With her hands tucked in the pocket of her wool coat, she walked with hurried strides along the sidewalk, past neighboring houses. Through a window, she saw a woman putting a tray of food on a table in the living room, where her family sat watching television. Eleftheria pressed on, past cars parked on either side of the street, and stopped where the street turned. She paused by a small stand of trees that stood bare but for the snow on their branches. Then she glanced to where the road rose slightly and met the highway. There, cars raced and sounded their hollow roar. With the wind pinching her ears and her face twisted with worry, she stayed in the same spot for ten minutes, praying to see her husband.

Back in the apartment, she removed a brick from the wall and from the hole pulled out a pack of cigarettes wrapped in foil. The last time she'd smoked was about half a year ago. She stepped out on the balcony, drew on the cigarette, coughed, and felt tipsy as her heartbeat quickened. Halfway through, she called her husband again. But she heard only the stupid answerphone message again.

Pacing and chewing on her lower lip, she finally decided to call the police. A woman at the other end of the line listened to her carefully and told her that there was nothing the police could do about it yet. She told Eleftheria that it was too early to draw conclusions and that they had to wait twenty-four hours to list him as a missing person.

"Ma'am, I understand how you are feeling, but you need to calm down," the officer said. "The best thing for you to do now is to wait patiently. Maybe your husband met an old friend, went for a coffee, and lost track of time. It happens. Maybe he lost his money and he's walking home as we speak. The city center is a long way away from where you live."

The smooth and reasoning quality of the officer's voice put Eleftheria at ease. She thanked her, rewrapped the pack of cigarettes in the foil, and went back inside to slid it back into the hole. She took a breath and felt exhausted.

In the bathroom, she washed her hands and face, brushed her teeth, and drank some water. As she walked into the living room, she heard the voice of her daughter coming from the boys' room. She went to the half-open door and gazed at her children. Philio sat on a stool between the boys' beds, reading from a book entitled *The Adventures of Tom Sawyer* by Mark Twain. Once Philio had read the tale to its conclusion and taken her leave, their mother moved into the room, kissed her boys, and told them she was sorry about being snappish with them earlier on. Their eyes were slightly red, and their eyelids looked heavy.

"Where is Daddy?" one of the boys said.

"He's on his way. When you wake up tomorrow, he'll be here, and we can all take a long walk in the woods, make another snowman, and see the birds and the squirrels. How is that for a plan, huh?" As the boys smiled, she pulled their covers to their chins, turned off the light, and went into the living room.

Philio sat on the sofa, propped up on some cushions as she read a book. Eleftheria put a log on the stove, settled on a stool, and fixed her eyes on the log as it caught fire. Then she looked at her watch. A knot formed in her stomach. It was now eleven.

Philio put the book down on her lap, and though she couldn't see her mother's face, somehow she sensed her worry.

"Mother, is something wrong with Father?"

Eleftheria wiped tears from her eyes. "What do you mean, honey?"

Philio gave her a look as if to say she wasn't stupid, moved over to her mother, and put her arms around her. "I'm sure Father is all right. He'll be home soon. You'll see."

Mother and daughter fell asleep on the sofa. Soon, Eleftheria was dreaming. In her dream, she heard a faint ringing. Little by little, as the ringing got louder, she told herself to wake up and forced herself to do so. She opened her eyes and realized with a touch of guilt that she had fallen asleep.

The embers were dying in the stove. With drowsy eyes, she pulled a blanket over Philio's shoulders and stood in the middle of the room, smoothing her hair and looking at her watch, which read one thirty. She was now certain that something bad had happened to her husband. A rush of worry and fear blew through her and sent her mind to pieces. Suddenly, her confused eyes turned to the balcony door. A car had come to a stop right outside the house. She rushed out onto the balcony and looked down. A hefty, gray-haired and bearded man crossed the beams of the idling Jeep's headlights, stopped, and peered up at her.

"Are you Eleftheria?"

The blood froze in her veins. "Yes," she managed to say. "What's the matter?"

"It's your husband."

As Eleftheria hurried back into the living room, eyes wild with worry, Philio raised herself on her elbows and watched her mother scurry to the door.

After a moment, Eleftheria spotted them coming up the stairs. Her husband had his arm around the man's neck and was limping. She called out his name in a trembling voice. He looked up and smiled at her, and her heart sank at the sight of his bruised and bloody face. But at the same time, a sense of relief lifted her spirits.

"What in God's name happened?"

"Two punks tried to mug me." His face was lined with pain.

Philio stood at the door with tears rolling down her face. "Dad!"

They helped Ioannis to the sofa and propped him up on cushions. Philio immediately demanded, "What's wrong? What happened?"

"Stop shouting. You'll wake the boys," Eleftheria said. "Look at me. Everything's going to be okay. Father's home now. That's what matters. All right, honey?" She wiped her daughter's tears. "Now put some firewood in the stove."

The bearded man stood by the sofa with his hands on his hips as Eleftheria checked her husband's face, took off his bloodstained jacket and woolen jumper, dropped them on the floor, and ran her hands all over his body.

"I'm not stabbed, darling. Just sore. If this gentleman hadn't found me, I might've frozen to death."

The two men looked at each other.

"Thank you," Ioannis said.

"Are you sure you don't want me to drive you to the hospital?"

"You've already done enough. I'm in good hands now."

The man smiled and gave him his business card. "Make sure you call me."

Eleftheria saw the man to the door, thanking him all the way.

"Sweetie, can you pour me a brandy?" Ioannis asked his daughter while his wife started pulling off his boots. As she took off his socks, five, ten, and twenty-euro bills fell on the heaped clothes on the floor. She picked up the money and stared at him in wonder.

"Those bastards just made off with my mobile." He touched her face. "Don't worry, darling. After a warm bath and a good night's sleep, I'll be as good as new."

Philio put the drink in his hand. He winked at her, drank a mouthful, then another. "Now, young lady, it's time for you to go to bed." He beckoned her over and kissed her on her forehead before she shuffled off to her room.

"Look at this," he said and handed the business card to his wife.

She brought it near her face and read, CHRISTOS PAVLIS, COURIER COMPANY.

"He offered me a job as a storekeeper or a driver."

They held each other's gazes and smiled.

Soon Ioannis was covered with hot water in the bathtub, making sounds both of pain and pleasure as his wife washed his face.

"Fucking bastards."

"Just relax," Eleftheria said and washed his forehead gently. She kissed his lips and began to soap his upper body slowly.

"Darling," he said, "you don't happen to have a cigarette, do you?"

"A cigarette?" she said in a strict voice.

He held her beautiful gaze a bit too long. "How are the boys?"

"They're fine. They made a snowman. You should've seen how proud they were."

When his eyes smiled, she kissed him on his lips again and told him that she was going to make him a bite to eat.

In their bedroom later, Eleftheria covered him with a thick duvet and looked into his red and drowsy eyes. "Now you need a good night's sleep."

He patted the space next to him.

"Just give me a minute. I've got one last thing to do."

Eleftheria went to the icon of the Virgin Mary, her eyes filled with disappointment. "Tell me why?" she demanded, anger rising in her chest. "Why did you allow this to happen? Tonight, my husband could've been killed. The past two years, we've been through hell." A knot formed in her throat. "We've always been good to others. Always. We never thought of changing the path we chose to walk on."

She picked up the icon and looked into the Virgin Mary's benign eyes. "I never feared your punishment or hoped for your reward. And despite all the obstacles you've thrown in our path, we endured. We endured, always hoping for better days to come, always praying." Her eyes brimmed with tears. "But now I'm sick and tired of empty hopes. I've had enough. You let us down," she said angrily.

She put the icon on the stool next to the stove and hurried about the room, pulling open drawers and picking up books and wooden crosses and other religious items. She gathered everything she could think of and put them in a pile with the icon. *How naive and stupid have I been all those years,* she told herself, throwing the items in the fire and keeping her eyes there as the flames enveloped them. A sense of peace grew inside her; it expanded to fill the house.

Eleftheria checked on her kids and returned to her bedroom. She stood near the bed and fixed her eyes on the calm, sleeping face of her husband. In the dim light of the bed lamp, his face seemed to her like it belonged to some saint in an El Greco painting.

She slid under the covers, snuggled next to him, and kissed him on the lips, softly. She closed her eyes and basked in the warmth of his body. Listening to his stable breathing and smelling the green soap on his skin, a glow of bliss brightened her face. And little by little, Eleftheria drifted into a peaceful sleep.

Got Any Milk?

THE RACKET woke Metaxas. He ran his tongue over dry lips and glanced at the clock on the side table. It was Monday, two o'clock in the morning. Under the cover, he clenched his fist.

In the kitchen, his bearded cousin opened and closed drawers, all the while singing a Greek song by Vasilis Karas "Άσ' την να λέει[1]" in a tobacco-rough voice while his girlfriend laughed loudly. His cousin continued, "δεν έμαθε ποτέ της να αγαπά.[2]"

"Motherfucker," Metaxas muttered and pictured himself getting out of bed and throwing his cousin and that woman out of the house and into the cold night. But he couldn't do that.

If not for his "auntie," as he liked to call her, he would never have signed up for this craziness. About a month ago, she called and asked him to let his cousin—her first cousin's son, with whom Metaxas hadn't spoken since the time of Noah—stay in his house until he found a job.

"Please, Metaxas," his aunt said. "Do it for me. He's having a tough time in the village. Who knows, he may get a job in Thessaloniki."

And what about me? Metaxas had wanted to ask her. *Don't I have a tough time working a job I hate and not getting paid on time? Don't I have a hard time making ends meet?*

But he couldn't turn his auntie down. She was the sister of his mother, and he was her favorite nephew. Unmarried and having no children of her own, his aunt had put the apartment in his name a few years ago.

---

1. *Let Her Speak*
2. She never learned how to love

As Metaxas rose on his elbows, a pocket of cold air snuck under the covers. He shivered and lay back down, mumbling.

Greek music and cheerful sounds continued to drift from the living room.

"You've got to put an end to this madness," his girlfriend, Agni, said in a sleepy voice.

Metaxas kissed his woman and sighed. He knew that it was high time to get rid of the monkey sitting on his back.

In the living room, the air smelled of alcohol and smoke. Half-filled bottles of retsina wine stood on a table. The music stopped playing, and in the middle of the room, the cousin stood barefoot, wineglass in hand and head tilted back as he blew a plume of smoke toward the ceiling. His shirt was open and hung over his trousers. From under his rolled-up shirtsleeve, the tattooed head of a snake slid out; its tongue was red, and its eyes were green, the same as his. The blond-haired, blue-eyed woman on the sofa sat up and began to peel her blouse off her slender body.

"Bad boy," she said, her lustful eyes inviting him over.

Agni and Metaxas lay listening to them go at it for over an hour. Metaxas couldn't understand what the hell a good-looking woman saw in his cousin. He was scrawny, didn't have a job, and didn't even have ten euros in his pocket. The first week, he had looked for a job; at least, that was what he told Metaxas. But after that, he seemed to forget why he'd come here in the first place. And two weeks ago, he started putting cigarettes and beers on Metaxas's tab at a kiosk and hanging out at a local καφενείο,[3] drinking beer and playing backgammon and cards.

Anger spread in Metaxas's chest. "That's it, Agni. I've had enough of this jackass. Tomorrow, after you leave, I'll put a stop to this madness."

---

3. A coffee shop where old people gather to play backgammon and cards, watch TV, and talk about politics and football

"It's about time," she said drowsily and snuggled her buxom body closer to his.

When they woke, it was still dark outside. An inch of powdered snow covered the city of Thessaloniki. Sleepy eyed, Agni and Metaxas stood shivering in the cold room as they pulled on their clothes. She was catching a bus to Veria, a town an hour's drive from Thessaloniki, where she lived with her mother and held a job as a saleswoman at a Cosmote store. She came to see Metaxas every other weekend. For over six months, she had been trying to get transferred to a Cosmote store in Thessaloniki, and her manager had assured her that as soon as a slot opened, she would be the first one to slide in.

Metaxas worked at a factory that produced the circuit boards used inside television sets, radios, and bus signs. Every day, he rode on two buses to work and back. He wanted to throw in the towel, but he didn't have any other option. Greece was on its knees, and so was he.

On the weekends Agni did not visit, Metaxas went up to the mountains to hunt wild boar. He was tall and muscular with brown eyes and hair the color of chestnuts. He had a strong memory, great knowledge of hunting and world history, and a good sense of humor. He was honest and loyal, but when someone stepped on his patience, he could turn into a raging bull.

Quietly, they moved into the kitchen and turned on the foot heater. While the coffee brewed and Agni put on her makeup in front of a tiny mirror at the kitchen table, he made toast with cheese, ham, and tomato. They ate the toast, drank the coffee, and talked about their plans for Christmas, which was a few weeks away.

"I'm glad we're spending the holidays with my mother this year." Her face glowed. She reached her hand over the table and knotted her slender fingers with his. "Honey, I appreciate it. It will be great."

Metaxas gave her a thin smile.

Outside, a bus roared up the street, and a line of cars dragged behind it. Someone leaned on the horn.

"Metaxas," Agni said and held his eyes. "Promise me that you'll not lose your temper with him."

"Don't worry, honey." He swallowed a mouthful of coffee. "I have the whole business under control."

At the door, she buried herself in his chest. He held her and kissed her on the forehead, softly. Her smell made him miss her already, and he hoped she would be transferred to Thessaloniki soon.

"I love you," she said.

"I love you too, honey."

She smiled and kissed him on the lips. As she made to go, he pulled her deeper into the kiss and felt as he had when he first kissed her two years ago outside a tavern in Veria, one week before Christmas.

"Have a safe trip. Text me when you get to Veria. And say hello to your mother for me."

Daylight broke on the horizon. In the kitchen, Metaxas turned on the radio. A woman journalist was sharing the news, saying that within the last year, thousands of economic immigrants had gone back to their countries and withdrawn their money from the banks in Greece.

Metaxas puckered his lips. His heart went out to all those people. Many years ago, they had come to Greece and gone to school to learn Greek in order to get jobs as plumbers, bricklayers, painters, and farmers, jobs the Greeks couldn't or wouldn't do. They paid taxes, and yet they never got permanent work permits. Thousands were exploited; even the hundreds who managed to set up their own businesses and save money couldn't buy property because of the rock-hard bureaucracy.

As Metaxas did the dishes, a sense of gratitude welled up in him, for he still had a job and a roof over his head. He dried his hands on a towel, poured coffee into a thermos, and put three tuna sandwiches in the knapsack, along with a bar of almond chocolate, a history book about the civil war in Greece, and a magazine about hunting. Before he moved into the bedroom, he broke off a piece of chocolate. He made a guttural sound as he put it in his mouth, then ate another piece before shoving the chocolate back into the knapsack.

After making the bed, he opened the balcony door a crack. The cold air smelled of snow. He grabbed a fresh towel from a drawer and moved into the bathroom to take a shower.

Afterward, he stared out the kitchen window at the pale light and imagined sitting at the kitchen table in his jeans and woolen jumper, telling his cousin the score. He thought of the words he would use. *That's what I'm going to tell him*, he decided as he crossed the hallway and pushed the living room door open.

At the sight of them sleeping on the sofa, the empty bottles on the table, the clothes scattered on the floor, and the smell of alcohol and tobacco—Metaxas drank but hated smoking—he felt something go off deep in his chest. He made another guttural sound and closed the door.

He gave his boss a call, telling him he would be late for work but not to worry because he would stay longer to finish the order the Athenians had placed on Friday.

From a local bakery, he bought brown bread and chatted with the bulky baker—also a hunter—about the weather and hunting wild ducks and boar. They discussed the law that prevented hunters from going after wild ducks in snowy fields.

"I wonder who passed such a stupid law," the baker said as he handed Metaxas a loaf.

"An idiot in a suit." Metaxas put the bread in his bag. "An idiot with no knowledge whatsoever about hunting and the balance of Greek fauna."

The baker nodded in agreement and welcomed another customer with a smile.

From a corner store, Metaxas bought Greek yogurt, feta cheese, lentils, olive oil, free-range chicken, and veggies. By the time he stepped back into the kitchen, it was past nine o'clock. He put the food away and strode into the living room. The woman, her hair disheveled and makeup runny, awoke and stared at him as though he were holding an axe.

"Wake up," he said, glaring at his cousin as he twisted and grunted. "Wake up!"

"Why?" he said, bleary eyed. "What time is it?"

"I want a word with you." Metaxas tossed the clothes from the floor to his cousin as the man sat up. "I'll be in the kitchen."

Hair uncombed, his cousin shuffled into the kitchen with his hands in the pockets of his jeans, hunched as though he were tired of carrying his shoulders. He looked at the coffee Metaxas had put on the table for him. Before the cousin sat down, he said, "Got any milk?"

Metaxas frowned.

Yawning, releasing a cloud of alcohol stench, the cousin said, "Forget 'bout it."

Metaxas worked his eyes over him. "You're a cupcake, aren't you?"

With a grin, the cousin lit a cigarette, drank from his coffee, and squinted at Metaxas.

As Metaxas opened the window a crack, he pictured slapping the cigarette out of his mouth. "I've got to leave for work soon, so I'll be quick."

The cousin dragged on his cigarette.

"You been here over a month now, and you haven't landed a job yet. At the local stores, you run tabs in my name."

His cousin pursed his lips as though he had eaten something sour.

"Even though you know I have to wake up early, not only you do bring women over, but you also make a racket, as though you lived in this place all by yourself." He held his cousin's sleepy eyes, hard.

"I'm sorry," he said. "Won't happen again."

"You say the same thing over and over again."

The cousin turned his eyes to the indifferent window and blew smoke through his nose.

"Hey," Metaxas said. "Look at me when I'm talking to you."

"Okay, okay," the cousin said in a tired voice.

"Nothing's okay, man. Since the day you arrived, my life has been turned upside down. You understand what I'm saying?"

The cousin nodded.

"Listen good. This isn't Hollywood. If you want to make it, you've got to go out there and plug it."

"It's very hard to get a job. As for the money, I'll pay you back soon."

"How the hell you going to pay me back? With pebbles?"

The cousin smirked, but seeing Metaxas's glare, he said, "I'm working on it."

Metaxas tore his eyes from his cousin. "He's working on it," he said, looking at the window as if a judge sat there. "How are you working on it, huh? By drinking beers and retsinas at the local hangouts?"

Metaxas felt like smashing his face against the wall as the cousin had done to a few puppies when the two of them were kids. Back then, this cousin had put the puppies into a plastic bag and swung them against a wall. When Metaxas tried to stop him, he ended up with scraped knees and elbows.

"Listen good, you jackass," Metaxas said, eyes wide with barely contained rage. "I don't want the fucking money back." He put a fifty-euro bill on the table. "It's the last one."

The cousin looked at the bill, but he didn't move a muscle.

"I let you stay with me because I owed my auntie a favor. But the favor runs out today. By the time I get back home from work, I want your ass out of here." He banged the table with his palm.

As the cousin put another cigarette in his mouth, Metaxas grabbed the ends of the table and rocked it. Thick veins stood out on his arms and his temples. Coffee sloshed over, and a box of matches fell on the floor.

The cousin sat up in his chair, startled.

"I'll be back at eight o'clock. Make sure you're gone by then. And give me the fucking key!"

The cousin fished the key out of his pocket and put it on the table.

And before Metaxas walked out of the kitchen, he added, "If you try any monkey business on me, I swear," he said and balled his fingers into a fist, "I'll track you down and break every bone in your good-for-nothing body."

By now most of the snow had turned to slush. Hands tucked in the pockets of his khaki parka, Metaxas marched along, his nerves cracking. Things hadn't turned out the way he'd planned in his mind. He got out the wrong words in the wrong order. He crossed under a bridge, cut left, and strode along a sidewalk by a tall wall sprayed with black letters spelling out, TROIKA GET OUT OF GREECE.

He climbed onto the bus and nodded to the driver. Passengers sat wrapped up in coats and scarves. He took a seat in the back by the window. He liked having his back against a wall.

As the bus pulled out into the traffic, Metaxas thumbed through the hunting magazine. Pictures of dogs with ducks in their mouths, dogs nosing at a downed wild boar, and hunters holding rifles and wearing boots, heavy jackets, and woolen beanies all paraded in front of his eyes. But his mind was on his cousin, who was capable of anything. He thought of going back, but the bus was already halfway into its journey. Metaxas assured himself that there was no way his cousin would find the four thousand euros wrapped up in foil and buried under the boar meat in the freezer. And if his cousin tried to make off with his CDs and the CD player or his television set, he would make him pay for it big-time.

Turning these thoughts over in his head, he shoved the magazine into his knapsack and let his eyes drift out the window. He saw an old man in torn clothes pushing a trolley with scraps of metal in it. He saw empty stores, run-down houses, and stray dogs outside food joints. Way back off the road, behind a fence, he saw a man smoking a cigarette in the door of an abandoned wagon with a blanket draped over his shoulders. Empty plastic coffee cups, cigarette packs, and sandwich wraps blew against the curbs.

The buildings and bridges gave way to fields and trees covered in snow. Standing at a bus stop near the arched gate of a cotton factory as the bus roared off, Metaxas replied to the message Agni had sent to him. *Sweetheart*, he thought. He huddled into his parka and headed along the edge of the road, thick breaths steaming in the air. The factory was a fifteen-minute walk, and this stretch was the best part of the journey.

On his side of the road were trees, and on the other, reeds swaying with the wind. Thick smoke rose in a steady climb from the chimneys of the factories in the distance. Farther down the road, a fox edged out of the trees with a bird in her mouth. Metaxas's eyes took on a glow, and a thin smile played on his face.

As he entered through the back of the factory, a Rottweiler chained to the fence started to bark.

"Bush," he said and whistled. "What's the matter, boy?"

The dog cocked his ears, wagged his tail, and whined. Metaxas stroked him and said a few doggy words.

Inside, it was warm, and the air smelled of metal and plastic. Metal clanks and voices came from the other end. He clocked in, then pulled on his uniform in the changing room and went into the office. A curvy woman with curly hair sat behind a desk, working on the computer. He greeted her and asked to see his boss.

"He's out."

"Did he say when he'd be back?"

"No, he didn't."

"Did he leave a message for me?

"No."

Metaxas walked out of the office with irritation marking his face. The boss had promised him that he would give him the thousand euros from the three thousand he owed him; with Metaxas's salary and the Christmas bonuses, he would be able to wire money to his parents, retired farmers who lived in the city of Ioannina.

He moved into a large, glass-walled cubicle and turned on a laser etching machine. Tapping a few digits on a keyboard, he placed a circuit board inside, closed the transparent door, and watched the machine engrave it. For the next three hours, he turned his eyes toward the office door every ten minutes.

A thin-boned, bearded man in dark-blue dungarees entered the cubicle and wiped his long fingers on an oily cloth. Without taking the cigarette from his mouth, he said, "How're you holding up, chief?"

"Not too bad. Yourself?" Metaxas glanced over his shoulder.

"I'll feel better when I get paid."

"Tell me about it."

"I heard the big man didn't get the loan from the bank."

Worry rose in Metaxas's chest. "Argiris, I'm getting paid either way. Enough is enough, man."

The man nodded his bald head. "See you at lunch."

As the workers were putting their empty lunch Tupperware away, the boss, a short man with a beer belly and floppy ears, rushed into the break room. From the way he looked at them, Metaxas figured out that something was wrong.

"Metaxas, can you come into my office, please?" he said and rushed off.

The men stared at each other in worry.

On the mahogany desk in the office were stacks of envelopes, an ashtray filled with half-smoked cigarillos, empty paper coffee cups, matches, and calculators. Faded photographs of Greek islands, ancient temples, beaches, and sunsets hung on the walls.

The boss sat at his desk and waved to him to sit down.

"I have to get back to work," Metaxas said, giving him a look that said, "Cut straight to the chase, man."

"The bank turned the loan down."

Metaxas's mind went to his family. "You promised to give me some of the money you owe me." He twisted his face. "You promised me."

"Of course I did. But as you know, many clients owe us hundreds of thousands of euros." He started to tap his pen on the desk.

"You mean, they owe you."

"Okay. They owe me. But nothing has changed."

"I want you to pay me the thousand euros you promised you would."

"If I do that, the rest of the crew will not get paid in full this month. And they have families and it's—"

Metaxas raised his hand. "Chronis, stop it right there. If you can't pay me," he said and pointed at his boss's wrist, "then give me your Rolex."

Chronis's brow creased. "My Rolex?" He laughed.

Metaxas's eyes narrowed to slits. He felt like grabbing his boss by his floppy ears and shaking him out like a rug. But instead, he said in a strict voice, "I been working for you for thirteen long years. I hardly ever call in sick. Many times, I work overtime and don't get paid for it. I don't care what you do, but I need you to pay me the money you owe me. You hear me?"

As the boss cringed at the irritation in Metaxas's eyes, the door flew open, and a man rushed in, catching his breath and saying, "Argiris cut his hand badly!"

Chronis sprang out of his chair as if he had been bitten by a snake. Metaxas pressed his eyes closed, sighed, and rushed after his boss as he surged out of the office like a hurricane.

In the break room, Argiris was slouched in a chair and cursing his luck, the bandage around his wrist soaked in blood. Metaxas asked how he was feeling. Argiris asked for a cigarette.

"What the hell happened?" the boss asked, wide eyed.

"A sharp piece of metal cut his wrist," one of the workers said and put a lit cigarette in Argiris's mouth. The injured man drew on it and let the smoke dribble out of his lips, his face creasing in pain.

The boss said, "His wrist?"

A second worker said, "Yeah. Close to the artery. The cut is deep."

Metaxas wrapped another cloth around Argiris's arm. "Hold it up." Then he walked him outside to the boss's car, with Chronis trailing along.

"What did the big man tell you?" Argiris asked as Metaxas opened the car door.

"Stop worrying about that."

"Did he get the loan?"

"Don't know."

Metaxas buckled him up and glanced at Chronis as the pudgy man climbed into the car and turned on the engine. The car sped off through the gate and roared down the road, snow billowing behind it. Bush's barks were answered by other barks in the distance.

Worry and fret spread through Metaxas's muscular chest. The thought that he would have to dig into his savings again drove him crazy. It had taken him several years to accumulate that amount.

Suddenly, he felt dead tired. *A cup of coffee will set me straight*, he assured himself.

His coworkers were still in the break room, smoking and making small talk. As soon as Metaxas walked in to get his thermos, they wanted to know what the big man had told him in the office.

"Will you give me a fucking break?" Metaxas growled as he dug his hand into his knapsack. "Argiris cut himself badly, and the only fucking thing you all wonder about is what the boss told me? I suggest we get back to work. Otherwise, on Christmas Eve, we'll have bread and butter for dinner."

Metaxas was the oldest employee, which gave him the right to speak in that manner.

After a couple of hours, the boss called Metaxas and told him that Argiris wouldn't be able to come back to work for at least ten days.

Metaxas clenched his teeth. *We're royally fucked,* he told himself. *A pair of good hands less.* Then he asked his boss how his colleague was doing.

"Ten fucking stitches. Would you believe that? Ten fucking stitches. The piece of metal cut him inches away from the main artery. He's on painkillers and sleeping pills. He's in the car, dazed like a puppy." Then he asked how it was going with the Athenian order.

"I'm about halfway through."

He heard his boss sigh. "Do your best."

Yeah, what fucking best, Metaxas thought.

At the end of his shift, Metaxas didn't feel like doing overtime. *I'll finish the job tomorrow*, he thought and went to change his clothes. One of the workers offered him a lift to the bus stop.

"Thanks, man, but I'll walk," he said, pulling the wool beanie over his head.

It was freezing outside. Two crows sitting on a wire looked at Metaxas and croaked. Bloody birds, he thought as he saw the wind in the trees and remembered that the weatherman had predicted more snow. He walked slowly against the wind and tried to drive the nagging thoughts out of his head. Holding a flashlight, he raked its beam over the snow-covered fields and reeds, hoping to spot an animal. When he heard a sound coming from the trees, he turned the beam of light toward them. But he saw nothing. Then he thought of his cousin, and an uneasy feeling began to settle inside him.

As he walked along the last stretch of the road, he saw the bus pulling up to the stop. He broke into a jog, but by the time he reached the main road, even though the bus driver had seen him waving, the bus had pulled out.

During the half hour Metaxas waited for the next bus to come, he paced and cursed. "Fucking monkey," he shouted again and again. He knew the chubby, bald driver. They'd had words once. Frequently, Chubby would pull off onto the shoulder in front of his own house, either to use the toilet or pick up a meal his mother had cooked for him. When Metaxas protested once, Chubby said that he was the only person that complained. "Sit down or get off my bus," he had said. On another occasion, he drove into turns so fast that Metaxas, who was standing and holding on to a handle, twisted his wrist. As the image of Chubby surfaced in his mind again, the anger that ran in his veins was hot and burning.

It was six o'clock when the bus pulled into the central bus stop. Metaxas immediately looked for Chubby. He asked a few bus drivers standing in front of a running bus as they shared jokes, smoked cigarettes, and sipped coffee from paper cups. One of them said he had last seen him in the station cafeteria.

Halfway to the cafeteria, Metaxas saw Chubby talking with another driver. "Hey, you!" Metaxas said sharply and felt a rush at his heart. Chubby looked over his shoulder but went on talking with his colleague.

"Aren't you supposed to serve the public, you piece of shit?"

"What did you say?" Chubby turned to face him.

"You heard me," Metaxas said and stood an arm's length away. He was a head and a half taller than Chubby.

"You better watch your mouth."

"Why didn't you wait for me?"

"I didn't see you."

"Do you see me now?" Metaxas held his gaze fiercely. Chubby smirked. As he turned again, Metaxas grabbed him by his elbow, squeezed hard, and whispered something in his ear.

Chubby made a squeak of pain. "Let go of me." He tried to shake off the grip on his elbow as his colleague stood startled, not knowing what to do.

Metaxas whispered in his ear again.

"Okay, okay," Chubby said. "Now let go of me!"

Two drivers ran over and asked what the matter was.

"I'll sue you." Chubby rubbed his elbow.

"Just make sure you see me next time around," Metaxas said before turning and leaving the station.

His breath clouding the air around him, Metaxas crossed a street heavy with roaring traffic and walked with lurching strides, hoping his cousin was gone by now. Outside a veggie shop in his neighborhood, the owner, a tall man in a black apron with an honest face, waved him over as he was putting red apples into a paper bag.

"Metaxas, I saw your cousin in an old jalopy with a dodgy-looking man."

"When?"

"About ten minutes ago."

Without saying goodbye, he stormed out of the shop and strode along the sidewalk, muttering. As soon as he rounded the corner of his building, he saw the old jalopy double-parked with its door ajar.

Metaxas felt like his head was on fire. He took a few steps ahead, set his knapsack on the threshold of a closed shop a few meters away from the entrance of his building, and waited.

In a few minutes, he heard the door open and the voice of his cousin, who stepped off the threshold holding one end of his kind host's flat-screen. If Metaxas had stayed at the factory longer, they would have made off with his forty-three-inch TV, the one he had bought in twelve installments. It was the TV he used to watch war and animal documentaries, good movies, and TV shows alone, with a few good friends, or with Agni. Metaxas's eyes clouded over.

"Hey, jackasses!" he boomed.

Both men froze in their tracks as if posing for a photograph. Beholding the towering Metaxas and his fierce look, the cousin's jaw dropped.

Metaxas balled his hands into fists and dashed forward, screaming.

Can You Please Stay Sober Tonight?

IT IS NOVEMBER. In the living room, a heavy-shouldered man with thick black hair and a beard lies on a sofa with his eyes closed and a newspaper spread out on his chest. Vangelis has just awoken from a dream he can't remember.

When he hears a hiss, he pictures his wife standing in front of the ironing board in the room at the rear of their apartment. From the window there, they can see part of the city, the port with its cranes, and the snowcapped Mount Olympus. And now and again, they see airplanes flying over wooded hills.

He opens his eyes and looks at the money for food shopping his wife put on the table before leaving in the morning. Mumbling under his breath, he gathers himself up and shuffles to the kitchen. His legs feel like they do after running up and down hundreds of stairs. Vangelis opens the window a crack, and in the wind, he smells pine from the patch of green down below. He yawns and sweeps his eyes over houses pitched next to one another on a hill. The sky is growing dark and dogs bark in the distance.

He fixes a strong iced coffee and traces his steps back to the living room. Propping his legs up on the table, he turns on the TV and begins to roll a cigarette.

Vangelis is unemployed. His wife, Dina, short for Konstantina, works as a secretary for a magazine called *Raft*. Unemployed and homeless people sell the magazine on the streets for three euros, half of which goes into their pockets. It isn't much, but it puts food on the table. When Dina tried to talk him into becoming a vendor, he thought she was joking. But she wasn't.

"Look, wife. I'm not cut out for this job," he said. "If I see a funny expression or scorn in people's eyes, I might bash someone."

Vangelis was once a taxi driver. When he drove the taxi, the car was spick and span, and so was he. He never spoke to customers unless spoken to and never overcharged. He worked nights and knew the nooks and crannies of the city and all the shortcuts. But three years ago, his boss, for whom Vangelis had worked for seven years, gave him the boot. "I can't afford to have another driver," he said. But Vangelis knew the reason was because out of all the drivers, he would get the smallest compensation.

Since then, he has worked part-time jobs hauling furniture, carrying fruit and veggie crates in the public market, doing touch-up painting, and working as a one-time deliveryman at a gyro joint.

Dina marches into the living room that evening. Seeing layers of smoke hanging in the air and the television going, she puts her hands on her hips and glares at him with scorn.

"What's the matter, wife?" he says, flipping through channels.

"Didn't you say you'd quit smoking?"

"I will."

"When?"

"On Monday."

"I've lost count of how many times you've said that."

"Will you stop nagging?"

"I will when you stop smoking that shit."

He blows a streak of smoke from his mouth. "I'll quit smoking when you stop nagging."

Dina bites her lower lip and sneers at the way he drinks his coffee through a straw.

Vangelis smokes his roll-up down to the nub and begins to roll a fresh one. Sensing her still there, he turns his head and regards her with arched eyebrows.

"What?"

"What what?"

"Why are you standing there like a scarecrow?"

"We've been married for twelve years, and I've never seen you in such a mess before. When I woke up this morning, you were passed out on the couch, snoring, and with the same clothes you've been wearing for days. The whole living room smelled of booze."

"It was Stelios's birthday."

"It's always something, isn't it? Holidays, birthdays, name days, football wins—you name it. Look at you!" She stands in front of the television, which is showing football highlights, and says, "What are you grinning at?"

"Honey, who stole your cookie today?" He leans back on the sofa, cigarette dangling from his mouth.

His wife reminds him that he has been living on that sofa for months now, drinking coffees, smoking roll-ups, reading the silly papers—that's how she views Greek politics—and watching the news and films with American gangsters until the sun comes up.

"We don't eat together anymore, and we've stopped talking and looking into each other's eyes. I'm the one who cleans the house, goes shopping, cooks, and does the dishes. I'm sick and tired of all this. From now on, clean up your mess." She points at the dishes in the sink. "I work every day so we can pay the bills. I can't take much more of this. I feel like I'm going to have a nervous breakdown."

She flaps her hand at a passing cloud of smoke and reminds him that if she hadn't spoken with the people down at the electricity company to pay the sum they owe in installments, he wouldn't be watching that stupid screen now.

"Fortunately, my parents left us this flat. God rest their souls." She looks at the icon of the Virgin Mary with baby Jesus in her arms that stands on a vintage dresser pushed against a wall. A tea light burns in front of it. Then, she scoops up the remote from the table and presses the off button.

Vangelis sighs.

"We don't even make love anymore. You better get your act together or . . ." Her voice cracks, and tears come to her eyes.

"Or what?" he says, staring flatly. "What're you going to do? Throw me out? Woman, you think I get a kick out of this shitty life? Haven't I tried to get a job? Tell me what the hell am I supposed to do?"

They stare at each other for some time.

"I'm too old to get a fucking job and far too young to become a pensioner. You understand?"

"Wash yourself, change into fresh clothes, get rid of that silly beard, and do what a man is supposed to do," she says and storms out of the room.

Cigarette in his mouth, Vangelis puts on his black parka and takes forty euros from inside a folded unpaid bill in a drawer. Then he winks at the icon and blows out the flame. Smoke rises to the hanging photograph of his wife's parents. In the front pocket of his denim trousers, he puts a little jackknife.

As he nears the door, he hears his wife's determined voice.

"In a few days, my sister is coming over to stay with us for a while."

His eyes pop wide open. "What?" He hopes he misheard. He pokes his head around the door to the back room and sees his wife facing him, iron hissing in her hand.

"You heard me right."

"What about her kid?"

She rolls her eyes at him. "Where will her kid stay? With her drunkard husband?

But who can blame him? Vangelis thinks. *His bitch wife can turn even Jesus into a drunkard.*

"He's going to jail soon."

"Jail? Why?"

"Dodging taxes." She turns her back and goes back to ironing.

Vangelis breathes a sigh. As he opens his mouth to say something, she cuts in.

"She cried her eyes out on the phone. Three days ago, that bastard went home drunk, and all hell broke loose. He told her words and broke things. I know she has faults, but she's my sister. I'm the only family she has. She says she wants a divorce."

Vangelis hides his creased face behind the door, draws in a long breath, and makes a fist. The word *divorce* does him in. Images of "the bitch and her brat," as he calls them, flash in his mind like the trailer of a horror movie.

Her sister lives with her son and husband in Kastoria, a lake city near the Albanian border. He is a loyal and devoted husband, a good father, and a first-rate car dealer with whom Vangelis has had a few good laughs over the years. Not long ago, her husband reached for the bottle. He started going to tavernas after work, eating appetizers and drinking ouzo with his friends, and then passing out on the couch in his office.

Three months ago, after an argument with her husband, she stayed at their place for two weeks. At the tail end of that ordeal, Vangelis wanted to hang her upside down. The woman took three showers a day, changed her clothes and shoes continuously, and filed and painted her nails every Tuesday and Friday. She read gossip magazines, watched Turkish soap operas, spoke on the phone with her friends, and acted as if she were Sophia Loren. Everything deserved a complaint: At restaurants, the chefs lacked skills and the waiters were clumsy. In shopping malls, the service sucked, and she always asked to see the manager. The polluted air ruined her creamy skin, and all the taxi drivers were rude. She called them lowlifes.

"How can she say that, huh?" Vangelis said to his wife. "That bitch hasn't worked a day in her life."

"Don't call her a bitch, please. She's my sister."

Vangelis finds it hard to understand how on earth these sisters came out of the same belly. As for his sister-in-law's brat of a son, he has every PlayStation game under the sun and doesn't listen to anybody. Vangelis dreads the time he will have to spend with them. He tightens his grip on the handle of the door and feels like tearing it off.

"Fuck me," he says between his teeth.

"Do this for me. If you love me."

Vangelis lingers. It has been a long time since he last heard the word *love* from her mouth. A shudder runs down his spine. As he pulls the door closed, he hears her say: "Vangelis, can you please stay sober tonight?"

It's cold and dark outside. Lights in the lampposts and the windows of apartment buildings are on. Two crows sit on a balcony railing, observing as Vangelis stands at the top of the sloping street, feeling like a raging bull. He thinks back in time. Not since he was a teenager has he known how it feels to be free of worries. If he had married that rich woman who was after him, he would have an easy life—but she lacked the looks.

High above the buildings, Vangelis sees an airplane, its blinking light suddenly vanishing behind the hills. *One minute you see it, and the next minute it's gone*, he thinks, and wonders what it is like to sit on a plane and look out the window.

He starts down the hill, letting the streets guide him. In his face he feels the wind that moves in the acacia trees on either side of the street. He soon finds himself on the main road, where the air smells of smog. Shops are everywhere he looks: confectioneries, burger joints, clothes stores, supermarkets, etc. People in scarves and coats move up and down the narrow sidewalks, and some of them jaywalk between cars and taxis roaring up and down the road. Vangelis wishes he were behind a wheel, just driving and listening to the news, the weather, and the night music on the radio. He misses his night breaks; in different hangouts, he would meet up with other drivers, have a bite to eat, drink coffee, smoke cigarettes, and swap jokes and funny stories.

A bus crammed with people pulls out of a stop, a cloud of smoke mushrooming behind it. In the bus windows, Vangelis sees many sets of eyes lost in thought. He walks past kiosks, pharmacies, and gyro joints.[4] The smells drifting out of the restaurants remind him that he hasn't eaten since breakfast. But he doesn't have the patience to chew food. What he craves is a drink.

He makes a stop at a καφενείο. Men sit at tables outside, talking about football and politics, smoking cigarettes, and drinking beer and ouzo. Inside, the air is warm. Some men play cards and backgammon, cigarette smoke hanging over their tables. At the far end, others watch the evening news on a flat-screen as a journalist and three politicians representing three different parties talk about how to get out of the economic crisis.

Each politician occupies a window on the screen. One of them, a man with thin glasses and a thick mustache, says, "The only way our country could see the light at the end of the tunnel is by renegotiating the debt with Troika. Only if the debt is adjusted will the Greek people begin to breathe again."

Vangelis smirks and turns to a man in a white apron standing behind the bar counter.

"Brandy, please." He sticks a roll-up in his mouth.

The man puts a glass in front of him and asks Vangelis, "What do you think?"

"About what?"

"About what the man with the mustache just said."

"What did he say?" He heard the politician's words but wiped them from his mind almost immediately.

The barkeeper tells him what the man said, verbatim.

Vangelis drinks the brandy down in two gulps and then nods for another.

"So, what do you think?" The man looks at Vangelis as though he has all the answers.

"Please, don't make me laugh," Vangelis says. "Even if them bastards wiped out our debt, we'd make a new one. Our eyes are hungry, and our pockets deep." He draws on his cigarette and blows a column of smoke. "What do you think, brother? Are we or aren't we sons of bitches too?"

A voice from a table calls for more ouzo and an appetizer. "Be with you in a minute!" the man in the white apron says and turns his attention back to Vangelis. "If you ask me, doc, I'd tell you that we're good at destroying things. We're masters at it. We modern Greeks have this thing in us that makes us do absurd things. And even if we wanted to, we couldn't get rid of it. And you know why? Because this thing feeds on us. Yes sir. It does. And the hungrier we get, the larger and stronger this thing grows. The setting is great, but the actors are amateur fucks."

Vangelis smokes, drinks, and thinks. He is disappointed and angry with his wife. He doesn't mind that she told him off about work and all. They both know the score. How can he find a job when every day one thousand people lose theirs? What hurts him the most is that she didn't even ask him if it was okay to have her sister stay with them. *I'm not fucking invisible*, he thinks and swallows a mouthful of brandy.

Divorce my ass, he assures himself and gives an ironic smile. *That bitch can't even fry an egg. In a week, her husband will send flowers, call her on the phone, take her to dinner, screw her in the car, and that'll be the end of it. At least that much I know.* When he remembers that her husband may go to jail, his heart sinks. *But who knows*, he thinks *maybe something will happen to her*, and washes away the regret of the thought with another mouthful of brandy.

"If you love me . . ." his wife said. He idly rubs his beard. Images of a blond woman come to mind. He fishes his cell phone out of the pocket of his parka and searches through names. Then he puts his cell phone to his ear, but before it begins to ring, he hangs up. "The hell with it." He pays the bill and leaves.

Five months ago, Vangelis worked at a gyro joint as a deliveryman.

Many low-income people in Greece moonlight in such jobs. On one of his night shifts, a regular client, a blond woman, gave him a piece of paper with her number on it and smiled. Her name is Eleni. She is thirty-three years old, seven years younger than his wife, and has a dog named Duke. Her boyfriend has been doing time for robberies. A few weeks rolled by, and after a heated argument with his wife, Vangelis made the call. They met at a bar, had a few drinks, and ended up at her place. Vangelis and Duke became good friends. About two months ago, he changed his mobile number and pulled out because things were getting out of hand. He told Eleni that he loved his wife. But does he?

Outside, the traffic has thinned out. The brandy has put a rhythm in his feet, courage in his heart, and confidence in his head. With the wind in his face and the night lights in his sharp eyes, Vangelis feels good and right. *Alcohol is medicine*, he thinks and stops outside a well-lit supermarket. When he was a boy, there was a cinema called Eve at this spot. Where the ticket box office used to be now stands a woman in a red uniform stocking the shelves. On Sunday afternoons when he was a kid, he would watch karate movies with his friends, and right after, they would go to a park across the street and practice punches and kicks on one another.

Now Vangelis finds himself walking the back streets. He hasn't been here in years. His schoolmates used to live in this neighborhood. A few blocks away, the school he went to still stands on a hill. He and his friends would ride their bikes down to the seafront, sit on the dock by cranes, and with the sun in their faces, they would toss bread in the water and watch the seagulls fight over it. He remembers looking at the big ships and wondering about the places they had traveled.

These neighborhoods are going to the dogs, he thinks. A sweet melancholy works over him. The colors of the apartment buildings, the streets, and the sidewalks are faded, patched up, and cracked. The lights in the windows seem sad to him. Some people sit at tables on their balconies, hanging out and talking in languages he doesn't understand. Further down the street, he hears a couple arguing. With all the years gone by and the way his old stomping grounds look, by the time he gets out of the neighborhood, he has sunk deeper into his frustration.

He strides across the street through the headlights of a bus. He stands outside the gate of Saint Mary's church, lights a cigarette, and glances at some foreign men on a bench, who are smoking and drinking beer from cans. The urge to drink comes over him like lightning in a dark sky.

The air in the gyro joint is warm and smells of roasted meat. Vangelis notices a young couple sitting at a table. They're drinking retsina wine, and "Παλιόκαιρος,"[4] a Greek song by Paschalis Terzis, comes out of the speaker. The woman is blond with blue eyes. They're both wearing denim shirts. From under the guy's rolled-up shirtsleeve emerges the head of a snake tattoo. The snake's tongue is red, and its eyes are green, the same as the man's.

Behind the counter, a man with a double chin sweats over a grill. Turning two burgers over with a spatula, he swipes the back of his hand over his forehead and throws looks at the occupied tables and a tiny TV hanging on the wall. The waiter puts a handful of glasses and plates into the sink, washes his hands, and stops to catch his breath.

"Stop stalling," Double Chin says. "The food's getting cold." He points his spatula at the plates lined up in front of him. "Move your ass."

Vangelis orders a small pitcher of ouzo, salty fish, and olives and goes to the bathroom.

He runs the tap and washes his hands and face. In the mirror, he notices gray hairs in his sideburns, and in his beard too. *When did this happen?* he wonders. As he looks closer, he notices wrinkles on his forehead and around his eyes. He sighs.

Halfway through his second glass of ouzo at the counter, a tall teenage boy with a clean look comes up to him and asks, "Sir, may I

---

4. "Bad Weather"

have two euros to buy a sandwich?" He looks into Vangelis's red eyes and waits. He's wearing a blue athletic uniform and has a knapsack on his back. "I haven't eaten all day."

While Vangelis studies the teenager, Double Chin leans a hand on the counter and glares at the teenager. "Stop pestering my customers."

Vangelis puts a five-euro bill on the counter. "Make the kid a sandwich and give him a Coke."

"Hey you! Didn't you hear what I said? Get the hell out of my shop!" He waves his spatula at the kid.

"Calm down. You'll have a heart attack." Vangelis winks at the kid. "He's with me."

Studying the kid again, it occurs to him that if not for his wife's second miscarriage, his unborn son would be this age, maybe slim, tall, and neat as this kid with kind brown eyes, the same as his wife's. A pang spreads in his chest.

Double Chin's face turns as red as the piece of meat he just threw on the grill. "Pay and get the fuck out, both of you!"

From the tables, eyes turn. The man with the snake tattoo sits up in his chair. Vangelis pours ouzo into his glass and says, "Hey you!" Before Double Chin opens his mouth, Vangelis throws the ouzo in his face, scoops up the fiver, and, taking the kid by the elbow, they surge out of the store. By the time Double Chin scrambles from behind the counter, they have turned a corner and are hurrying along a narrow street. They laugh and run. They run and laugh.

Vangelis puffs and huffs and feels heavy in his chest. They go to another gyro joint and sit across from each other at a table. Vangelis drinks a beer and watches the kid devour his sandwich. Between bites, Vangelis learns he is a runaway and that he lives in Vasilika, a village on the outskirts of the city.

"I don't do that," the kid says.

"What don't you do?"

"Beg for money."

"I know."

"How do you know?"

"You look like a schoolboy who plays basketball."

The kid gives a thin smile and drinks from his Coke. His face turns serious. Holding the gyro in both hands, he says, "My mother works at a supermarket and my father drinks. He doesn't beat us, but lately, he shouts and breaks things around the house." He tells Vangelis that he is going to stay with his sister, who studies psychology at Aristotle University. He shows him the piece of paper with her address penned on it.

"She's a good sister. She asked me to meet her at the restaurant where she works as a waitress. I'm supposed to be there soon." He glances at his watch.

After a while, Vangelis puts him in a taxi, gives him the twenty-euro bill left from the forty that was meant to pay the apartment bills, and tells the driver where to take him. He also makes the boy promise that he will call his mother.

The strong wind feels good on his wobbly head. Vangelis goes through the gate of an old Byzantine church, the Twelve Apostles, moves on along the yard, stops under a tree, and settles his eyes on a lit window in the apartment building across the narrow street. When he sees a shadow behind the curtain, his eyes narrow to slits. Images come to his head of all the nights he spent up there. He sighs. Then the light goes off. It's ten o'clock. *This time of night,* he thinks, *Eleni usually walks Duke to the park just around the corner.*

Vangelis watches Eleni come out of the building, Duke wagging his tail and dashing ahead of her. She's wearing faded jeans, boots, and a black duffel coat. Her blond hair is held loosely with a rhinestone pin. When Duke noses the base of a tree, she fires up a cigarette and looks around as though she is expecting someone to show up.

Vangelis feels an intense desire to smell her shampooed hair, touch her soft skin, and hear her moan. As he looks on, his mobile rings. He knows it is his wife. He silences the phone and hides behind an acacia tree.

Eleni takes a few steps forward. Duke comes and stands next to her, raises his muzzle, and smells the air. He begins to trot toward where Vangelis stands. But in a moment, the sound of two cats fighting sends Duke dashing in the opposite direction. Calling after him, Eleni runs toward the corner of the church. Both Eleni and Duke disappear from sight.

Vangelis buys a beer from a kiosk, sits on the threshold of an apartment building, drinks, and watches the cars pass at low speed. He sees a woman with white hair and worn-out clothes pushing a cart with wonky wheels. She stops at a rubbish bin and rummages around. He watches her pull out a few empty beer cans and drop them in the cart.

The sound of a siren cuts the air. Cars pull over, and an ambulance speeds through, followed by a police motorcycle and two cars with rotating lights.

Vangelis shivers. All at once, images come to him from the night he and his wife rode in an ambulance, heading for the hospital where she had her second miscarriage.

Now he stands at the curb and observes the passersby who have gathered around the police vehicles and the ambulance. A bald man with a beer belly and a cigarette wedged between his lips rushes out of a nearby kiosk. "What the hell happened?" he says, face scrunched in curiosity. Both men now stand at the curb and stare at the small crowd that has assembled.

As a gust of wind moves in the acacia trees lining the narrow street, Vangelis passes a few cars. Vangelis passes a line of cars, the drivers standing behind open doors, craning their necks to see beyond the cluster of people as tension fills the air. The ambulance and the police cars have their doors open too, and a policeman talks on his radio. Two uniforms are on the ground, trying to keep things in order, and another two uniforms stand on a balcony and talk with a woman as they jot down details on their notepads. People stand at the entrances of apartment buildings and on balconies.

"A man jumped from the fourth floor," Vangelis hears a woman say with shock in her voice as he elbows through the crowd. "Good God," another woman says while a third woman adds that the man was married with three children and that he lost his job recently.

When Vangelis sees the body lying wrongly on the sidewalk, his heart clenches. He looks up at the fourth floor and then down to where the man lies; strangely, he supposes he feels the way the man felt the moment he hit the ground.

A cold sweat breaks out over his body as a wave of nausea kicks in. Buildings, cars, trees, and people start to spin. He tears away from the scene, thoughts rushing through his head like galloping wild horses. All at once, he has an indescribable need to go to a church. The feeling takes him by surprise and is so strong that he cannot shake its grip on him. Save for the few times he went to church for baptisms, weddings, and funerals, he has never felt the need to be inside one.

Head whirling, he puts a hand on a tree and empties his stomach. He gasps for air. A woman approaches him. "Are you okay?" she says with concern in her eyes.

He nods and vomits some more. "Hold on a second," she says and goes off. In a minute, she comes back and hands him a bottle of cold water. "Here."

Vangelis feels weak. He drinks from the bottle, splashes his face, and looks at her. She reminds him of his wife—the way she stands, her beautiful lips, the way her eyes care for people.

"Thank you."

She smiles.

Now Vangelis moves along the sidewalk, past closed shops, cafés, and burger joints, their smells turning his stomach again. "I'm sick and tired of everyone and everything," he says, and hastening his pace, he pictures the dead man. "Goddamn bitch life."

He pays no attention to the ancient open-air market, the square with the tall trees. For a few minutes, he feels at a loss. *Am I losing my fucking mind?* He pictures his wife. *I've lost hold on things. Look at me. I'm a mess. I slope about all day, doing nothing but drinking. Fuck me.* He grinds his teeth. *We're still young. Maybe we can convince ourselves again that it's never too late. Maybe we ought to begin to believe.*

He trudges up a steep street, crosses over St. Dimitrios Street, and climbs up the steps leading to the yard of a church. It is not just any church; it is St. Dimitrios, the protector of the city of Thessaloniki.

When he was a teenager, he experienced a vision. It was autumn and it was night, he remembers. He stood at the curb of a road busy with traffic and heard the galloping of a horse as clearly as if he were in a movie theater, watching a spaghetti Western. Right across from where he stood was a huge brown horse. He couldn't make out the rider, who was shrouded in bright light. In a moment, the huge horse and the bright rider vanished into thin air. Years later, when he revealed his experience to his grandmother, she told him to go to church and light a candle. She told him that the rider was Saint Dimitrios, his protector.

Inside, the church is quiet. The air is cool and smells of burned candles and incense. A wave of calmness washes through him. He drops a few coins into the slot of a wooden box and picks up a candle, lights it, and sticks it in the sand next to other lit candles. Their flames flare in a draft, casting trembling shadows about.

Vangelis kisses his fingers and puts them on a large icon of the Virgin Mary holding baby Jesus. He feels his heart slowing down. Then, he passes a row of wooden benches where a few people sit with their eyes closed and stands in front of a large icon of Saint Dimitrios. The relics of the saint lie in a decorative case, and pilgrims travel from the world over to view them.

Vangelis raises his weary eyes and gazes upon the slim image of the saint for quite some time. With a feeling of shame washing through him, he puts his hand on the icon and closes his eyes. *I promise to be a better man*, he tells himself. *Please, help me.*

Unexpectedly, Vangelis senses an indescribable relief and elation, as though he has elevated a few inches off the ground. An indefinite glimpse that patience, courage, and hope are mankind's only weapons against adversity fills his eyes with tears. With his gaze fixed on the image of his protector, he says softly, "Please, help me."

The Way You Look Tonight

PARIS KIRIAKIDIS felt like he was coming down with the flu. His bones ached, his throat was sore, and he had a splitting headache. *I can't afford to get sick*, he told himself and swept his feet out of bed. By the time his new job as a factotum had picked up speed, he had already fallen a few months behind with the electricity and telephone bills and run up a tab at a small family-run food store in the neighborhood.

Sighing, he shuffled to the bathroom and opened the cabinet. With a mouthful of water, he swallowed two pills, one of which was a placebo. He thought of his ex-girlfriend. The evening before, she'd called him on the phone. "Don't ever bother me again," he said and hung up on her.

Crossing the hallway, he heard the couple from next door fighting again. He often saw the girl's boyfriend killing time at a local καφενείο, drinking beers and playing backgammon and cards.

In the kitchen, a draft circled his ankles and put a shiver in his spine. Paris pressed his lips together at the sight of the sink filled with unwashed dishes. Then he stood in the chill of the open fridge as he stared at the sum total of his vittles: a jar of strawberry jam, two slices of yellow cheese, and a carrot. *Goddamn it*, he thought. *I forgot to buy eggs.*

He put a piece of yellow cheese on a slice of bread, spread a teaspoon of strawberry jam on top of it, and brewed coffee. He ate standing and staring vacantly at the wan light in the window.

It was a cold February morning. The fog that had settled over the city of Thessaloniki in the early hours began to dissolve. Wearing a pair of summer shorts and a creased T-shirt that read, Just Do It, and with a blanket draped over his broad shoulders, Paris stood before the balcony door. He peered out at the bus stop, where a few people stood huddled in their coats, breaths fogging the air. A small dog crossed the street, and Paris muttered, "Little shit." Each time he walked past the food store, the dog barked at him.

Many moons ago, he said to a friend, "Don't get me wrong, Dionisis. I agree: dogs are fine animals. But I love cats more." The truth was that he was afraid of dogs. When he was twelve years old, Paris had been chased by a sheepdog, and to escape he scrambled up a tree.

Now he glanced at the yard of an abandoned gas station. On the broken sign sat two crows. Smudged napkins, empty coffee cups, and beer cans lay scattered across the bases of the dusty pumps. A man with a beanie, a brown coat, and a backpack moved into the yard. Halfway through, the man stopped and looked up at Paris as though he had heard his name called. Paris took a sip from his coffee. If I hadn't owned this apartment, I would be like that poor guy, he thought and felt a shadowy gratitude.

Eight months ago, he had lost his job as a courier driver after working for the company for ten years. Following endless hours of waiting in line and filling out useless forms at the job centers, and with Dionisis's words—"You're good with your hands, brother"—playing over and over in his head for days, he decided to work as a factotum. He did plumb work and carpentry, replaced broken windows, and because he was sturdy, he hauled furniture. He landed the jobs by word of mouth. Paris Kiriakidis was punctual, meticulous, and quick. Working as a factotum earned him enough to put food on the table and pay the bills.

Part of the money he earned came from helping an old lady with her chores on Tuesdays and Fridays. And it was one of the jobs, if it could be called that, he loved the most. It put his soul and mind at ease. The old lady was a retired literature teacher and didn't have any children. Now she gave classical piano lessons to kids. And since she suffered from cataracts in one eye, one of his tasks was to read stories to her.

His apartment was on the first floor of an apartment building located near the main train station. He had inherited it from his mother, who had lived in it for years with his father, his older sister, and himself. His father, an even-tempered man and a top-notch painter, had fallen from a twelve-meter scaffolding when Paris was fourteen. He fell into a coma for months, and despite the doctors' best efforts to bring him back to life, he never opened his eyes again.

After months of mourning, the family gradually came to see the bright side of life again. Their mother, an ample woman with thick dark hair and brown eyes, started working at a local bakery. Every day, she brought home-baked bread, spinach or cheese pies, and cookies. She never invited any man to the apartment and never got married again.

She took loving care of her children, but she could be overprotective. Even when her children were old enough to look after themselves, she always wanted to know where they were and who they were with. She called them on the phone every day, and when she met with them, she always found something to say about their health. "Paris, my son, you need to put some meat on your bones." And to her daughter she would say, "Angeliki, my sweet darling, you look pale. Are you sure you eat enough?"

When Paris came back from the army, his mother moved into her family home in Nea Pella in the valley. "I can't live in the city any longer. I feel suffocated. Especially with the air pollution and the smog from the pellets people burn these days," she said, putting her hands on her throat and rolling her eyes.

Every other week, Paris half-heartedly drove his rattletrap to the village, where he stayed with her a day or two at most. He once said to Dionisis, "Don't get me wrong, my friend. I love my mother. I owe her my existence. But she thinks she knows everything and talks like a machine gun." With his hands, he mimicked a machine gun, pointed it at his friend, and pretended to fire away, making rattling sounds. His friend broke into laughter. "Yeah, man. Laugh all you want."

When he stayed with her, eating out was out of the question. The food at restaurants was never good enough for her. But Paris didn't mind because she was an excellent cook. He believed her food could even bring back the dead. He had yet to taste better burgers with roasted potatoes, fried fish, veggies, bean soups, and casserole dishes, let alone her syrupy dessert, ραβανί[5] .

In winter, mother and son would sit at the kitchen table or in the living room, and if it was summer, they would spend time together on the patio. She liked solving crossword puzzles daily, listening to psalmodies on the radio, talking about the mishaps and wrongdoings of the villagers, and trying to talk her son into finding a better girlfriend than whichever one he was dating at the time. In his mother's eyes, every woman he dated was worse than the one before. They were either too skinny or short, tall, or flashy. They talked too much or too little or didn't talk at all.

"The right woman hasn't walked in your path yet, my son. When I'm long gone," she would say, lowering her eyes to a cup of coffee or a piece of pie, "you'll nod and say to yourself, *My mother was right.*"

The only woman she spoke well of was Maria. And that was after they had broken up. "Maria wouldn't do that" or "Maria was prettier," his mother would say and make his sense of regret swell up. When Maria wanted to have kids, Paris hadn't felt ready. Sometimes, he wondered what it would be like if the three children she had now were his.

As for his sister, Angeliki, save for a few squabbles here and there, it all went well between them. For over five years, they had lived

---

5. Ravani is a delicious Greek wet cake made with semolina, ground almonds, yogurt, lemon zest, and sugar syrup

together in the apartment until she fell in love with a Greek guy who owned a Greek restaurant in Munich, Germany. When Paris lost his job, she invited him to come work in the restaurant. But he turned her down flat.

"Thank you, sis, but I'm good. I'd rather die of hunger than come over there and work for your son-of-a-bitch husband," he told her over the phone. He didn't like her husband much. And it wasn't because their political views differed, nor because they supported different football teams—Paris was an Aris fan and her husband a PAOK one; it was because he exploited his employees. He made them work long hours, gave them one day off a week instead of two, and didn't pay them enough. On the flip side, though, Paris was happy with the way the man treated his sister and their two teenage girls, whom loved Paris dearly. His brother-in-law was an excellent provider.

Paris sat on the sofa and put his legs up on the table, next to the remains of the chicken he'd sent out for last night and two crumpled cans of beer. *Playboy* and *Hustler* magazines lay on the table too, along with porn DVDs.

He searched his mind for any jobs he needed to deal with today. Yes. He remembered that a woman had asked him to replace her bathroom window at three o'clock. He liked her voice on the phone and was curious to meet her.

In the living room, furniture was crammed with books on philosophy, psychology, photography, history, religion, and literature. Books were stacked on the floor against the wall, too. On a central table sat the clay bust of a man screaming. Paris had studied fine arts for five years at Aristotle University, but even though he graduated at the top of his class, he rarely practiced what he'd learned.

It was quarter to one. He rose from the sofa and moved over to the bust. The air smelled of paint and clay. As he studied his creation, his eyes clouded. "Son of a bitch!" He grabbed hold of the bust, threw it on the floor, and kicked the cracked head angrily.

In the steaming shower, he closed his eyes and tried to picture scenes from the porno he had watched the night before. He took hold of his penis and began to work on it rhythmically. When he felt it getting stiff, he started to get his hopes up. But as soon as his penis reached full erection, it went limp again. "You bitch! You ruined my life."

It had all started after he lost his job. By and by, his relationship took a nosedive—especially in the bedroom. Paris knew that he was in a serious fix because of all the things his most recent ex-girlfriend, Popi, had loved, the most important for her was sex. She was a medium-sized woman with dark hair, green eyes, solid hips, and an ample bosom. For the three years of their relationship, they'd had sex every day. One night, when he was out of sorts, she asked him if he still found her attractive. "Baby, give it a rest, will you? Don't get me wrong, but I'm drained of energy. Even Captain America needs a break. Do you understand? Popi?"

But once he was unemployed, they hardly did it. And when they tried to go at it, he performed poorly. The doctors told him he suffered from erectile dysfunction. They told him it happened to many men his age, being over forty. They put his problem down to stress and suggested he seek psychological counseling. But he didn't have faith in that. Running her fingers through his rich hair, Popi had said, "I love you, hon. We'll weather it."

Weeks dragged into months. They tried all the tricks in the book, but his penis stayed down, as though it had a mind of its own. The only time Paris got a proper erection was when he first woke up, but whenever they tried to take advantage of that, it went up in smoke.

And so, six months ago, Popi had pulled out on him. All that "Don't worry, hon; I love you" business jumped out the window. Standing in the living room, suitcases by her feet and a slim cigarette between her fingers, she said, "Since I don't want to cheat on you, I've decided to leave you. I have needs you can't fulfill."

Paris had been sitting on the sofa, staring at her in stunned disbelief, and not because she was leaving him—he had anticipated her departure—but rather because of the way she behaved. She was suddenly a stranger and not the woman he had spent the past three years of his life with. And that was that. No getting drunk, no phone calls, no nothing. That day, he took a long walk along the seafront and decided that he would never forgive her. *She isn't worth fretting over*, he told himself, as he gazed at the tankers anchored far out at sea. *I'll be just fine*. But her words—"I have needs you can't fulfill"— remained wedged in his head.

It was never easy for Paris to forgive people who hurt others. Once, over supper, he told Dionisis, "Don't get me wrong, my friend. Yes, I can forgive a child or a young person, but not grown-ups. A true character, my friend, is shown through hardships." He also told his friend that forgiveness was a Christian act, and Paris didn't like the priests. "It's their fault we're morally limp. They forgive sinners too easily. And who the fuck gave them the right to do so, eh?"

The last thing on his mind when he went to sleep and the first in the morning when he awoke was neither the lack of jobs nor the bills he had to pay, but rather his freaking erectile dysfunction.

After his shower, he headed out of the apartment. He walked past the food store with his hands tucked in his black duffel coat, and the shapely woman behind the register inside looked out at him as if to say, "You've got to clear your debt soon." But she couldn't force him to do it; many in the neighborhood ran tabs as well.

Inside the jalopy, he blew into his cold hands and shivered. He looked into the rear-view mirror and finger-brushed his long hair back, then turned on the ignition, impatient for the engine to warm up so he could turn on the heater. The yellow car, a Fiat Seicento, rolled for a few meters and then stopped. He turned the ignition again. "Come on, you," he said. "Come on!"

At a traffic light, under the gray sky, an acrobat with a tall hat, black circles around his eyes, and a white-painted smile was juggling five balls. Before the light turned green, he held out his hat, and some drivers dropped in a coin.

Paris doubled-parked, put on the blinkers, and hurried into a warm little glazier shop that smelled of freshly baked cookies. He heard a woman on the radio talking about the earthquake on Kefalonia Island and all the families that would have to live out in the open for God knew how long. Behind a desk was an old man sporting a thick, gray mustache and a head full of gray hair. A floor heater glowed near his feet.

"Paris! How are you, my son?" He smiled. "Been a spell."

"How you been these days?"

"Since I'm still breathing . . . Coffee?"

"No, thank you." He noticed with curiosity the suitcases at the base of a ladder leading up to a loft.

"I moved to the loft two days ago. It's big enough for an old man like me."

"Nice move." Paris smiled. "Many people work from home."

The old man smiled too and asked what had brought Paris to his store. Paris handed him a piece of paper with the measurements of the broken window. "I have to be there in half an hour."

"Don't worry about a thing. I'll have it all cut and wrapped for you in two shakes of a lamb's tail."

Half an hour later, holding the window glass in one hand and his toolbox in the other, Paris spotted the woman's name on the intercom. He pressed the button and waited, his breath visible in the chill.

"Hello. Who's this?"

"This is Paris. I'm here to fix your bathroom window."

The intercom crackled. "Who?"

He cupped his mouth with his hand. "This is Paris. I'm here to fix your bathroom window."

"Oh. Take the elevator to the third floor. It's the door at the end of the corridor."

The corridor was dark, cold, and smelled of french fries. Paris switched on the light, and as he walked, from various apartments he heard a television, a woman telling her kids it was time to eat, and a dry cough.

After he buzzed the bell, he heard shuffling sounds and saw a moving shadow under the door.

"Who's this?" the woman said.

He wanted to say it was Santa Claus. "This is Paris." He heard a dog whining. "I've come over to fix your bathroom window."

"Can you step back so I can see you?"

With his ear against the door, he said, "Lady, you got a dog?"

"Yes. Why?"

"Look, lady, can you put your dog on a leash?"

"Could you move back a bit so I can see you?"

Paris stepped back and lifted the glass just below his chin, feeling as though he were posing for a photograph.

At the other end of the corridor, a man in a black coat started to bang on a door. "Open up. I know you're in there. Open up!" He waited for an answer. Then he put his ear against the door and banged again. "Neoklis, listen carefully. If I don't get my rent by Monday, I'll throw you two out. Do you hear me?" The man turned and looked at Paris.

Poor guys, Paris thought and felt a sense of gratitude for not having a pimp breathing down his neck.

As the woman opened the door, saying, "You can't be too careful these days," Paris saw a white dog trying to get past her feet.

"Lady, can you put your dog on a leash?" He stepped back. "If it comes near me, I'll kick it."

Seeing his expression, the woman laughed. Then she took the dog by its collar and put it into a room. As she was closing the door, the dog barked at Paris, who had his eyes fixed on it. *What a stupid creature*, he thought and moved into the apartment.

The space was clean and warm, and the air smelled of baked bread.

"Laika doesn't bite." She gave a nervous smile.

In a few breaths, he felt relieved. His eyes swept over an armchair where a book lay open, then over two loaves of bread under a towel on the kitchen board and a basket with bananas and apples on the kitchen table.

The young woman tucked a strand of hair behind her ear and crossed her slim arms across her chest. He liked the smell of her shampooed hair, the way she held herself.

"My name's Anna."

Anna, he thought. Since he didn't see a ring on her finger, he wondered if she was single. "My name's Paris."

"This way." She took him to the bathroom.

He put his gear down, took off his coat, and got to work.

When he was placing in the new window, he felt Anna at the door.

"Would you like a cup of coffee?"

"Sure. Coffee sounds good."

When he finished the job, he put away his tools and began to wrap up the broken glass.

"Coffee's ready," she said, standing at the door.

As he joined her, he felt as though they'd known each other for a while. He didn't know whether she was married or had a boyfriend. *Maybe she's a widow*, he thought and hoped, but when his eyes glimpsed the cup with multiple toothbrushes, he cursed his luck.

They sat drinking coffee at the table. He asked her where she got his number, and she said he had been recommended by a friend of hers, Meropi. Paris nodded. They talked about this and that. Moments later, she glanced at the clock on the wall and reached inside her bag.

"How much do I owe you?"

"Twenty-five euros."

Paris noticed nervousness in her voice, heard a key turning in the lock, and a pudgy man came in with a questioning expression on his tense face.

Anna said, "This gentleman is the glazier."

"You don't say." The man moved closer, his breath smelling of tobacco and alcohol. "Anna, what have we got here? Maybe we should ask the gentleman to dinner. What do you say, huh?" he said and gave a wicked grin. "Mister, do you like desserts?" He lifted the box he was holding. "I've brought cupcakes."

What a jerk, Paris thought.

The man continued, "But before we do that we should check if Mr. Glazier"—he dragged the last word—"has done a decent job," and he started for the bathroom.

"Please," Anna said with worry in her eyes. "Don't say anything. He's a good man. He lost his job recently."

"Will you be okay?"

She nodded and showed Paris to the door.

When he got home, it was dark, and his place was cold. He flipped on the lights and put away the food he had bought from the store. In the living room, he brought the floor heater nearer the sofa and turned on the TV. Paris made a face at the sight of Greek politicians and flipped to another channel. But the same images came on. Journalists and politicians were holding forth about how they would reduce the debt, how they would bring prosperity, and how much better they were at achieving things than other politicians belonging to different political parties in Greece. *Empty rhetoric*, Paris thought and switched off the flat-screen.

Lying on the sofa with his arms tucked behind his head, he stared at the ceiling. He couldn't get Anna out of his head. He still smelled her shampooed hair. In a moment, his mobile began to ring. It was his mother. She always rang at the same time every single day. Paris didn't feel like talking, but if he didn't answer it, she would be worried sick.

The next day was a Friday, and he looked forward to it. He had already chosen the short story he would read to the old lady. It was entitled "A Good Man Is Hard to Find" by Flannery O'Connor.

At ten the next morning, the old lady stood at the threshold of an old neoclassical building, under the indifferent sky. She wore her hair in a bun, red lipstick on her lips, and a brown coat, the color of her good eye. The cataract had made the other eye look like a scuffed marble. Her fingers were long, and her nails were painted red. She lit a cigarette and tucked her wrinkled hand into the pocket of her coat.

"Ermioni!"

She smiled. "Paris, my son, you'll catch your death out here."

"How's Ermioni today?" He kissed her softly on her cheek.

"I am better than yesterday."

He took the shopping trolley and let the old lady grip his arm. They walked and talked. They were going to an old market called Modiano just a few blocks away.

"What's on the menu today?" he asked. The only times he ate well were when he visited his mother and when he spent time with Ermioni.

"I thought of baking salmon in the oven with spinach and mashed potatoes. How does it sound to you?"

"Divine!"

The market was in the middle of the city. Narrow alleys crisscrossed the space in front of roofed stores. The smell of meat hanging from hooks and fresh fish lying in cases filled the air, along with the scents of spices and herbs, tea, and coffee. Bare bulbs shone over fruit and veggies. The baritone voices of the sellers with long aprons and galoshes boomed in the space. They called out how good, cheap, and fresh their products were. Ermioni and Paris picked their way through people in the alleys, talked with shop owners, and put bags into the trolley. She smoked, nodded at their comments, and laughed at their jokes. The shop owners called her by name.

At the tail end of their shopping excursion, they went to a cafeteria near the market. They always sat at a round table in a corner by a window, drank espresso, and talked about their latest news. Paris enjoyed watching the old lady. So precise and gentle, so slow and subtle were her movements that in his eyes, the rest of the world seemed as though it were in a perpetual race.

Before they left the coffee shop, Ermioni said, "What's troubling you, my son?"

"I was just thinking."

"Would you like to share your thoughts with me?"

Paris turned the coffee cup on the saucer. "I was just thinking about a woman I met yesterday. I went to her place to fix a window."

Ermioni waited for him to go on, but he didn't.

"And?

"I can't get her out of my mind."

"Why don't you text her?"

"I can't do that."

"Why not?"

"Because she's with someone."

"I see."

There was silence.

Ermioni finished smoking her cigarette, and they stood and moved along. As they turned the outside corner, a woman seated on the ground with a child in her arms held her hand out. Ermioni put a two-euro coin in the woman's dirty hand.

The old lady's apartment was on the fourth floor of her building. The air inside was pleasantly warm and smelled of oranges. Her apartment had high ceilings and three bedrooms along a long hallway, a spacious living room and dining area, and a good-sized kitchen. The first time Paris entered the apartment Ermioni was born in, he felt as though he had stepped sixty years back in time, especially when he looked at the black-and-white photographs standing on the heavy, antique furniture in the living room—photographs of the old lady as a young woman, of her parents, of her dead brother, and of a Thessaloniki he never knew.

On the walls hung images of the city at night: people holding umbrellas and crossing traffic lights, a taxi with a man and a woman in the back, the docks, an empty bus stop, two men on bar stools hunched over their drinks. Ermioni's father had been a photographer.

Thick curtains hung behind armchairs and sofas upholstered in faded blue and crimson velvet, and candleholders, thick with wax, were sprinkled about. Behind the piano stood a wall-to-wall bookcase. Papers, books, pencils, and ashtrays lay all across the dusty furniture.

In the kitchen, Ermioni put on the kettle. Paris sat at the kitchen table, listening to Schubert's Allegretto. She prepared the food, put two mugs of herbal tea on the table, lit a cigarette, and coughed.

"Ermioni, don't get me wrong, but you should throw your smokes in the bin." Seeing the concern on his face, she gave a thin smile. "It's not funny."

"Paris, my son. Thanks for caring about my well-being, but smoking is a part of me. If I quit, a part of me will surely wither away, and the rest will follow suit. Smoking is like a ritual for me. It is solace. Besides, in a year, I will turn eighty."

They looked at each other.

"Now, would you like to tell me about that woman?" She blew a cloud of smoke toward the ceiling.

"Ermioni, I've got nothing to say, really."

"Are you sure?"

"Of course I'm sure."

They stayed quiet, drinking their tea and listening to classical music on the radio.

Night started to darken the windows. After they ate, he did the dishes, put out the rubbish, and brewed coffee. Ermioni sat in an armchair, her legs propped up on a stool and covered with a woolen blanket, and closed her eyes. She liked to listen to the sounds Paris made as he busied himself about the place. She had told Paris that this was the way she wanted to go. "Just drifting away into those wonderful sounds."

Holding a book, Paris sat on the sofa. He was glad to have found a soul who loved stories as much as he did. The arrangement was that on Mondays, she would pick a story, and Fridays would be his turn. Last time, she had chosen a story by Chekov, "The Lady with the Dog."

"I'd like to read to you a story I very much enjoy," Paris said, thumbing through the book. "It's called 'A Good Man Is Hard to Find.'"

"It sounds like a delightful story." Cigarette between her fingers, she got out of her chair. "But I had another story in mind for today." She ran her finger over a row of books and drew one out. "Have you ever read anything by Raymond Carver?"

"No, I haven't. But I've heard the name. Is he any good?"

She handed him the book and sat back down in the armchair. "He's one of my favorite American writers," she said. "I'd like you to read me a story entitled 'The Cathedral.' Would you do me the honors?"

Frowning, Paris studied the cover and read the author's bio. "Hmm. What's the story about?"

"It's about a blind man who pays a visit to a married couple. The husband has never met the blind man. But he has heard about him from his wife. For many years, his wife and the blind man keep in touch by recording tapes and writing letters to each other. The husband is not looking forward to meeting the blind man, but to please his wife, he promises to behave. At the end of the story, something extraordinary happens between the blind man and the husband, which will change the way the latter looks at life."

"Sounds interesting."

"It certainly is." Ermioni closed her eyes, and a peaceful expression came over her wrinkled face.

Paris cleared his throat and began to read. "This blind man, an old friend of my wife's, was on his way to spend the night. His wife had died . . ."

Paris enjoyed reading aloud. He used to read to a few of his girlfriends. He had a rich and confident voice, a voice that could be trusted. Halfway into the story now, his voice was steady and sonorous, rising and falling and then rising again to the flow, rhythm, and music of the prose.

"My eyes were still closed," Paris read. "I was in my house. I knew that. But I didn't feel that I was inside anything."

When he read the last sentence, he drew in a deep breath and stayed still for a while, deep in thought. The story was written in such a way that he felt as though he were part of it. He smelled and ate the food they ate, heard the sounds, smoked the joint, and saw the cathedral. Before he stood to go, he sat for a while, contemplating the story's message.

"That was a remarkable story," he said excitedly and glanced at Ermioni. But she was fast asleep. For a moment, he observed her serene expression and wondered how it felt to be an old person. Then he pulled the blanket up to her neck, made sure that everything was in order, pulled on his jacket, and walked out the door.

As he drove home, the story stayed with him. That night, he fell asleep reminiscing about his life—the things he'd done and the things he shouldn't have done. "The Cathedral" made him realize some truths about life, existence, and himself.

A few days later, while he was having coffee, his face took on a glow. He rushed to his feet and began to pace. *The blind man couldn't see with his eyes*, Paris reminded himself, *but he could see with his mind*. It was sight versus vision. "How could I be so stupid?" Through the blind man and the suspicious husband, Paris realized that a person didn't need eyesight to see the world. He also realized that change comes from within.

He did the dishes, cleaned the kitchen, threw the *Playboys*, the *Hustlers*, the porn CDs, and the broken clay head in a box, and put the box out on the balcony next to the rubbish. *I've been my own worst enemy*, he thought.

Days rolled into weeks. It was late March. Paris decided to pay off the debts, starting with the family that ran the food store. He couldn't stand the woman's sharp glances any longer. And so, he kept his nose to the grindstone. He painted apartments, hauled furniture, went to see his mother, and met with the old lady. Every day, he would wake up early, have a full breakfast, go to the library to borrow books by Raymond Carver and other authors, and take walks along the seafront or uphill toward the fortress.

One day, Paris woke to the sound of his mobile. He had fallen asleep on the sofa with the television on. He opened his eyes and saw sunlight streaming into the living room through the balcony door. His shoulders, back, and arms were stiff from all the furniture he had hauled the day before. At the other end of the line was a woman who was wondering if he could fix the clogged pipe in her kitchen.

"Ma'am, who gave you my number?" He raised himself on his elbow.

"Anna."

"Anna?"

"A few weeks ago, you—"

"I remember," he said and heard her light a cigarette. He wondered how things stood for Anna.

"Paris, can you fix it?"

He glanced at the clock; it was twelve. He wrote down her address on a piece of paper. She lived in Panorama, an affluent suburb of the city.

"Does four work for you?" she said.

"I'll be there at four then, Mrs. . . . ?"

"Martha. My name's Martha."

"See you soon, Martha."

"Okay."

Her tobacco-rough voice excited him.

The sun was high in the sky, and the nippy fresh air smelled of spring. At a traffic light, a lanky man with dark skin, thick black hair, and worn clothes sprayed water on the windshield of a car and began to wipe it down.

In half an hour, Paris got to the Panorama district and parked the car in front of an iron gate of a two-story house. He smelled burned wood and pine in the air. After speaking his name into the intercom, he walked through the gate into a yard where sunlight streamed down onto the pine trees, casting long shadows over the nearby vegetable garden and flower beds.

"Mr. Fixit, come on in," Martha said from the front door, holding a small ashtray and flicking the ash of her slim cigarette. She wore a crimson robe, her hair was in curlers, and her fingernails were painted red.

The furniture in the living room was modern. The space was spick and span and smelled of the roses in the vase on the dining table. Paris studied Martha and thought that the wrinkles about her black eyes and her full lips made her attractive. Smoking and talking, she led him to the kitchen, where the voice of Edith Piaf drifted from the radio.

"Look at this mess!" She pointed at the unwashed dishes in the sink. On the floor was a large wet towel. "I hate mess."

Paris put down his toolbox, kneeled, and put his hand on the siphon as water dripped into a bucket right under it.

"Is it serious?"

He raised his eyes past her slender legs. "Yes, it suffered a heart attack."

They laughed.

"Would you like an Americano?" she said cheerfully.

"Why not," he said, moved things from under the sink and lay down on the floor on his back. When he heard the espresso machine going, a rush of positive energy spread in his chest. In a few minutes, she came and stood by his feet, and as she bent slightly, Paris saw the curves of her breasts against her robe.

"Mr. Fixit, your Americano is ready."

They sat at the kitchen table by the window. Martha brought her cup to her lips and kept her penetrating eyes on him.

"How's the heart operation going?"

Paris smiled. "The patient needs a new valve. But he's in good hands."

"I don't doubt it." She smiled playfully, opened the window a crack, and lit a slim cigarette with a silver Zippo. They drank the coffee, made small talk, and took quick looks out the window. One of the things Paris loved about being a factotum was meeting different people every day.

Beyond the fence, a woman was shaking out a blanket on a balcony.

Martha said, "Do you see that woman over there?"

"What about her?"

"She was a good friend of mine. She has two kids and a prick of a husband. On the first floor of that house live her parents, and on the third lives her sister with her husband and her two kids. If I were in her shoes, I'd simply die. I mean, I love my parents and my brother but . . ." She drank from her coffee. "Don't you agree, Mr. Fixit?"

He nodded yes.

They stayed silent for a while.

"So, where was I?" Her eyes searched for an answer.

"You were talking about your friend over at that house."

She half rolled her eyes and sighed. "Yeah, as I said, Stella and I were very good friends, but her prick husband ruined our friendship. One night, they were throwing a party. In the kitchen, he put his hands low around my waist and tried to kiss me. After I considered my options, I decided to keep quiet. But guess what?" She blew smoke toward the window. "He told Stella that it was me that made a pass at him. Can you believe that prick?"

Paris caught sight of a man stepping out on the balcony, now stretching his arms and yawning. "Is her husband that man over there?"

"Speak of the devil."

"He looks like a weasel."

"Tell me about it."

"What happened after that?"

"I tried to convince her that he was lying, but she wouldn't listen. She couldn't believe that her husband would do such a thing. That weasel put our friendship in the ground."

"Don't get me wrong, but in every job, group of friends, or family, there is always a weasel or two. I know that much."

A quiet moment passed as they listened to the music on the radio. Martha sighed. "Anyway . . ."

Paris thanked her for the coffee and got back to work.

Since it was Saturday, it took him two hours to find a gasket for the siphon. When he got back to her place, the sun had started to set on the kingdom. The space smelled of cooked food, and ambient music came from the speakers. Paris caught Martha cooking in the kitchen. She was wearing a black skirt and crimson shirt, and her black, wavy hair fell to her shoulders. *She's so beautiful*, he thought.

Martha put a pie dish on the counter, and the way she looked at him made Paris feel as though they were a couple.

"I made roasted chicken with potatoes and an apple pie."

He made to speak, but she beat him to it.

"I've got white wine as well." She lifted a bottle she had opened.

Paris knew where things were going, and only an idiot would turn down such an invitation. But hesitation crept up on him.

"What's wrong?"

"Nothing's wrong. Why?"

"Okay, I get it. Mr. Fixit has a girlfriend."

"No, I haven't."

"So, what's the problem then?"

"Who said there's a problem?"

"Here." She put a glass of wine in his hand. He smiled faintly and held her warm and smiling eyes. "White wine is my favorite drink."

They touched glasses and drank a mouthful. Paris said it was delicious and set the glass on the kitchen table. "I'll get on with my work."

Once he'd fixed the siphon, he tidied up the mess and put away his tools. The day grew darker outside. Martha had dimmed the lights and lit candles. They ate at the kitchen table, talking, drinking, and laughing. She asked about his life, and he told her mostly about his work. He shared stories about different people and how he enjoyed spending time with the old lady. She found his work interesting.

"Can you please get us another bottle of wine?" Martha asked cheerfully.

Paris rose and moved to the fridge.

"Not that one. Bring the one next to that. Bingo!"

He sat back down and filled their glasses. Now it was his turn to learn a few things about her life. She told him that she had been married for five years.

"He's as handsome as you are." She took a sip from her wine, all the while holding his gaze. "The marriage was arranged. I agreed to it because I wanted to help both of us." She told him that they had known each other for a few years before they got married; the man was a homosexual but didn't want his parents to find out. "We slept in the same bed, but that was that. I felt like I was sleeping with my brother. Once, we tried to do it, but we ended up playing cards." She laughed as if she had just watched the scene from the dark window. "Oh, God!"

Paris gazed at Martha in amazement.

Rolling the end of her cigarette on the edge of the astray, she continued, "We were best friends. His family own a winery and real estate offices all over Greece. Fanis and I traveled the world. We were good at acting and covering up our affairs. But after a few years, we got tired. When we went to Tokyo, he fell in love with a Japanese man, and now they live together. When he told his parents about it, all hell broke loose. His father turned against me and tried to throw me out of the house and take back the car and the jewels his son had given to me, along with two flats and money in the bank. But they couldn't do anything because it was all in my name. Fanis took good care of me."

Paris rubbed his beard. "That's some story you got there."

Running her finger along the rim of the glass, she said, "That's life. We talk every week on the phone, but his parents still haven't come to terms with him being a homosexual."

She also told him that the money she made from renting the flats was just about enough to make ends meet. "Bloody Troika," she said. "I'm thinking of selling one of them."

"Bad timing."

"I know. But it looks like I'll have to do it pretty soon."

They opened another bottle of wine and moved into the living room. On the way, she put her hand low around his waist and smiled. "That's one of my favorite songs," Martha said as Frank Sinatra sang, "The Way You Look Tonight."

She peeled her hand off him and lifted it gracefully in the air.

Listening to Sinatra sing, "Someday, when I'm awfully low, when the world is cold, I will feel a glow just thinking of you and the way you look tonight," Paris sat on the soft sofa and watched her take a few dancing steps toward the center of the room, holding her glass by its rim. She swirled around slowly, now looking straight into his eyes, wiggling her hips and snapping her fingers in perfect sync with the rhythm of the music.

His whole body electrified, and feeling a sweet tipsiness, Paris got to his feet as Frank sang, "Lovely, don't you ever change."

He slid his hand around her waist and pulled her toward him gently. He felt her velvet touch, her warm, sweet wine breath on his neck, and smelled her perfume. When she slid her leg between his and pressed her bosom against his chest, he felt his manhood stiffen.

They danced slowly, effortlessly. His gaze sneaked through the half-open door of the bedroom and fell on a duvet and two pillows bathed in the soft bedside light. Paris closed his eyes, and with Martha's mesmerizing aroma, he let himself drift to the melody of the music.

Eyes That Hold Nothing at All

A DARK-SKINNED man in a denim shirt sits at his kitchen table, next to a dark window. A floor heater burns by his feet. On the table is an ashtray filled with cigarette butts, a bottle of brandy, and a baseball hat with the initials NYPD. Between his fingers, a cigarette burns. The man's brown eyes are pensive.

Costas is at the end of his rope. In the past weeks, worries have started to wear him down. If he doesn't pay the loan installments to the bank and clear the debt to the suppliers of his καφενείο, he will have to sell a plot of land he inherited from his parents for next to nothing and maybe still lose his business. Such a scenario would surely finish him for good.

After weeks of unsuccessful attempts to gather the money, his mind offered a solution that baffled him beyond all reason. Since then, he has eaten and slept little, and drinks and smokes more than usual. The hard truth is that, whether he likes it or not, he must do the unthinkable. And the sooner he does it, the better.

I've planned it down to the last detail, he thinks *and knocks back the rest of the brandy in his glass. On Thursday night, I'm going to the cemetery.*

After his wife was killed in a car crash two years ago, he couldn't land a job as a bricklayer—a skill his father had taught him and a job he enjoyed working for years. But no one in this town or anywhere else he knew was lifting so much as a pebble. The economic crisis caved in the construction industry and buried the Greek dream. At the time, his wife's small bookstore in Giannitsa brought in most of the money needed to support himself and their daughter, Thalia.

Following the passing of his wife, Costas made an effort to keep the shop running, but the economic crisis forced him to close its doors.

Half a year after the funeral, fearing he would never be able to find another job, he mortgaged his house to the bank and bought the shop he now owned from an old man. "If you look after the shop," the man said to him with his rough voice, "the shop will look after you too." To give Costas a good head start, the old man stayed on for a few weeks and showed him the ropes.

In the following months, Costas poured all his energy into his business. He worked from dawn to dusk seven days a week with unbending persistence and patience. He is a lean and strong man, solid as a rock, who has never known how it feels to have the flu, run a fever, have a toothache, headache, or cigarette cough. When he turned fifty, his wife convinced him to have a checkup at the hospital. All the tests came out fine, and when he told the lung specialist that he had smoked a pack of cigarettes a day since he was in the army, the doctor said, "It must've been someone else's lungs I just examined." Save for a few scrapes and scratches here and there, Costas has never had an accident of any kind.

In the beginning, the shop went well. But with the economic crisis hanging over Greece like a bad smell and his customers running tabs, things took a nosedive. Some of his regulars, mainly cotton farmers and pensioners, stopped coming to the shop every day; others came in once instead of twice a day; and most of them cut down on the ouzo, brandy, and appetizers. Now and again, when Costas cleaned ashtrays and picked up empty glasses, saying, "We got bills to pay," his patrons said they would go home soon. But most of them stayed on. Fortunately, there were customers who still spent money, but it wasn't enough to make up for the loss.

The bills kept coming all the same and on time. Every month, Costas had to pay back an installment to the bank and his maxed-out credit card. At the same time, he had to give money to his daughter for rent, food, and other expenses and, every so often, to his mother, who had moved in with her first cousin in an apartment in the city after his father died ten years ago.

When Thalia mentioned that she was thinking of working at a local bar on the weekends, Costas was dead set against it. "Work at a bar? Forget about it. Sweetheart, if you want to get good grades, you must keep your nose to the grindstone. You wouldn't wanna end up like me."

Besides, when she came back home for Christmas, Easter, and summer holidays, she always helped her father on busy nights. Thalia was studying philosophy at Aristotle University in Thessaloniki.

The idea about the diamonds came to him on a sleepless night three weeks ago. Smoking and drinking brandy, he had sat in an armchair by the living room bay window and gazed out at the wonky swing and the wind in the walnut tree. The pale light of the moon revealed his facial features. His wife had loved to trace her fingers over his sharp jaw, his broad forehead, and his strong nose. Under the Hilux Toyota sticking out of a carport, he spotted the eyes of his black cat. He had found her in a ditch the day of the funeral and named her Artemis after his wife.

While Costas mulled over the state of his life, he felt as if someone's eyes were on his back. Then he thought he smelled a whiff of the rose-and-violet perfume his wife used to wear. Images of Artemis— in a white dress, a straw hat, and a smile, or in denim shorts and a white T-shirt, bent over her plants in the garden, or lying next to him and holding his gaze—flashed before him and swelled his chest with emotions. He looked over his shoulder, but save for the dusty bookshelves crammed with literature, nothing was there.

"What the hell," he whispered.

Even though Artemis is buried in a cemetery next to her parents, in a plot where he too will one day be buried, he still imagines, as he did that night, that the door to his house will open, and in she will walk. He can't get his head around the thought that one day they were together and the next they were not. Death to him is an unsolved mystery. No matter how hard he contemplated it when he was a young man, and no matter how many long conversations he had with friends, he has never understood it. "There're plenty of hypotheses around death and the afterlife," he said to his best friend, Lefteris, once. "But there are no concrete facts."

As he peered behind him for some evidence of a spirit, he caught a glimpse of a family photo album. He rose and went to run his gaunt fingers over its spine, then opened it at random. Looking at a photograph of himself, his wife, and their teenage daughter, he sat back down on the armchair with sadness in his eyes.

The photograph had been taken on a sunny winter day at the seafront of Nea Paralia in Thessaloniki. They stand smiling with the wind in their hair in front of the statue of Alexander the Great riding his horse, Voukefalas. It was a Sunday, he remembered. They had driven to Thessaloniki early in the morning and walked along the seafront. He could still feel his wife's soft touch, her happiness, and her wholehearted love.

Later the same day, they drove to Hortiati, a town built on the wooded hills with a view of Thessaloniki and its suburbs. They sat on the terrace of a taverna near pine trees, had traditional dishes, and drank local wine. Then they drove to the Panorama district, drank coffee, and enjoyed syrupy delights in one of his wife's favorite places.

With a bittersweet melancholy and a sense of loss rising within him, he closed the album with a snap. The void left by his wife's absence behind was unbearable, still. He thought that the whole world and especially Greece was guilty of her death. Instead of speeding ahead for an Olympic gold medal, Greece crawled like a hundred-year-old tortoise. Where were the things life promised him when he was a teenager? Where was the collective spirit that could drive Greece toward a brighter future? Where were the incorruptible politicians and the impartial judges? By now, vehicles should have voice recognition technology to detect drunk and drugged-up drivers.

By now there should be automated ambulances equipped with high-tech medical machinery as well as highly trained personnel.

By now Greece should be living in such abundance that poverty, hunger, debt, and human suffering would sound like a dreadful old wives' tale. That night, he decided that the whole country was to blame for his wife's death, including himself for doing absolutely nothing to change the old ways. And he felt it in his heart that if the Greeks didn't act the way they should, there would be no end to their suffering.

His eyes settled back into their usual state of soft sadness.

Since the funeral, not only has he not gone to the cemetery, but he also refuses to drive by it. "My wife hasn't died," he'd say to Lefteris, patting his heart. "She still lives in here and not in some place up in the sky."

But his sister, despite Costas's objections, goes to the cemetery, puts flowers on the grave, lights candles, and talks to his wife as though she were sitting right across from her. One day, about three months ago, Costas got furious. "What the hell are you trying to prove?" he said to her when she delivered cooked food to his house. "When Artemis was alive, you often bad-mouthed her. Please, stop going over there and stop bringing me fucking food." He closed the door in her face and hasn't spoken to her since.

On that sleepless night, his face pinched in thought, he lit a cigarette and started to look at the photographs again. Long-forgotten feelings unfolded inside him like an expressionistic canvas evoking smells and sounds. When he came across a picture of his wife and himself playing with snowballs, he smiled faintly. He looked at another picture, and his eyes slightly brightened and then clouded over.

In the picture, his wife wears a diamond necklace around her slender neck. The largest of the diamonds is the shape of a large tear. The earrings and the ring are cut in the same fashion. Her mother gave them to her before the old woman died—a gift for her wedding day. Artemis intended to pass them on in the same way the day her daughter got married. A few relatives were against burying Artemis with the jewels, but Costas thought it an act of respect and love toward his wife.

He paced in the semi-dark living room. *What the hell am I thinking?* he asked himself over and over again and pictured himself standing by his wife's grave with a spade in his hands. "Fuck you!" He put the album away and reached for the bottle of brandy.

In the weeks since, he has tried to find a better solution, but nothing has come of it. When the banks rejected his application for a personal loan, Costas turned to his ex-boss—a construction foreman for whom he had worked many years and who owed him a couple thousand euros; but the man's sister told Costas that he had moved to Australia. She promised to have her brother call him back, but he never did. And when Costas called again, no one picked up the phone.

As things stand, the only solution to his problems is to dig up his wife and get the diamonds. After it first occurred to him, this idea stuck to him like a leech, made him drink a lot, sleep little, and hate the world even more. Finally, in his despair, he reconciled himself to the idea.

Besides, he thinks, *in a few years from now, I will have to dig up my wife anyway.* But to put his plan into action, he needs help. What he needs are strong hands to dig and shovel. He could sure use a set of eyes to act as a lookout, but he doesn't want to involve too many people. *The fewer, the better,* he thinks. Apart from him and whomever he hires for the job, no one else should ever know about it. No one.

On Wednesday, under a cloudy sky, the wind moves in the pine trees in the square. Beneath the benches, stray dogs curl up next to empty beer cans and paper coffee cups. A man with a round face and a black coat lumbers past a statue smeared with graffiti spray. He walks into the yard of the καφενείο, where the aluminum tables and chairs are covered with dust.

Costas is behind the bar counter. He wears black clothes and a black apron. Thick veins stand out on his lean arms as he wipes the counter down and watches the man enter the shop. A pocket of air smelling of damp soil sneaks in.

The man picks up a backgammon board from the counter, makes a *V* sign with his thick fingers—indicating two Greek coffees—and starts for the table next to a window where a man in a red baseball cap, jeans, and mud-caked boots is waiting for him.

Costas sets the coffee and two glasses of water next to the backgammon board. Without lifting his eyes from the game, the man says, "Put them on my tab."

Fucker, Costas thinks, for the round-faced man behaves as if life owes him a favor, and he is often on a short fuse. But he is Costas's best customer. He will drink his coffee and then order ouzo and appetizers for himself and his friends, and at the end of every month, he will settle his tab like clockwork.

I wish I had more customers like him, Costas thinks and opens a notebook. Next to the word COFFEE, he draws two lines. Then he lights a cigarette, leans an arm on the counter, and glances up at the television set mounted on the wall.

He sees men in berets and bulletproof vests, their pistols in holsters and clubs hanging from their belts. Men and women with children in their arms are sitting on the ground and huddling in shabby jackets. *Poor people*, Costas thinks. Plastic bags filled with food, bottles of water, cans, and blankets lie at their feet. A journalist says that the situation with all the refugees and immigrants in Athens and on many of the islands is spinning out of control.

A man with a brown hat who is playing cards with a friend says, "Poor people. They came to Greece hoping for a better sun on the horizon. But how can we help them when we're stuck in shit up to our neck? Tell me how. But nobody can blame them for being here. We went to their countries, plunder their resources, and—"

His friend throws down a card over other cards. "Come on. Stop watching the silly screen. It's your turn."

Costas opens the door to air out the space with its ten tables and the old mirrors advertising spirits, beers, and coffee. In the cold air, he smells pine and chimney smoke. Lights have come on in windows and house patios. In the square, a few of the lampposts are burned out. A dog missing a hind leg crosses the road. Costas steps out and lights a cigarette.

In a moment, he hears the bell of a church. Vespers is up. Beyond the pine trees, Costas sees the church's dome and its cross and pictures the stocky priest with his long, gray beard and kind eyes—the same priest who has been trying to convince him to come to the church. The same priest will start the Holy Mass before the devout eyes of the women who are now crossing the square with scarves tied around their heads. With the words "Blessed is our Lord," he will raise a sense of awe and hope in their hearts.

A feeling of irritation comes over Costas. He can't understand people who believe in and pray to this all-powerful, all-knowing, and invisible being who sees, feels, hears, and judges everything.

As he smokes, his mobile signals a text message: How are you, Papi? I'm coming back on Sunday and I'm so looking forward to coming home for a few days next week. Please, go and visit Grandma. She's worried about you. Persephone says hi. I love you, Papi, followed by a smile and a kiss.

His daughter is in Athens to visit her cousin, who studies law. Costas hasn't seen her for a month; she has been studying for her June exams. He looks forward to spending some quality time with her. He loves when they take long walks together, either in the forest of Seyh Su or along the seafront of Thessaloniki, listening to her speak with great passion about Plato, Pythagoras, Nietzsche, and Carl Jung, about her life as a student, the parties, the flirting, and generally the crazy staff all students pull. Costas doesn't worry too much; he and his wife gave their daughter a proper upbringing based around the belief that a child needs to be composed and responsible.

The last time she was home, they relaxed in front of the fireplace, drinking red wine, playing cards, and teasing each other. When he thinks of how absentminded and clumsy Thalia is, he smiles faintly. But when his plans for tomorrow come to mind, the brightness in his eyes fades away.

He sees himself at the wheel of his Toyota, driving to Thessaloniki; sees himself talking with a man in the square right across from the main train station, where foreigners gather to land casual work; sees himself driving at night and parking the car in a cluster of trees near the cemetery. As the images parade before his eyes, he draws hard on his cigarette and flicks it toward the road. The cigarette bounces off the curb, sparks scattering into the wind.

Back inside, two men approach the counter, pulling on their jackets. One of them brings out a handful of coins. "How much for the Greek coffees?"

Costas looks at him as though he is an idiot. "One hundred euros."

The man breaks into a grin, revealing a few missing teeth. He pays for the coffee and moves along.

That night, when Costas is done sweeping and mopping the shop, he pours himself a glass of brandy and waits for his friend to show up. The last time Lefteris looked after the shop, he almost burned it down. Part of the wooden floor, the working space, and a wall burned. Lefteris wanted to pay for the damages, but Costas refused. In the end, they split the expenses.

Lefteris is the only one he can trust. Costas knows that nothing bad will happen under his watch again, and when he sees his bearded friend coming into the shop, he pours him a generous glass of brandy.

"How's your day been?" Lefteris asks as Costas rubs his nape.

"It's been a slow night. It's not even eleven yet, and I'm closing for the day. March has been the worst month so far."

"Tell me about it. People are laid off at the factory."

"So I heard."

"Who told you?"

"Words travel fast."

"Kiriakos was fired today."

Costas arches his eyebrows. "Was he?"

"When the manager broke the news to him, he turned into a raging bull. They had words. Kiriakos broke a chair and turned a table over."

They sip from their drinks.

"Who could blame him," Costas says. "Working for them leeches for fifteen years hasn't been easy."

"Fifteen years," Lefteris repeats and runs a hand through his dark hair.

"Do you think they'll compensate him?"

"I hope them bastards do. He has two kids and a pregnant wife at home."

"I saw her today at the bakery," Costas says. "Angeliki and my wife were good friends." He drops his eyes between his feet and digs his toe into the floor.

A moment of silence passes. Costas lights a cigarette.

They stay in the shop for another hour, smoking, drinking, and talking about the weather, politics, people moving abroad, Lefteris's new love, and Thalia's progress. When they step out into the cold night, Lefteris says that he will take over at around four o'clock the following day, as soon as he gets off work at the factory.

Before they part ways, Lefteris puts his arm on Costas's shoulder. "And don't worry. I won't burn the place down this time." He smiles.

Costas was on the verge of revealing his plan to his friend twice during the conversation, but fortunately, he didn't.

When the colors of dawn fall over the cotton and grass fields, over barns and houses, glinting on trucks and tractors wet with dew, Costas opens his eyes from a dreamless sleep.

He sits up in bed and feels a draft of air around his feet. Rubbing his face, he grabs the pack of cigarettes from the side table, lights one, and moves out of the room, leaving a cloud of smoke behind him.

He takes a shower and puts on black clothes. Drinking a cup of filtered coffee, he looks out the kitchen window. A light wind moves in the trees, and dark clouds bank on the horizon. He lights another cigarette, and in the morning light, he writes a letter to his daughter.

Dear Thalia,

I hope that after you have read this letter, things will become clear to you. And I hope that you will find it in your heart to forgive me for what I did. But believe me when I say that there wasn't any other way for me to get out of the woods.

He stares out the window, then goes on writing and explaining in detail how and why he will execute his plan. When he reaches the bottom of the page, he rubs his forehead and concludes: I hope I haven't left out anything of importance. If something happens to me, please give this letter to the police. I'm sorry I've let you down, sweetheart. I truly am. I want you to know that I love you very much.

Papi.

He slides the letter under her pillow and fondly regards the bed as if she were there sleeping. In his bedroom, he reaches under the mattress, brings out a handgun, and shoves it in the pocket of his black parka.

After tossing a spade, a pickaxe, and a heavy sack into the bed of the Toyota Hilux, he backs out of the carport and drives through the gate.

Soon he eases the truck to a stop right in front of his sister's house and sees her car parked under the carport. He knows she is already awake, getting ready for work at a supermarket in Giannitsa. Since the day he closed the door in her face three months ago, she has called him several times, but he never answers. He makes to kill the engine, but instead, he throws the car into gear and slowly drives away.

Outside his shop, two of his patrons stand talking. They're wearing thick jackets, muddy boots, and woolen beanies.

"You late," one of them says.

"You guys came early."

The men move into the shop, rubbing their hands, and Costas turns on the television. A journalist is saying that a man walked into a florist shop in Thessaloniki, shot his wife twice in the face, and then turned the rifle on himself. A camera follows a few men in blue uniforms and hard hats into the shop, brushing past flowers, and all the way to the bloodstained floor. "Both of them are in the hospital in critical condition," the journalist says.

"Thessaloniki's turning into Chicago," one of the men comments.

"If you have too much time on your hands, your mind wanders off easily," his friend says.

Costas serves them two double Greek coffees and a couple of biscuits. Then, he prepares a coffee for himself.

In a while, more people will trickle in for coffee, tea, toast, and omelets. When things start to slow down in the afternoon, Costas will pop over to the bakery and get bread, and from Ilias's grocery store, he will buy pickles, smoked fish, olives, ham, cheese, and butter. When Lefteris comes in later, Costas will have the place well stocked and ready for the evening shift.

Afterward, he will drive for about an hour to the city, go to the square opposite the central train station, and try and find a man. But it will not be easy. Over the stretch of an hour, and though he will offer a hefty fee, four men will turn him down. But in the end, he will find a man who does not ask questions and will arrange to pick the man up at ten o'clock that night from the same spot. Next, he will pay a visit to his mother and her cousin in the apartment near Saint Sophia's church in the heart of the city. He will have dinner with them, and a few glasses of brandy.

It's 21:30. Costas stands in the hallway, pulling on his parka as his mother approaches to say goodbye. The dimly lit space smells of the roses standing in a vase in the hallway. His mother's cousin stands next to a long mirror near the door. She's wearing a flowery dress and smiles at him.

His mother, her gray hair tied in a neat bun, takes his hand into hers, looks into his eyes, and says, "Be careful. And start eating. You will disappear soon."

"Please, Sophia, don't worry." He smiles at her softly and kisses her forehead.

Outside, the wind is stiff and cold. The pork steak, the mashed potatoes, and the spinach salad set him straight, and the brandy smoothed the edge of his worries. He looks up at the sky and hopes it doesn't rain.

In the car, he takes a pull from the bottle of brandy he keeps in the car and puts it under the seat. He drives along Egnatia Boulevard; the construction site for the metro has turned traffic bumper to bumper. He eases the car to a stop at the traffic light in Aristotelous Square, and people cross the street in front of him, alone or in pairs. He watches them talking, laughing, and speaking on their phones. *How fragile we all are*, he thinks.

He parks at the curb next to acacia trees and lights a cigarette as he watches three foreigners seated on a bench; they drink beer from cans and smoke as they chat. In a moment, the heavyset man he hired for the job rounds the corner, dressed in black and with dark eyes and thick hair that peeks out from under his black beanie. Traces of doubt cross Costas's mind. But there is no turning back now. He flashes his headlights and fires up the engine.

With a joint wedged in his lips, Faris opens the door and, wrinkling his forehead, asks in broken Greek, "Can I smoke in car?"

A gust of cold wind enters the vehicle. Costas nods yes and watches him slide in. Smelling marijuana, he drives up the road and turns sharply at the traffic lights. The car fishtails but settles in its frame.

The man holds out his hand. "Want a smoke?"

As Costas overtakes a bus, he says no, and notices that part of Faris's left thumb is missing. When he met with him earlier today, he saw the scar on his face but didn't notice the finger.

"How far is village?" Smoke surges out of the foreigner's mouth.

"About an hour's drive."

"And you drive me back to city?"

"Yes. I'll drive you back to the same spot I picked you up."

Faris nods, tosses the joint out the window, and sticks a toothpick in his mouth.

Costas wonders why the man hasn't asked about the job yet. Of course, the 150 euros he offered was a hefty amount, and he has already paid him half of it, but Costas assumed that at some point Faris would ask what it is they are going to dig up—especially at this hour.

They drive under a bridge, past empty shops with knocked-out windows, billboards with shredded posters, abandoned factories, neon-lit hotels, and gas stations.

"Faris, where are you from?"

"Me Bosnia."

"Sarajevo?"

The Bosnian nods yes.

Heavy silence builds. Costas turns on the radio and picks up a news channel that reports the weather. When he hears "light showers," he lights a cigarette and opens the window a crack.

The traffic starts to thin out in the industrial zone of Sindos. A few kilometers out of Halkidona, Costas notices that the oil lamp symbol is on. He slaps the steering wheel and frowns.

Faris turns his red eyes at him. "What is problem?"

Costas points at the red light. He pulls into a gas station a few kilometers down the road. Inside the shop, an old man sitting on a stool by the register watches the television mounted on the corner of the wall.

Costas asks Faris if he wants something.

"Coffee and chocolate."

Emerging to stand by the truck, Costas smells earth, manure, and gasoline in the air. He rubs his nape and gazes out over the road and beyond into the dark fields. In the distance, the lights of houses glitter in the open flatland, and he imagines people watching television, playing cards, or reading books. He imagines them eating, talking, and laughing at the kitchen table, and pain grips his heart.

It's warm inside the shop. Costas gets two cups of coffee from the dispenser and a bar of chocolate and moves up to the counter, where he asks for a bottle of motor oil. The old man gives Costas the change, then glances at the television and says with a grimace of indignation, "We should throw our politicians into the sea."

Halfway to his car, Costas's mobile rings. He listens to Lefteris tell him that it has been a slow night and that the television has gone bust. "It's just my luck."

Costas clenches his teeth. "Stop worrying about the television, and close the shop soon."

He and Faris drive, drink coffee, and smoke in silence. Costas glances sideways at Faris as the Bosnian breaks off pieces of the chocolate and shoves them in his mouth, letting out satisfied sounds. Further down, they see a dead dog lying on the shoulder of the road with its guts spilled out. The lights of Pella appear in the distance.

"How far is village?"

"About ten minutes.'"

Soon Costas drives over a dirt road and parks behind a cluster of trees moving in the wind. He kills the engine, leans back in his seat, and draws in a long breath. *You can do this*, he thinks and feels a knot forming in his stomach.

He looks at Faris. "Aren't you afraid?"

Faris stops working the toothpick around in his mouth. "I not afraid."

"Why haven't you asked me about the job yet?"

"You pay good. You promise we not harm anyone."

"I might've lied to you."

"You no liar. You good man."

"How do you know?" He frowns. "How do you know that I'm a good man?"

Faris makes a *V* sign with his fingers and points them toward Costas's eyes. "Your eyes clean and kind. Faris knows."

Costas takes two good hits from the brandy and hands it to Faris. When Faris sees him pulling out the handgun from the clove compartment, he grabs his hand.

"No guns."

"Let go of my hand."

They stare at each other.

"No guns."

Costas lets go of the gun. Faris hands him back the bottle of brandy. He drinks another mouthful, looks into the darkness, and, before he puts the bottle under the seat, drinks some more.

The air smells of dirt and pine. They grab the tools and the bag from the bed of the truck and set off along the road, the wind numbing their faces. Grass fields line either side of the road. Lights from far-off windows glisten under the dark sky.

Halfway down the road, Costas feels like giving up this crazy idea. He can simply stop in his tracks, turn around, and walk away as if nothing has happened. But his feet keep moving, keep crunching hard on the dirt road as if they have a mind of their own.

They now stand in front of the arched gate of the cemetery, which is encircled with tall cypresses and a tall wall. Costas pushes the rusty gate open and waits for Faris. But the Bosnian doesn't move a muscle. He just stands there and works his suspicious eyes over Costas.

"What's wrong?"

"What we do here?"

Costas motions him to keep it down. "Here's where we're going to dig." He waves him over. "Come on in, my friend, before someone sees us."

Faris hesitantly obeys. Closing the gate, Costas cocks an ear. He hears a truck on the road and a dog barking far away. He empties the bag and coils a chain around the gate, puts a padlock on it, and moves to where Faris stands leaning on the pickaxe and raking his eyes over the graves. Most of them are marked by white-and-gray marble, others just have a tombstone with a cross on the top, and a few are built with iron. In a few tombs, tea lights flicker before photographs.

Alcohol running through his veins, Costas draws in a deep breath and meets Faris's eyes, which tell Costas that the Bosnian knows what they are about to do.

"Yes, we're going to dig up a grave."

"What grave?" He frowns.

"We're going to dig up my wife."

"I do many things in life, but I not dig up people."

"You told me that you could do anything. We're not going to harm anybody," Costas says and moves behind a marble grave where he can't be seen from the road, waving him over.

Faris spits on the ground and does as he is bidden.

"Without your help, I can't do it," Costas says in a low voice. "That's why I paid you good money. Do you understand what I'm saying to you?" He creases his forehead, eyes fixed on Faris.

Faris produces a cross with Jesus set on it and brings it before

EYES THAT HOLD NOTHING AT ALL

Costas's perplexed eyes. "In war Sarajevo, he save my life. I promise not do bad things. You good man, but dig up wife not good."

Costas cannot believe what he's hearing. He tightens his grip around the flashlight until his fingers go white. Looking into Faris's eyes, he tells himself that the man is either stupid or crazy.

"Why dig up wife?"

"You'll see when we open her coffin."

A gust of wind moves in the cypresses.

Costas puts his hand on Faris's shoulder. "You promised to help me if we wouldn't harm anybody. If I don't do it, my daughter and I will have a hard time."

"You have daughter?"

"Yes, I have."

Faris rubs his chin.

"My wife . . ." Costas points toward Artemis's grave down the path. "My wife has been dead for years. I'm her husband. And that gives me the right to do this thing." He can't believe he has spoken these words.

"Not right to dig dead. Only priest do it."

"Look, Faris. We don't have much time. Here is the seventy-five euros, plus another fifty." He counts out bills of tens and fives. "That's all I have."

Faris opens his mouth to speak, but he doesn't.

"Please, take it." Costas puts the money in his large hand. "You said I was a good man." Then he shares how they will carry out his plan. Faris listens carefully as he works his toothpick.

They move quietly after the beam of light on the ground. Images of his wife from the funeral come to Costas's mind.

"Here is where we'll dig," he says and sees withered red roses lying on the ground.

Faris makes the sign of the cross and watches Costas pick up a photograph from his wife's tombstone and bring it near his face. He watches as Costas clenches his jaw and rubs his forehead.

Costas breaks out in a cold sweat. Tears come to his eyes. But he doesn't cry. He kisses the photograph, puts it back, takes the flowers from the ground, and lays them carefully next to the tombstone.

Faris shrugs out of his coat and picks up the pickaxe. Costas squats on his heels five graves away and fixes his eyes on the gate. For the next half hour, the only thing he hears is the blows of the pickaxe, Faris's labored breathing, and the wind in the trees.

They take turns digging and shoveling and keeping watch. Costas is almost two meters down in the hole. His clothes are wet with sweat. All the pain and the agony, the anger and the frustration, and the tears he was supposed to cry the past years are now oozing out of his pores, uncontrollably. When the blade scrapes the coffin, his heart clenches.

He draws in a deep breath and wipes the sweat off his forehead with the back of his hand. His body aches, and his stomach and chest burn. He hears a rush of feet on the path, and then Faris reports that he heard voices.

Crouching, both men move to the wall of the cemetery and peer over the edge at an old house with a lit window fifty meters away. An old man lives in the house with an old dog. Costa knows him. Since the man's wife died last year, he often walks with his dog in the village and speaks to himself. Costas wonders whether he heard them. *It's impossible,* he assures himself. The old man is looking out the window and toward the cemetery, but a moment later, he draws the curtain and turns off the light.

After Faris has brushed off the last soil from the coffin, Costas hauls him out of the grave and, flashlight in hand, jumps in. Heart pounding, he pulls back the lid. A heavy, out-of-this-world stench breathes out. Faris flinches as the beam of light falls on the remains of Costas's wife.

His stomach turning, Costas takes a hesitant look inside the coffin, leans a hand on the earth wall, and tries to catch his balance. A moment passes. When he looks closer at his wife, it takes a few panicking and painful seconds for his mind to register what has already happened. And as the hard realization sets in, he feels like he has lost the ground under his feet.

Costas looks up at Faris with eyes that hold nothing at all, eyes so empty that Faris's heart sinks. The diamond necklace, the earrings, and the ring are gone.

Faris watches tears stream down Costas's face. He watches as Costas lets out a long, drawn-out sound that causes Faris's blood to freeze in his veins. He watches him as the Greek starts to laugh out loud, as he falls on his knees and puts his hands over his face.

Cold wind whips through the cemetery; whips through the cypresses; whips through the grass fields; and dies in the darkness as a silent drizzle begins to fall.

I Called Home Today

THE NIGHT was freezing cold. In a shack, a young man with a woolen beanie lay in his sleeping bag. Thick blankets covered an old man in a corner. A dead fire and a barbecue rack propped on four bricks sat in the middle of the space. Outside, in the yard, the stiff wind moved some clothes hanging on a slack line and rattled sheets of rusty metal.

The man with the beanie coughed. With each breath he took, his chest hurt.

"Marcus, are you okay?" the other man asked.

"Go back to sleep." He coughed again, pulled on his thick coat, and rummaged around for a bottle of water. But he found none. From his rucksack, he pulled out a crowbar and cough syrup he had shoplifted from a pharmacy. He swallowed a mouthful and pushed the crowbar up the sleeve of his coat.

Marcus went out to the yard and pushed aside the sheet metal that served as a gate. Right across from the yard was a tall wall, and over it a rail bridge. The wind whistled in his ears. Coughing, he turned up the collar of his coat and hurried past a large plane tree, past an open kiosk, and between empty buses standing at bus stops. A hooded man lay on one of the benches, scrunched up in a sleeping bag. Marcus wished the buses were running. On cold days, he liked to get on different "warm worms," as he liked to call them, and ride across the city, and when a thought came to his mind, he jotted it down in his notepad. Recently, he wrote,

In the city center, I saw my ex-fiancée. A man dressed in a suit and a coat was holding her hand. She was wearing

him on the head, stepped back, and watched the man fall over.

Marcus's chest burned. "Motherfucker!" he coughed, cold sweat breaking out all over his body. Thinking he heard voices, he jerked his gaze to the door and then turned his panicked eyes back to the man, whose hair was soaked with blood. Marcus dragged him into a stall, propped him up against the wall, and put two fingers to his jugular. Fortunately, the man was alive. Marcus mopped the bloodstains from the floor and, hearing voices again, rinsed the blood off the crowbar and shoved it back inside the sleeve of his coat. As he stepped through the doorway, he saw a man coming down the stairs. Coughing, he put his chin down, and up he went.

A few days after Marcus had settled in the shack, he sat in a dilapidated armchair by the fire and wrote the following account:

I've had enough of everything and everybody. My little printing business went belly up. People owed me money and I owed money to people, too. I was about to blow a gasket. What I needed was to escape from all the hustle and bustle of city life and its people.

I needed time to think of my next steps. Since I couldn't afford to pay the rent and other expenses, I decided to live on a plot with pine trees my old man owned in Halkidiki near the sea, half an hour's drive from Thessaloniki. It was a hard business to talk my old man into letting me stay on his property, but with my mother's help, he gave in.

With the money my grandfather had given me before he died, I bought an old caravan from a dealer. I'll never forget him. In the shade of a plane tree, we drank coffee and talked about life and the strange and inexplicable things that happen to people all over the world every day. I'm glad I met him. He was a man who didn't look at the world with his eyes, but with his mind.

When I moved into my new home, it was midsummer. For two months, my fiancée stayed with me. Every day, we swam in the sea, went fishing, barbecued, had dinner under the stars, talked about things, listened to the radio, and slept in each other's arms. In September, she landed a job as a secretary at an architecture office and took most of her things to her parents' house in the heart of the city. When she was staying with them, I didn't like the silence between us. In the beginning, she drove out to my place every day, but by and by her visits began to thin out.

By mid-October, we'd already had a few arguments about the way I lived and the way I saw things lately. I told her that we were both still very young, just over thirty. I told her to stop worrying. On her last visit, after we had a heated argument, she drove to her parents, and a week later she called me and broke up our engagement. She said she couldn't see us having kids together. I didn't say anything. What could I say? I kind of knew there was something fishy in Denmark. For a week, I was as drunk as a skunk.

My old man, a retired brigadier, turned against me. He didn't approve of most of the things I did in my life. He wanted me to work for the army, as my brother did, and not as a typographer. One afternoon, he drove over to see me, and we had words. Quite often, he was on a short fuse. He told me that if I had listened to him, I wouldn't have been in this muck. He said that if I didn't move back to that little shitty town they lived in, he would disinherit me. I told him I didn't give a damn. He said I didn't deserve to be his son and wanted me off his land by the next day. It was then that something hardened inside me.

The next day, I went and stayed with a friend in the city center. I crashed on the couch. He worked in a fish market, left for work at dawn, and came back home in the evening smelling like a fish. I slept on the couch for half a year, and I worked different jobs. For a month, I worked as a night security guard in a parking lot, but I quit because the owner tried to cheat on my salary. Then, I worked a job on the grill of a cantina near Aristotle University. The first days were difficult, but I learned the ropes. I sold souvlaki, burgers, fries, beers, and ouzo to students, taxi drivers, partygoers, hustlers, pimps, and prostitutes. People called me John because they thought I looked like John Turturro, the actor.

I worked a ten-hour shift and got paid for eight. But I didn't mind. I liked my job; it kept my mind busy and got me tired. When I returned home, I'd usually find my friend at the kitchen table, drinking coffee. He'd tell me that I smelled like a burger and smile. Things were looking up for me. I'd managed to save a bit of money, and I was thinking of renting my own place in a few months. But two weeks into my contentment, the state shut down the cantina because it didn't have a license. After that, things took a nosedive for me. My friend and his ex-girlfriend got back together, she moved back to his flat, and a week later I moved out.

I made a phone call and managed to find another couch in a flat on the outskirts of the city. My friend collected unemployment benefits and sat in front of his laptop all day, lived on junk food, smoked pot, played video games, and made silly and meaningless posts on his Facebook. I called him Facebookowski. The flat was a mess and smelled stuffy. I spent two weeks looking for a job, but nothing came of it. It was then that I started smoking again and drinking a bottle of cheap wine every day.

One evening, I went home and found my rucksack in the hallway. Facebookowski looked at me with his little red eyes, went into his room, and shut the door behind him. That beat it all. Had I done something that might've offended him? I searched my mind, but nothing. I had even paid the month's rent and bought the junk food the fucker ate. I spent the night at a cheap hotel, and the next day I hit the streets.

Frankly, I was confident that I'd be just fine. In the past months, I'd read articles and watched documentaries about homeless people who said that the problem with living on the streets starts on the second or the third day. Homeless people talked about the fear, danger, and cruelty of the streets. They talked about the insecurity, anxiety, and panic they experienced every day. On the streets, your imagination runs wild, they'd say. You begin to fear because you lack basic human needs, and you always think of the worst possible scenarios. In other words, homeless people are held to a dark view of things.

I agreed with them, but my situation was different. I didn't have a family to support, and I was neither old nor sick. I had two hundred euros in my pocket, and it was early spring. This is not America, I told myself. In Thessaloniki, people don't carry guns. Ironically, what I felt when I found myself on the streets was freedom and relief. Yes, I may have lost the comfort of my basic human needs, but I didn't have to think about how to pay the fucking bills. All my belongings were in my rucksack.

The first night, I slept on a corner outside the church of St. Dimitrios. I was dog tired, fell asleep easily, and woke to the sound of morning traffic. I drank a coffee, ate a spinach pie, and set off to roam the streets. I wanted to see how badly the crisis had affected the people but also the city itself. And so, I took myself to the west side.

In these quarters, the air smelled of burned rubber and the smog the factories spew out every day. Fortunately, car pollution was reduced slightly because people had begun to use public transport. The stigma of the crisis was evident in the streets. Roads and sidewalks were cracked and patched up, and zebra crossings were nonexistent. Empty cans of beer and soft drinks, plastic bottles of water, and cigarette packets were blown against the street corners. You could see cats in dumpsters with missing lids. Many stores were for rent. Schools, parks, and squares with bronze statues looked bleached in the spring sun. Stray dogs, solo or in packs, wandered in parks and hung around outside food joints.

Despite the media talking about millions of unemployed and thousands of homeless people, in my ten-hour walk, what I saw was a different picture. In my wandering, I only stumbled upon a few scavengers. In every neighborhood, people sat at cafés and gyro joints and popped in and out of shops, carrying bags. I remembered I'd seen a program on television about a famous female photographer who had come to Greece to take photographs of people in crisis. But she found the mission very difficult because the statistics didn't hold up to the visual reality.

Early the next morning, I picked up a travel guide with all the services the city provided to people who suffered from the crisis, and as I was reading over it, I realized that since so many spots were available, there should be a comparable amount of people that kept these services going. And so, I went to check on a soup kitchen run by the city. I stood outside, looked through a window, and saw well-dressed people sitting and eating together with people in tattered clothes. What really stayed with me that day was their silent eyes.

Outside a church, I saw a line of people; some of them came out holding bags with cooked meals, and others sat on benches, eating out of plastic bowls. I felt sad, but at the same time, I blamed the little man for this misery—the short-sighted little Greek man who just thinks for himself. The little man does nothing to change the state of the things that torment and torture him daily.

I spent the night in an abandoned neoclassical house near the port. Before I went to sleep, it dawned on me that the homeless population included all the people who didn't have a job or money to buy food and lived in apartments without electricity, water, and heat. It also dawned on me that the main problem for people living on the streets twenty-four seven was all the hours of the day. When you're homeless, time slows way down.

In the morning, I counted my money. I had about one hundred and eighty euros in my pocket. Right away, I

remembered a man, Anestis, whom I'd met about a year ago
through my printing shop. At the time, he lived in a village
near the sea outside Volos. I'd printed his menu for a beach
bar he owned.

On the phone, he said he had a job for me. The same day,
I rode a bus to the city of Volos. Anestis picked me up, and
we drove to his beach bar that stood twenty meters off the
sea. On the other side of the road, you could see pine trees,
and farther away were wheat fields and olive trees. That day,
the sky was blue, the air crispy, and the sun felt warm on my
back.

It was early in the season, and Anestis was getting ready to
open. For two weeks, we touched up paintwork, carpentry, and
set up the bar. The man didn't speak much, and his face was
often pinched in thought. Two days before the opening,
he offered me a job as a night guard. I couldn't believe my
luck.

From midnight until nine in the morning, I sat in a chair
in a room I was also sleeping in. I had good meals and took
long walks. Listening to the sound of the sea, I read books
and looked out the window. The books that made a lasting
impression on me and changed my way of thinking were
THE ART OF LOVING by Erich Fromm, THE
UNDISCOVERED SELF by Carl Jung, and THE ROAD
by Cormack McCarthy.

Right by my feet, I had a shotgun. Each time I heard a funny
noise, I'd walk out of my room with the shotgun, feeling like
Clint Eastwood. Except for a few passersby, stray dogs, and
cats digging into rubbish bins, nothing much ever happened.

By the end of September, when the bar closed for the winter, I'd saved three thousand euros. My boss asked me if I wanted to go with him to America to work in a fish factory, but I told him I didn't feel ready to leave my country yet. I wanted to give myself a chance in Athens.

"Athens?" he said and frowned. He told me that if he were me, he'd think three times about that decision. That place is a war zone, he said. But I'd made up my mind.

In Athens, things started to fall out of place again. On my fourth day, I was walking through a district and thinking of renting a flat when it started to rain. I took cover under an overhang of an apartment building and waited until the rain eased up. Then, I set off walking again and ended up in an alley.

Suddenly, I felt a pull from behind. Three men broke my jaw and two ribs and busted three of my fingers. I woke up in a hospital bed with my body aching from head to toe. I had trouble breathing. Outside it was still night. It took me a few minutes to come to my senses and understand what had happened to me. A nurse told me I was out for a whole day. For the first time, I found myself feeling afraid. But later, I realized that the fear of death that troubled me from time to time was beginning to diminish. Death is nothing but the absence of life.

The first days, I was fed with a straw, and my anger burned inside me like yellow fever. But seeing the man who lay two beds away from me, I felt lucky. His body was covered with bruises and cuts, he had his leg and arm broken, and on his shoulder and back were knife wounds. Also, his spleen was ruptured. I heard he was a foreigner and had been in the hospital for ten days.

About a week later, I pushed his wheelchair into the cafeteria of the hospital. We sat outside with the warmth of the sun on our faces, and over coffee and cigarettes, we talked about one thing and another. Ervin told me was jumped by men with baseball bats. He told me that although he had been living in Greece for over twenty years, he still hadn't managed to get his papers in order. Each time he applied for a residence and work permit, they were rejected, and he was asked to reapply again. This had been going on for over ten years.

Ervin spoke fluent Greek. He had a degree in economics but worked as a bricklayer. He said that from over a hundred thousand applications for citizenship that were submitted in the year 2011, only ten thousand were approved. His parents moved back to Albania as a thousand others had done. Before the crisis, those people served a purpose in the exploitative and tax-evading Greek society.

That day, something went off deep in my chest. I had read of their plight, and had watched the news and the programs, but the impact of his words on me was a totally different matter altogether. I sensed rage running in my veins. I felt embarrassed and ashamed for being Greek. Of all people, the Greeks ought to know fucking better.

I spent ten days in the hospital and felt lucky to be breathing. The men who mugged me also made off with most of my savings. The police could not find them as I couldn't remember their faces. I blamed myself for not leaving my money in the room at the hostel I had checked into.

Disappointed, and with three hundred euros in my pocket, I hitchhiked my way back to Thessaloniki, where I drifted for a few weeks. I slept in abandoned railroad cars and in a run-down beer factory near some brothels. One day, as I was going to catch a bus to see about a downtown squat, I stumbled upon a shack. The place was huddled in a unique spot; it was within reach of the central train station, the port, food joints, and nightspots. Right behind the shack was a church.

Over a few days, I observed an old man living in that shack. He was of medium build, wore a tattered coat and a woolen beanie, and walked with a limp. On a sunny day, I went to see him. I brought him some food supplies, and we sat by the fire, drank coffee, and talked about things.

He told me he used to be a lorry driver transporting wine to Europe. But four years ago, he'd lost his job because of the economic crisis. His employers got rid of the older drivers. The old man dragged them to court because they cheated on his insurance, but he was still waiting. The justice system in Greece sucks, he said. He also said he had a daughter and a son who had families of their own and lived and worked in Halkida, near the sea. They didn't know anything about his situation. When I go to see them, I put on my dancing shoes, he said. I wanted to ask him about his wife, but I didn't. Since the space in the shack was big enough to house four men, I asked if I could stay with him. He stroked his mustache and said he didn't know. He was six months away from becoming a pensioner and didn't want any trouble. He said he'd think about it and asked me to come back the next day. But as I was walking toward the bus stop, he called out my name.

When Marcus opened his eyes, the sky was gray, and the air was cold. So deeply had he slept that he didn't hear the traffic, the workers drilling and shouting at one another, the trains going over the rail bridge.

What he heard now was music on the radio. The old man, Apostolis, was sitting in an armchair with a thick blanket draped over his shoulders, warming his hands over the low-burning fire. Marcus wondered about the man he had beaten unconscious, but when his attacker's image came to his mind, he told himself that he deserved it.

"How you feeling?" the old man asked, pouring coffee into a tin mug.

"As though a truck ran me over. What time is it?"

"It's noon." Apostolis put the coffee mug in his hand. "This'll set you straight."

Marcus took a sip. A nice warmth flooded his chest and stomach and filled him with a sense of satisfaction while he sat by the fire and shook the bottle of cough syrup.

Apostolis started to roll a cigarette. "Go easy with it," the old man said. "You don't wanna get high on it."

"Better high than sober."

"I'm going to the office today to sign some papers. On my way back, I'll bring us water."

"Sounds good."

"You go over to the soup kitchen and get us dinner. On today's menu, it's lentil soup."

Marcus drank his coffee, brushed his teeth, and washed his face with ice-cold water in a makeshift sink in the yard. He put two Tupperware bowls in a plastic bag, and as he made to leave, the old man said, "Bring some extra bread." In the evening they usually made sandwiches with yellow cheese and tomato and sat by the fire, eating and drinking tea.

Marcus joined a line of people huddled in their warm clothes at the rear of the church. Small talk and sporadic laughter surrounded him. An old man in frayed clothes and with crooked and dirty hands stood in front of Marcus. Street smells hung on him like leeches.

A disheveled middle-aged woman with black roots showing in her blond hair rushed past the line. But when she tried to go through the entrance, the supervisor, a hefty young man, put his arm out and said, "Lady, you must wait for your turn."

She stared at him. "You've got to be shitting me, right!" With her bosom, she pushed against his stretched arm.

"Please, lady. Don't make any trouble. If you like to eat, you must wait for your turn."

"Go and fuck yourself," she said and stormed off, muttering.

The supervisor greeted and smiled at the people walking in and out of the room. Inside, the air was warm and smelled of cooked food. Marcus approached a young man sitting by a large straw basket. The man put a loaf of bread in his bag and, wrapping up two spinach pies, said, "Here is a treat for you and Apostolis. Send him my regards."

Marcus thanked him and moved to a window that looked like a ticket booth. A buxom lady stood behind the counter, wearing surgical gloves and a shower cap on her head like the other three ladies busying themselves in the space behind. They were all members of a volunteer crew that came in twice a week and cooked.

Marcus pushed the Tupperware toward the lady. "Eighty-five and one hundred and fifty-eight."

One of the ladies put the numbers down on a list of names while another one dipped the ladle into the hot lentil soup. "Here you go, young man," she said and smiled.

Later, as it grew dark, sporadic raindrops spattered against the metal sheets of the shack. Marcus sat in the armchair and stared at the fire. A sudden sense of solitude blew through him like a blizzard wind. He lit a cigarette and thought of his mother and of his ex-fiancée, whom he had dreamt of a few nights ago. In the dream, he had caught her in bed with another man. But when he grabbed him by his shoulder and yanked him around, he saw that the man was himself, only much younger. Marcus wondered how it would have been if they hadn't broken up.

The fire crackled and sparked. When he heard a dog bark, he grabbed the crowbar, moved out in the yard, looked over the metal gate, and saw a stray black-and-white dog trotting toward the old man as he returned.

"Scotty!" Apostolis patted the dog and produced a bone wrapped in a piece of newspaper. "Take it."

The dog leaped up and grabbed the bone out of the old man's hand.

"Good boy," Marcus said and laughed.

They warmed up the lentil soup, and with blankets draped over their shoulders, they ate listening to Nick Papazoglou sing, "Αχ, Ελλάδα σ' αγαπώ."[6*]

Halfway through their meal, Apostolis told Marcus that he might have to wait until October for his pension. "I had a row with my lawyer today."

"Why don't you hire a new one?"

"What's the point?"

Marcus shrugged.

"It's not worth it. Been with her for over a year. She's a good sport and a good lawyer," the old man said, chewing.

---

6. * "Oh, Greece, I love you."

There was silence.

"By the way, the cleaner found a man in the toilets of the train station today. He was smashed up bad."

"You don't say."

"Pavlos told me."

"The guy who gives us the cheese pies?"

"Yes. A few hours before daybreak, the cleaner found the man unconscious and covered in blood. He's in the hospital in bad shape. But he'll pull through."

A gust of wind sneaked under the sheets of metal, blew across the fire, and moved the ends of their blankets.

"Stop looking at me like that," Marcus said.

"How am I looking at you?"

"You know how."

"You don't have anything to do with that business, do you?"

"What you mean?"

"The uniforms are looking for clues."

"Let them look all they want." He stared past the old man and out of the window at the drizzle falling in the light of the lamppost.

"Hey, son. I don't want any trouble. They know I live here. If you did it, come clean. And if you ask me, that scumbag had it coming. He beat people, stole things, the works."

Marcus put down his plate and stood up, sighing.

"Sit down and tell me about it."

Marcus told him the truth.

Apostolis drew in a deep breath and got to his feet. "I don't want to sound like your old man, but in my book, you've got two choices. Either you turn yourself in or move your ass out of here."

"Listen, I don't want to turn myself in. That move would throw me off my path."

"Your path?" Apostolis chuckled. "What path?"

"I like the way I live."

"You got to be shitting me, right?"

"It was my choice."

"Whatever."

"Listen, old man. I told you, I like the way I live."

"I don't like the way I live and neither do you. But you're too damn stubborn to admit it. I can't wait to move out of here. This place sucks."

Marcus was shaking his head.

"Look, son, it's high time you got your act together. I know it, you know it, and Mr. All-Knowing knows it." He pointed at the ceiling.

"And what about you, huh? Look at you."

Apostolis' eyes turned angry. He grabbed him by the sweater and lifted his fist. The blanket fell to the floor.

"Go on, hit me! What are you waiting for? Fucking hit me!"

"You only know half my story. So shut your mouth!" Veins stood out in the old man's temples.

"You're a bitter old man living in a shack."

He let go of Marcus, slowly sat down in the armchair, and lit a cigarette, frowning.

A heavy silence fell.

"Listen—" Marcus said.

"Forget about it."

The men sat by the fire, smoked, and listened to the sounds of the city. Then Apostolis began to talk. He said that when he lost his job, he started to drink. At first, he drank a couple of ouzos at dinner, and before he knew it, he was drinking almost a bottle a day. He said it went like that for about a year.

"My kids and my wife were worried. I slowed down for about a month, but then . . ." his voice trailed. "I drank, but I wasn't raising hell." He studied the fire as though he were reading from it. He said that three days after his second granddaughter was born, he had a few ouzos with friends to celebrate the news. "I was feeling good about things."

On the same day, he and his wife decided to drive to the hospital to see the newborn baby. She asked him if he was fit to drive, and he assured her he was. "Halfway into our journey, my eyes closed. When I opened them again, I was in the hospital. My wife didn't make it. The car had skewed off the road and slammed into a pole. And I've been driving trucks for thirty-five fucking years." He shook his head. "Since then, I've been homeless. I never drank again. My kids asked me to go live with them. I can only be grateful they don't hate me. But they remind me so much of Athanasia."

The drizzle eased up. Marcus went out to let Scotty in, and the dog lay down by the old man's feet. Stroking him, Apostolis said, "Marcus, you're half my age. You've got to get your things in order. I like you being here. The past four months have been good. I enjoyed our walks and talks, the laugh and the bus rides. I loved it all. But this is my home until I get my pension. You can stay tonight."

When Marcus woke up, it was early afternoon, and the sky was cloudy. He lay in the sleeping bag and listened to the wind on the metal sheets. He didn't want to leave, but he had to. *And it's all because of that scumbag*, he thought.

Just before he woke up, he had dreamed of his mother. She stood at the entrance of the shack, wearing a white dress, but her face was solemn. *She wanted to tell me something*, he thought and decided to call her later today.

On top of the armchair, Marcus found a note. I HATE GOODBYES, the note said and offered good wishes along with twenty euros. Sadness traced the edges of his eyes. At the door, he threw a last look at the place and felt his sadness grow. "Good luck to you too, old man," he said and slung his backpack over his shoulder.

He headed down Monastiriou Boulevard, which was heavy with traffic, walking against the wind blowing in off the sea and feeling the cold in his bones. He remembered the run-down neoclassical building where he could spend a couple of nights. But what he needed now was a warm place to sit and have a cup of coffee. And he knew a place in the heart of the city where he could get it free of charge.

He crossed the road at the traffic light. Foreign men in woolen beanies stood in clusters in a little square, drinking coffee and smoking cigarettes, waiting to land a job. They were great bricklayers, painters, carpenters, and plumbers. They were cheap, punctual, and worked hard.

With the wind now howling in his ears, he moved to Politechniou Street and walked past an empty spot where, a few months ago, he had met a lanky, soft-spoken man with kind eyes who was living in his car. But he wasn't there now. One day, they had coffee and a long talk at the place where Marcus was heading now. The man said he was thinking of moving to Crete.

Halfway down Tsimiski Avenue, where people begged for money on every corner, he turned left and rounded the Olympion movie theater. Before he turned onto Proxenou Koromila Street, he glimpsed the rough sea.

In the cafeteria, the air was warm. Young people sat by the windows with their coffees, surfing on smartphones. The voice of David Bowie came from the speakers: "A little piece of you, a little piece of me will die (this is not a miracle), for this is not America."

Blowing into his hands, Marcus stepped up to a corkboard hanging on the wall. Pinned to it were two stamped papers representing coffees that had already been paid for by customers.

He walked to the bar counter and handed it to the gray-haired man. "How are you?" the man asked.

"I'll feel better after I've drunk one of your tasty Americanos." The man winked at him.

Marcus sat at a table, took off his beanie, and ran his hands through his long hair.

The man set the coffee down on the table, along with a glass of water and a mini croissant. Marcus drank from the strong coffee and ate the croissant. Little by little, he began to feel better.

Then he flipped open his notebook and wrote:

I've reached rock bottom. Things have gone from bad to worse. I'm very angry. It was an interesting ride, but being voluntarily homeless is unforgivable. It's the lowest of the low. Of all the people I've met, none of them decided to live on the streets of their free will. And the ones who did it failed immensely. Being homeless is like doing time. I don't know. I feel I'm not myself anymore. I've done things I'm not proud of.

He lit a cigarette and sipped his coffee. Deep in thought, he went on writing.

I'm thinking of moving abroad. This thought has been turning in my head for some time now. I need to get out of this country. I have a friend who lives and works in Chicago. We were in the army together. Last year, he offered to help me. He said that I could stay at his place until I found a job. Amerika is a country with plenty of opportunities. The pace over there is tough and fast, and your limits are put to the test. Also, the transition from the idiosyncrasy of one country to the other is very difficult. All the above may be true, but I don't care because my future in this country is bleak. The last time I spoke to my friend, he was on a holiday in San Francisco. San Francisco! I'm thirty-two years old and where the fuck have I been?

He shoved the notepad back in his rucksack and counted his money: €47.50. *I need to get more*, he thought. But where would he find it? And what was he willing to do to get it? He said goodbye to the gray-haired man, and as he pulled the door of the café open, an idea was stoked in him. An element of risk was involved, but first, he needed to let the idea ferment.

The wind had eased up. Marcus stood outside the door of the soup kitchen. He came over here a few times a week to take a shower, wash his clothes, and have a hot meal. He climbed down a few steps and looked through the door at two women preparing the food. One of them had a round face and red cheeks; her name was Maria. A month ago, she had talked to him about the benefits of believing in Jesus. The other lady, slim and with large brown eyes, came to the door as Marcus took off his beanie.

"We open at six."

"Let the young man in," Maria said in a cheerful voice. "It's freezing outside."

Marcus thanked her and stepped into the warm space smelling of fresh bread, chicken soup, and oranges.

"How are you, Marcus?" Maria asked him.

"I'm still standing."

The other woman began to put pitchers of water on the tables.

Marcus said, "I know that the showering day for men is on Friday, but because I'll be out of the city, I was wondering whether I could take a shower today."

"We are not allowed to break routine." She turned the cooker down a notch. "But I'm going to make an exception for you." She smiled.

He went upstairs to the first floor and entered the bathroom. The hot water and the soap felt good on his skin. Marcus started drawing up a plan on how to get the money. When he was a teenager, he worked as a waiter at a cantina in a tall building near the port. On each floor were offices that belonged to accountants and lawyers. Some lawyers stayed late. Now and again, they would go to the bathroom or visit a colleague in an office next door and leave the door of their office unlocked. The only problem was that in the evening, the entrance of the building was usually secured.

He put on fresh jeans and a thick, woolen, black jumper as he heard Maria welcoming people downstairs.

When he came back down into the dining area, women and men

had begun to file in. Most of them were elderly. Maria and Christina stood behind the counter, dipping their ladles into the steaming pots. Slices of warm bread were stacked in straw baskets. After a short prayer, they started to eat, keeping their eyes mostly on their food. Some made small talk. Marcus felt a sense of kindness wash through him, and the image of the old man came to him. The fact that he would never see him again made him sad.

The air was cold and damp when Marcus arrived at the tall building that once housed the cantina. It was 19:27, and the entrance was locked. Marcus lingered there and remembered Maria's words: "Young man, make sure you pick up your rucksack at nine o'clock sharp. I have kids at home."

He waited, lit a cigarette, and noticed two crows sitting on an electrical wire right across the street. He glanced at his watch again: 19:55. He decided to burn another cigarette and then leave. When he heard something clank inside, he took a set of keys out of his pocket and faked that he was trying to unlock the door. Out of the elevator came a well-dressed couple. When the man opened the door, Marcus stepped back, mumbling.

He started at the top of the building. The seventh floor was quiet. On either side of the corridor, the doors were closed. Someone was on the phone in one of the offices. Two floors down, Marcus turned a knob, but the door was locked. He tried a few more doors, but nothing again.

On the fourth floor, he sneaked into an office through its half-open door. The room was carpeted wall to wall, and the lights were dimmed. Over the reception desk hung a painting of Lady Justice. A picture window offered a view of the buildings across the street. Black leather sofas and armchairs sat heavily on the floor, and on the tables were magazines and glass ashtrays. Behind an open sliding door, a lamp cast its light on a desk. Marcus smelled cigar smoke.

He swiftly rummaged through the pockets of a blazer. *Where the fuck do you keep the money?* he thought just as he spotted, in a half-open drawer, a revolver. Then he looked at a framed photograph with a black-haired woman and a young girl on the desk. They were smiling. A crystal glass stood next to an almost empty bottle of bourbon, and a pen lay on a piece of paper. Marcus began to read:

> I've been thinking about writing this letter for a while now. At first, I tried to move on with what was left of this life of mine, but I can't go it another step. I feel you deserve to know how things stand. I'm aware that this may come as a shock to you, but I'm tired of lying. I'm sick and tired of everything and everybody. . .

Marcus opened the top drawer and found a manila envelope filled with hundred-euro bills. Glancing at the door, he shoved a handful inside the pocket of his coat, put the envelope back, and closed the drawer. As he was tucking the revolver under the belt of his jeans, he heard steps.

A bit earlier, a man in a black shirt had been on his knees before the toilet bowl, his stomach in spasms, retching. He vomited again and again. He was now trudging along the corridor. His hair was clammy, and his eyes were red. Feeling light-headed, he entered his office and raked his eyes about. Marcus stood behind the door of an office on the other side of the room. After a few breaths, the man plopped down in the chair and poured himself another glass of bourbon. Marcus peered from behind the door. Taking small, catlike steps, he slithered against the wall and snuck out the door as the man wrote. Inside the elevator, he took a deep breath and tried to calm down. He glanced at his watch. It read 20:33.

Outside, the siren of an ambulance cut the air. He threw the gun in a back-alley gutter and the bullets into a rubbish bin. Walking along, he decided to have a drink, but first, he had to pick up his rucksack and make a phone call.

After stopping by the soup kitchen for his belongings, Marcus walked through Aristotelous Square and up Archea Agora (the Ancient Market), found a public phone, and dialed a number.

The voice on the other end said, "Where the hell are you?"

"On the phone talking to you."

"We've been looking for you."

"Why?"

"You must come home."

"Is Mother okay?"

Marcus heard his brother call out to their mother. "Okay, okay," he heard his brother say as he passed the receiver to her.

"Mother, what's wrong?"

"What's wrong? I haven't heard from you for over a month. I've been sick with worry. Where are you?"

"I'm okay."

"Listen, your father is in the hospital. The doctors ran tests. They say it's in his head."

Marcus tried to speak, but his voice caught. He never thought his old man would get sick. He went to bed early, woke at dawn, took long walks, and ate healthily.

His mother sniffled into the phone. "They gave him three months. Three months, you hear, son? You must come home. He's been asking for you. Are you there? "Marcus?"

Later, Marcus sat on a barstool. Three stools down the bar, a man and a woman were drinking beers, talking, and laughing. In the orange light of the bulbs hanging over the counter, cigarette smoke moved like a jellyfish.

He thought of his father and felt ashamed of the things he had done in the past six months.

A woman with black eyes put a drink down in front of him. From the speakers, Johnny Cash sang, "The Man Comes Around." Marcus knocked back his bourbon, raised his glass for another, and counted the money again: 1,750 euros—enough for a trip abroad. Now his mother's words waged a war inside his head. He pictured his father lying in bed. *How little and unprotected he must be feeling now*, Marcus thought. *But now, old man, it's too fucking late. You behaved as though you were immortal.*

When he left the bar, the lights of lampposts blurred his woozy eyes. Feeling wiped out, he decided to check into the motel where he had slept the night before he rode the bus to Volos last spring. He put on the beanie and headed down the sidewalk.

Just a few blocks away from the motel, from the corner of his eye, he caught sight of a man tumbling out of an abandoned neoclassical house, then running up the street and turning a corner. Despite the eerie feeling hanging around the place, Marcus decided to go into the house.

His crowbar in one hand and a Zippo lighter in the other, he stepped past the main door. The smell of urine and feces turned his stomach as he moved into a large room. In the corner, he saw a gasoline lamp burning low, and on a torn and smeared mattress lay a young woman.

"Lady, are you okay?" He shook her. "Fuck me. Lady!"

He pulled the syringe from her vein, put his finger on her jugular, and felt her weak heartbeat. He slapped her face, talked to her, and slapped her again. "Motherfuckers," he said, pulling up her jeans. Then he heaved her up into his arms and got out of the old house.

While he looked for a taxi, he talked to her, clouds of breath forming in the air. People stopped and stared. In a moment, a car screeched to a halt in front of him. A young woman asked what the matter was. Marcus told her.

"Get in!" she said. "Get in!"

He climbed into the car. "Hold on," he said to the unconscious woman. "You can't die tonight. Hold on."

The driver raced through the city, leaned on the horn, and drove through a red light, drawing lots of attention.

Later, when Marcus emerged from the emergency room, he

crossed in front of the lights of an idling ambulance and moved to where the woman had parked her car. He stood outside her open window as she smoked a cigarette, biting her lower lip.

"How's she?" she asked with traces of agony in her voice.

"I don't know yet. They're trying to resuscitate her."

"Fucking bastards," she said angrily.

"I know the feeling." Marcus produced a fifty-euro bill and told her that the police were on their way and they'd most likely want to ask him a few questions.

"What's this?" She frowned at the money.

"Take it."

She looked at him like he was crazy. "I'm not a taxi driver, man. Please, don't insult me." She tore a piece of paper from a notepad, jotted down her name and number, and handed it to him. "Here. I'd appreciate it if you'd call me and tell me about the girl."

He studied the note. "I'll call you, Dimitra."

"I'll be waiting."

Walking back inside, Marcus felt spent. He bought a coffee and sat in the waiting room. The fluorescent lights hurt his eyes. People leaned against walls or slumped in chairs. One man had his arm in a makeshift sling, and a woman sat with a bandage wrapped around her head. Nurses and doctors busied themselves, bustling in and out of rooms. A digital screen mounted on the wall displayed changing numbers. "Two hundred and nine," a voice over the speaker said. An old man on crutches hobbled to reception.

A big-bellied paramedic rushed through. "Move out of the way!" A young woman lay on a gurney, breathing through an oxygen mask, eyes closed.

Marcus thought of his father again. He knew that tough days lay ahead for the whole family. He pictured his mother standing on the threshold of the house, throwing her arms around him.

Then he remembered his father teaching him how to ride a bike when he was five years old. It had been a warm spring day. He could still feel the joy he felt the moment his father let go of the bike. He felt his shaky feet on the pedals, his little hands on the handles, trying to keep the bike steady, the sun on his back, the wind in his hair, and the thrill in his heart. He still remembered his father's cheering and his warm hug.

The female doctor who had asked him to wait outside called him.

"How's she?"

"She's still unconscious, but out of danger."

Marcus breathed out a sigh.

"If it hadn't been for you, she would've left us by now."

"May I see her?"

"Only relatives are allowed."

Marcus held her gaze and frowned, and the doctor relented.

The room was warm and quiet. The young lady lay in a bed near a window. The curtains were drawn, and a drip hung by the side of the bed.

"Her parents are on their way, but you can take a seat." The doctor gave him a thin smile. "I'll be back soon." She made to go. "Oh, by the way, her name is Chrisanthi."

Marcus sat in a chair. Hearing the rain on the window, he huddled into his coat, leaned back, and fixed his eyes on the young lady. He focused on the spot where her blanket rose and then fell again. It rose and fell. Then, with a wave of sweet warmth flowing over his body, his eyelids grew heavy, and, bit by bit, Marcus drifted off to sleep.

The Doctor

THE DOCTOR WOKE with a start. His heart pounding, he wiped the sweat from his forehead with the back of his hand. He sat up on the bed, threw a worried look around, and drank a mouthful from the glass of water next to the bed as images from his nightmare played in his mind.

In his nightmare, his wife was sitting on the Persian carpet in the living room. She wore a white tunic and looked straight into his eyes as a seductive light shrouded her face. When he tried to touch her, he could neither move nor speak. The last thing the doctor remembered, and the thing that scared him the most, was when his wife's face began to fade away, screaming soundlessly all the while.

Four months ago, his wife, Dimitra, had kissed him good night and gone to sleep in his arms. In the morning, the doctor put a mug of coffee on her side table only to realize in the next moment that his wife was dead.

"The autopsy showed an aneurysm in the head," said a neurosurgeon friend. His words sent the doctor into the permanent dumps. Dimitra was sixty-five years old, twelve years younger than him.

About a month prior to her death, now and again she'd complained of splitting headaches. He'd tell her to take a painkiller and lie down. "Lie down, honey; it'll pass." He did not know that one afternoon, when she was moving things about in her organic store in downtown Thessaloniki, she had felt a pain in her neck and all the way down to the fingers of her right hand. The pain was so severe that she had to close the store. But she didn't say anything to her husband.

Since the funeral, she often came into his dreams and messed with his mind. The doctor blamed himself for her death. *I should've taken her headaches more seriously. I'm a doctor, for Christ's sake*, he told himself again and again. As time dragged by, his sadness grew bigger, and in a few months, the only thing that brought him out of his house was his practice. He was a retired gynecologist, but he kept seeing patients at his office on Egnatia Boulevard, in Thessaloniki.

The doctor realized that there was only one way to put an end to his pain. That way was suicide. He pictured himself cutting his wrists, swallowing a box of pills, or jumping off his balcony, as a neighbor of his had done a year ago after his business failed. But he had not the heart to do it, nor did he want to hurt his daughter, Iphigenia, and granddaughter, Dimitra. *What kind of a man would choose such a way out?* he asked himself, only to answer, *An idiot and a coward.* And so, it dawned on him that the most honest and silent solution was to stop eating, gradually.

A month ago, he put his plan into action and tried to stand by it with a religious reverence. For breakfast, he drank a double Greek coffee and a glass of water, for lunch he ate a spinach pie, and for supper, when hunger plowed through him, he'd drink a few glasses of bourbon and smoke cigarillos. The first three days were the most difficult ones; his stomach rumbled all day, his mouth got dry, and the mood swings got the better of him. On the tenth day, instead of feeling weaker as he had expected, he felt much better than before. He went to sleep easier and woke in a better mood. His energy levels rose, his skin felt softer, and his mind became sharper. But within three weeks, his clothes began to bag on him, and the veins on his hands stood out. "If I keep at it, I'll die soon," he said, heaving up his pants in the mirror.

His daughter lived with her husband and their daughter in a comfortable apartment a block away. Since her mother's death, knowing that the only food her father could prepare was eggs, she brought food to his place every day: meatballs with roasted potatoes, Greek salad, flat beans, spinach with rice, moussaka with lettuce salad, and pork steaks with french fries and beet root salad. But the doctor fed it all to the strays in the neighborhood.

One afternoon, he said to his daughter: "Your moussaka was delicious. Thank you, sweetheart." But the weakness made his knees feel rubbery.

"Father, are you sure you eat the food I bring over?" She studied him. "You could sure play Count Dracula."

The doctor kissed Iphigenia on the forehead and told her not to worry. He also told her to stop bringing food over because he liked to eat either at a local restaurant or at a hamburger joint located near the church of Saint Sophia, in the heart of the city.

"Father, one day you can eat out, and the next day at home." She gave him a stubborn look.

Once a week, she cleaned his place and did his laundry. Whenever his granddaughter was back in the city, on a break from her studies in Ioannina, she would give her mother a hand.

By the time the doctor drove to his office and began examining his patients, he felt untied. The nightmare had rattled him and enhanced the despair that circled him like a hungry hyena.

Late in the cloudy afternoon, during his last examination, a patient asked him, "Doctor? Are you okay?" After what seemed a long, embarrassing silence, the woman looked past her bent legs at his white hair. In a more alarmed tone she asked, "Doctor, are we good down there?"

The doctor stood and looked at her, but his gaze was blank, as if he couldn't see her.

"Doctor?"

He dropped the surgical gloves into a bin. "Eleni, there's absolutely nothing to worry about."

Now he sat in his chair with his fingers knotted on his desk as the patient reached into her purse for her wallet. He raised his hand. "Eleni, there's no need for it. Please."

To patients who could afford to pay, he asked for twenty euros, enough to cover office expenses. But from patients he knew were in a tight spot because of the economic crisis, he didn't take any money. In a country where doctors in public hospitals accepted payoffs from their patients—known as φακελάκια [7*]—to perform their duty, he was seen as a traitor.

Many moons ago, when he was working in a public hospital, he'd caught his colleague sliding an envelope into the pocket of his trousers as a patient left his office. They had studied at the university together. "I just bought a new house," he blurted out. "And we just had a baby. How can I make ends meet on my salary alone, eh?" The doctor glared at him with anger and contempt and never spoke to him again.

If things were up to him, he would build a health system where people had their annual checkup at a high-tech clinic and where they would run tests from head to toe. It would be like the MOT test for cars. The doctor believed this would either prevent serious health troubles or catch them at an early stage. If the individuals didn't show up for their tests—unless, of course, they had a good reason for their absence—they would get a firm fine for their irresponsibility. Their medical history would be recorded on a card like a driver's license, and they would have to always carry it on them. To his wife he once suggested, "My love, if people score high results on their tests, they will be rewarded with a two-month supply of spirulina and omega-3 fatty acids fish oil."

Eleni put a twenty-euro bill on his desk anyway, then turned to go. At the door, the doctor put the money in the pocket of her black coat. "Next time."

"Doctor, you said the same thing last time."

"Say hello to your husband for me." He smiled.

The woman thanked him and went out the door.

Since Eleni was his last patient for today, he poured himself a

---

7. ˙ Meaning small envelopes

generous glass of bourbon, lit a cigarillo with his Zippo, and turned his chair toward the dark window. He let the smoke dribble from his lips and worked the bourbon in his mouth as though the sorrow he felt were a toothache that could be numbed by the alcohol. But the harder he tried to ignore the pain, the stronger his sorrow and sense of regret grew.

He drank another bourbon and smoked another cigarillo. Images of his wife from the nightmare surfaced again. And as time passed, he didn't want to go back home.

When his wife was alive, he couldn't wait to return home. He couldn't wait to smell all the sweet and spicy scents from her cooking. Dimitra enjoyed baking brown bread and spinach and leek pies. She loved to cook casseroles and oven dishes, apple and milk pies. Most of the products came straight from her store, which was now being run by their daughter. The doctor enjoyed eating with his wife, sipping wine, and holding long conversations about their jobs, movies, and literature and about all their travels around the world and the places they would like to go. He missed all that, but what he missed the most was her laughter and the way she made him laugh. Her face had been made to smile. He even missed their passionate arguments and the silences that followed, as well as her soft touch and her warmth under the bed covers.

It started to rain. The round headlights of the Mercedes Benz swept over cars parked on either side of the acacia-lined street. On the radio, a woman was saying that the government had managed to put together a long list of Greek businessmen and politicians who had made large euro deposits in banks in Zurich. "It's too late now," the doctor said. He parked between two cars, killed the engine, lowered the window a crack, and heard the two men passing by on the sidewalk speaking a language he couldn't understand. Most of the foreigners who lived in Thessaloniki were Albanians, Russians, Armenians, and Georgians. Thousands of Albanians had gone back home after the construction business caved in.

An old couple walked under the light of a lamppost, holding hands as the rain pattered on their umbrella. "You bastard," the doctor said, agony creasing his face. "Of all the women in the world, why my Dimitra?"

The doctor retrieved a paper bag filled with bananas, oranges, and green apples from the passenger seat. His wife had always preferred a nice bowl of fruit in the middle of the kitchen table to flowers.

With the rain soaking him, he locked his car and swiftly headed down the sidewalk. Empty drink cans rolled in the wind at the doorsteps of shops, along with crumbled paper sandwich wrappings and cigarette butts. Signs on the windows read, FOR RENT.

Two crows on the balustrade of a school right across the street watched the doctor turn the key at the entrance of the apartment building. As he pushed the door open, a slight hesitation worked over him, as if someone were watching him. He turned and looked about. *It's just my mind playing tricks on me*, he assured himself.

The doctor got out of the elevator and made for the door of his apartment, then paused, thinking he'd heard something. He took a few steps toward the stairs at the end of the hall and stopped again, then held his breath and listened, unable to shake the faint feeling of being followed. If the doctor had taken a few more steps toward the stairs and looked around the corner to his right, he would've seen two men pressed back against the wall, holding their breaths.

He returned to the door of his apartment and heard bickering on the third floor below—between two siblings, a man and a woman, who lived with and took care of their father, who suffered from dementia. Their mother had died many years ago. He could hear the siblings argue when he took showers and when he listened to the radio or as he lay on the sofa in the living room. Once, their voices woke him in the dead of the night.

The doctor was their family friend. Mother had been his patient, and the daughter still was. A week ago, he had gone to see their father, with whom he played chess a few times a week. Together with their wives, they used to go to dinners at tavernas and have good times. That day, the old man lay helpless in his bed, staring at the doctor as if he were an alien. *Look at how we end up*, the doctor thought and felt sad. He knew the family was strapped for money. The old man had been a construction worker but spent most of his wealth on the roulette table.

As the doctor nudged the door open, he heard a rush of feet. Before he could turn, he felt a strong push on his back. The doctor fell into the hallway of his apartment, slamming his elbow and knees on the floor. The bag tore open, and the fruit scattered.

One of the robbers flipped on the ceiling light. "Don't fuck move," a voice said in broken Greek. When the doctor tried to stand, the robber came down hard on his back with his wet boot.

"You bastard!" the doctor grunted.

"Shut mouth!"

"Let go of me!" The doctor twisted and turned his body.

The robber put a gun to his temple. "Shut mouth. If you scream, I shoot."

"Go on, you bastard! Shoot me!"

"Go easy on him," said the second robber, who was standing behind his partner.

His back and elbow aching, the doctor turned his head to the sound of moving feet and saw the second robber making his way into the living room.

"Where is money?"

The doctor gritted his teeth.

"Where is money?"

"Get out of my face!"

"Don't scream." The first robber grabbed the doctor's hair and pulled hard. "Where is money?"

"What money?" the doctor said with pain in his voice.

"We know you have money. Yesterday you go to bank. You put money in bag."

The doctor was stunned. *They must have been following me for some time*, he thought with horror. And when his daughter and granddaughter came to mind, fear shot through him like an electric current.

"Let go of my hair!"

"Where you put money?" The robber's eyes turned ugly.

The doctor heard the opening of drawers in the living room, the sound of objects being swept off surfaces and glass breaking. "If you let me stand up, I'll tell you."

The robber let go of the doctor's hair and called out for his partner. In a moment, the other one moved back to the hallway. "Help the old man stand," the robber said in fluent Greek.

"I can manage by myself," he snapped.

Both men were younger, taller, and stronger than him. "Aren't you ashamed of yourself?" the doctor said to the Greek man with as much contempt as his words could carry. "Is that what your parents taught you?"

"No, I'm not ashamed of myself. If our boss had paid us the money he owes us, we wouldn't be here now. We broke our backs building summer houses for fucking doctors, lawyers, bankers, and CEOs." Veins bulged in his temples. "You wanna know what the fucker did? He moved abroad with the ten thousand euros he still owes us. I'm sick and tired of this fucking country. I wanna go to America. We saw you taking money out of the bank."

"You should be ashamed of yourself."

His face stiffened. "Where is the fuckin' money?"

I'm not afraid of them, the doctor thought. *If they kill me, they'll never find the money.* "Come on, shoot me and get it over with."

The foreign robber looked at his partner and grinned. Holding the gun, he moved closer to the doctor.

"Old man," the Greek said, "we don't want to hurt you. Just give us the money. We know you hid it in the apartment."

The foreigner grabbed the doctor by his clothes and shook him good. A few shirt buttons fell on the floor.

"Let go of me." The doctor threw a few clumsy punches. One of them caught the robber on his chin. He swore in his own language and bashed the doctor's nose with the back end of the gun. The doctor tumbled to the floor.

When he came to, he found himself in the living room armchair. He heard rain tinkling on the railing of the balcony, and through his blurry vision, he saw the robbers standing in front of him. He wondered how long he had been out. His face and his head hurt, and his mustache was soaked with blood. Drops had stained his shirt and trousers. He tried to focus.

His mind again went to his granddaughter, who called him twice a week and talked to him about her studies and asked him to promise her that he would eat more because the last time she had seen him, he looked thinner than before, something which made her worry. She looked so much like his wife.

The thought of dying rattled him. Everything had happened as fast as the crackle of the thunder he had just heard. His hands trembled. He gathered himself to stand, but then plopped back down on the armchair as spots of light danced in his vision.

The Greek handed him a wet towel.

With an unsteady hand, the doctor pressed the towel to his nose, which stung and throbbed. *What the hell was I thinking*, he thought and felt foolish about the idea of committing suicide.

The foreigner moved closer. "Where is money?"

"If I give you the money, how do I know that you will not shoot me?"

The Greek said, "We aren't killers. But if you don't give us the money, we'll send you to the hospital with broken bones and ribs." He wrinkled his forehead. "You understand?"

About two years ago, a robbery had taken place in the apartment building next door. The robbers managed to make off with jewelry and thirty thousand euros. Two days before, at the news that Greece might pull out of the euro currency, the neighbor who was robbed had withdrawn most of his money from the bank and brought it home. When he tried to stop the thieves, they shot him in his leg.

The doctor had brought home six thousand, planning to give a small part of it to the siblings and the rest to his granddaughter. Luckily, he split the money in three stacks.

"Outside on the balcony, you will find pots with plants." He pointed to the balcony door.

As the Greek opened the door, a chilly wind that smelled of rain and leaves gusted in.

"Dig in the pot without a plant in it." He watched the foreign robber with the gun as the nervous man's eyes skipped between the doctor and his partner digging into the pot.

"Bingo!" the Greek said and took the money out of a black plastic bag. He thumbed through the fifty-euro bills, and his face grew serious. "What the fuck's this?" The Greek shook the money near the doctor's face. "You think we're stupid?"

The doctor tried to act normally.

"Old man, where is the rest?" He put his large hand on the doctor's shoulder and pressed so hard that the doctor cried out. "This is your last chance. Where's the rest?"

"Get out of my house, you bastards."

The foreigner pushed his partner aside and lifted his hand. "Where is money, old man?"

The doctor's mobile rang. The robbers stepped back and glared as he pulled the phone out of his pocket. "Who is it?"

"It's my daughter. She calls at ten o'clock every day to check on me."

"Answer it. But if you as much as breathe a word . . ." The Greek made a fist.

The doctor cleared his throat and spoke calmly. "Hello, darling."

"Hello, Father. How are you today?"

"I'm good."

"Did you eat the dish I brought over? It's your favorite," she said and asked her husband to turn down the television.

"I know; I'll eat soon."

"Father? You sound strange. Are you okay?"

"I'm fine. Why?" He tried to keep his voice from cracking.

"You want me to come over?"

"No, I'm fine. I'm in the bathroom. You caught me with my pants down."

"Oh!" She chuckled. "I'm sorry."

"Look, darling, I must go now."

"Good night, Father. I love you."

"I love you too."

The Greek approached him. "You did good, old man."

The doctor raised his eyes to meet his. He hoped to see a hint of kindness in them, but in vain. Those eyes were the fiercest he had ever seen. Now the doctor felt hollow and sick. He wanted their stench out of his house. "The other half is in the fridge." He dropped the bloody towel on the floor between his feet. "Inside a carton of milk."

"I'll be damned," the Greek said and rushed to fetch it.

Once he'd retrieved the money, he crushed the doctor's mobile with his boot, put him in the bathroom, and locked the door. Darkness gathered around the doctor as he heard them exit the door of the apartment. His hands trembling, he turned on the light over the mirror and examined his swollen eyes and nose. Both eyes were bruised. He set his nose with a quick movement of his hand and a bark of pain.

Breathing heavily, he took off his clothes and stood under the shower. The steamy water felt good. He wrapped a towel around his waist and opened the medicine cabinet, grabbing the iodine, which he dabbed on the cut on his nose before bandaging it. Then he put the lid of the toilet bowl down and sat on it, trying to cope with his feelings of helplessness and humiliation. *Nobody needs to know about it*, he told himself. *If my daughter asks, I'll tell her I tripped and fell.* The doctor knew that even if he went to the police, nothing would come of it. They still hadn't caught the men who robbed his neighbor. *I hope you lose the money, you bastards*, he wished with his whole heart. At least they hadn't found the last two thousand.

He glanced at the line of light under the door. Then he took a wire hunger from the top of the washing machine, straightened it, and slid one end into the keyhole.

Out in the apartment, the doctor put on a tracksuit, swept the floor of broken glass, tidied up the living room, and then put the bruised fruit in a bowl. He poured himself a drink and sat in his armchair. Sipping his bourbon and smoking a cigarillo, he listened to the rain. He tried to push the horrible experience out of his head. Surprisingly, he felt an urge to eat.

He set everything out on the kitchen table and dug in. He tore the bread, forked flat beans and feta cheese into his mouth, and went back for the Greek salad. The food felt right and good in his mouth and stomach. Chewing, he took quick breaths through his nose, swallowed, and continued. Little by little, he began to regain his strength. Wiping the dishes clean with a piece of homemade bread, he leaned back in his chair and sighed. He felt as though his stomach would burst open. Then he gazed at the empty seat across from him and let sadness wash over him. This was the first time since the funeral that he had sat at the table and eaten alone.

In the living room, he reached under an armchair and picked up the framed photograph that had been standing on the sideboard. He took a long look at it as rain continued to drum in his ears. It was of the day he and Dimitra had driven to a beach called the Boats in Afitos, a village in Halkidiki. The day had been a sunny one, and a sweet September wind was blowing. In the photo, she poses in her yellow bikini just where the waves are breaking, her hand on the top of her straw hat, blowing him a kiss. Behind her, white and blue boats bob in the water. That day, the doctor remembered, she told him she was pregnant with what would be their only child. *It was a beautiful day*, he thought. He closed his eyes and heard her laughter.

Pandelis Karagiannidis ran his thumb over her face in the photograph, and his eyes welled with tears. He kissed his wife, and in a sad, soft voice, he said, "My sweet love, I'm afraid you have to wait until my time is up," and set the photograph back in its place.

An Honest Man

THE KNOCK on the apartment door is strong, determined. Kiriaki stands in the hallway of her apartment, petite in her purple robe and slippers. She tucks a streak of disheveled black hair behind her ear and looks at her husband, who stands barefoot by the door. He's wearing boxer shorts and a white T-shirt.

"Who is it?" she asks.

Neoklis looks through the peephole, then puts his index finger to his mouth. He is of medium height, with rich-brown hair and eyes. He is muscular, the result of many years at sea and his status as a member of the Coastal Rowing Club Thessaloniki.

Outside the door stands a stocky man of around sixty years in a long black coat and a flat cap. His thick finger over the peephole, he puts his ear against the door, waits for a few seconds, and bangs on it again.

"Open up! I know you are in there! Open up!" He sighs. "Neoklis, listens carefully. If I don't get the rent in a week, I'll throw you two out. Do you hear me?" He looks over his shoulder at a man in a black duffel coat at the other end of the corridor, a toolbox by his feet. Mumbling, the stocky man barrels down the stairs.

Through the peephole, Neoklis can now see all the way to the end of the corridor, where their neighbor Anna stands at her door, talking with a man holding a big square of glass.

In the kitchen, the scent of freshly brewed, chestnut-flavored coffee fills the air. Kiriaki puts two mugs on the table by the window and sits across from her husband. Between them burns a floor heater.

"We're fucked," Neoklis says. "We've hit rock bottom. What are we going to do?" He puts his hand around the mug and shivers.

"Kiriaki, I don't understand." He puts a cigarette in his mouth.

"Neoklis, you don't need to be Einstein to understand. Our landlord wants his money. We owe the man five months' rent." As she fishes a cigarette out of the pack, her gaze falls on a large shell on the window ledge, which they found on a beach on Amorgos Island on their last vacation—three years ago.

Neoklis drinks his coffee and blows a streak of smoke toward the frosty window, from which they can see the ruins of the Ancient Market, Aristotelous Square, and all the way down to the Thermaikos Bay, where tankers are anchored.

"A week ago, I called and told him that we would pay the rent at the end of the month. You remember that, right? We have ten days until then."

"And where the hell will we find the money, huh? On the streets?" she says with irritation in her voice and flicks ash in a glass ashtray in the middle of the table. "Neoklis, come to your senses. We don't have jobs, and we spent most of the money we got from selling the car to pay the bills."

"How much money we got left?"

"Five hundred euros and some change."

There is silence.

"What's on your mind?" she asks.

"Nothing."

"Neoklis, what's on your mind? Tell me."

He raises his eyes to meet her questioning gaze. "I was just hoping . . ."

"Go on."

"I was hoping . . ." He turns the lighter in his hand. "Look, I want you to ask your parents for a small loan."

She widens her eyes and leans forwards. "Neoklis, have you lost your freaking mind? How can you even think that I would do such a thing? Have you forgotten that my father is still paying back the bank loan he took out to help us, huh? You forgot?" She glares at her husband, who is now staring out the window. "Neoklis, I'm talking to you."

"I'm listening," he says, shaking his leg nervously under the table. "Go on. I'm all ears."

"Just forget about it. They help us enough with food and all. We've been milking them dry, and one more loan would crash them." She stubs the smoke out in the ashtray. "Our baby girl is fortunate she was never born." Kiriaki's voice cracks.

Seeing tears in her eyes, his heart sinks. "Honey?" He reaches a hand across the table. "Don't talk like that, honey."

"Don't *honey* me." She wipes her face with a handkerchief and holds his hand. "Light me a cigarette."

He puts two cigarettes in his mouth, fires them up, and gives one to her. It has been a year since her miscarriage on that cursed night. Kiriaki was in the fourth month of her pregnancy when she felt something trickle between her legs as they ate supper. When she saw the blood in the bathroom, she lost the ground under her feet. After a few days and several tests, her gynecologist tried to calm them down. She called it a spontaneous abortion and explained to them that it was caused by chromosomal abnormalities of the fetus.

"You shouldn't worry; it's a common phenomenon. This happens when the egg or the sperm doesn't have the right number of chromosomes and therefore the fetus isn't viable. Thus, mother nature provided and rejected it." She also told them that it happens to one in four women and that many of her patients became pregnant again and gave birth to healthy babies.

Neoklis knows that his wife is right. "Kiriaki, don't worry. I'll think of something." He strokes her hand.

"Tell me that everything is going to be okay."

"As long as we have each other, everything's going to be okay. You'll see. I still have some irons in the fire." He gives her a reassuring smile.

Adjusting her robe, she stubs out the cigarette and stands. "Okay," she says numbly. "I'll take a shower, clean the apartment, and cook dinner."

He hears the water in the bathroom. As he smokes, he thinks about whom to call that might owe him money.

For many years, Neoklis ran a florist shop at the end of Saint Dimitrios Street, in the city center. On a rainy day eight years ago, Kiriaki popped into the shop to ask for directions. He instantly realized that she was his soul mate. They hit it off right from the start. They respected each other, saw truth and beauty in everyday things, and had the same taste in food, clothing, music, and films. Six months into their relationship, she moved into their apartment on Olymbou Street and since that day they have been inseparable.

When the couple got married four years ago, they were rich in plans. But when the economic crisis ran through Greece like a tsunami, one by one their plans were swept away. This happened in 2010, exactly two years ago. The florist shop started to lose money. But stubborn as he was, he wouldn't listen to Kiriaki, who warned him to sell the shop.

"Honey, we'll be fine. You'll see. We can't give up everything with the first storm." But Kiriaki, who had studied economics, expected the worst-case scenario; and she was right. The florist shop went belly up, and as if that disaster weren't enough, Neoklis had used up most of their savings in trying to keep it afloat.

They stood in long lines at job centers, filled out forms, went through job interviews, and made endless phone calls. But nothing came of any of it. Through a friend, Kiriaki found a job as a saleswoman at a lingerie store in the Kalamaria district for about a year. After that, she drew unemployment benefits for five months.

When some of Neoklis's friends suggested they come work at a Greek restaurant in Stuttgart, Germany, Kiriaki reacted as if he had asked her to move to the North Pole. "Neoklis, have you lost your freaking mind? Don't you remember the time we went to Munich?

We couldn't wait to come back home. For five days straight, it poured down like mad. The sun came out one day, and the next it rained again. Just forget about it."

She told him she would rather live on bread, olive oil, and Greek salad and have the Greek sun shining on her face than move abroad. And about two months ago, she said, "If our situation doesn't improve, we could go and live with my parents till we can stand on our feet again. Why do you look at me like that, Neoklis?"

Now it seems this scenario is in the cards. If they can't produce the money to pay the rent, they will become one of the many couples in Greece who have had to move back to their family home.

This is what Neoklis fears the most. When he heard the words "We could go and live with my parents," the blood froze in his veins. Her parents, with whom he gets along quite well, live in Ptolemaida, a town Neoklis hates. He hates its smell, doesn't much like its people, and since he neither has parents—they were killed in a car crash when he was a teenager, and his grandparents raised him—nor siblings to assist him, he is determined to do everything in his power to prevent his wife's words from becoming a reality. But so far, all his efforts have failed.

For dinner, Kiriaki prepares lentil soup and beetroot salad to accompany the smoked mackerel, a luxury they allow themselves occasionally. Since she is unemployed, she has time to cook, and she enjoys it. She says, "Cooking relaxes me and makes me forget about things." As always, they eat in candlelight, but this time mostly in silence.

In the high-ceilinged living room, they sit on the khaki corner sofa. Green curtains cover the wooden balcony doors, posters of movies they watched at the International Film Festival in Thessaloniki hang on the walls, colorful rugs cover the faded wooden floor, and red and green cushions sit on the sofa and on the armchairs.

Neoklis promises Kiriaki that come Monday, he will make a few phone calls and meet with people who owe him money. "Everything's going to be okay." He decides to try to put her at ease by doing the things she likes the most.

On Saturday, it rains like hell. Neoklis downloads a few movies: *Shame*, directed by Steve MacQueen, *The Master* by Paul Thomas Anderson, and Wes Anderson's *The Royal Tenenbaums*. He buys a bar of her favorite chocolate, flavored with ginger and orange, and two bottles of red wine. After supper, they play Scrabble, drink wine, and fall asleep halfway through the second movie.

On Sunday, the sun shines in a blue sky. With coats on and scarves about their necks, Kiriaki and Neoklis take a walk along the seafront and all the way to the White Tower, the city's most significant landmark. They buy coffee, sit on a bench, and gaze out at the sea.

Huddling in their coats, and with the wind smelling of salt and iodine, they drink, talk, and smoke.

In the evening, they eat crackers and cheese, drink the rest of the red wine, play cards, and listen to a song called "Αμερική"[8]* by Socrates Malamas.

Neoklis feels fortunate to be with a woman who doesn't nag and isn't miserable. She is so easy to please. They have had arguments, of course, but mostly over trivial matters.

With a satisfied expression after winning at cards, Kiriaki says, "Neoklis, I'm thinking of going to my parents' for a few days." She writes *22* on a piece of paper under her name. "On Tuesday, my sister and her kids will also visit them."

He shuffles the deck of cards. "That's a great idea, honey. A change of scenery will sure do you good."

Later, they make love on the sofa. Kiriaki falls asleep on his chest, but Neoklis stares at the ceiling. Now and again, he hears a car driving past or a dog barking. He has been thinking about how to come up with the money throughout the weekend. He has many

---

8. * America

acquaintances but only a few friends, and many of them owe him money from when the florist shop was doing well. Half of them, though, are unemployed, and the other half hold jobs that barely make ends meet. *How can I ask them back for the money they owe me?* he wonders. And when he thinks of all the money he put into the florist shop when it was collapsing, he feels frustrated. That money amounted to many arduous years of working hard and saving up.

Monday is a pale day, and a chilly wind blows through the streets. Neoklis and his wife have just arrived at the bus stop on Egnatia Boulevard. Two crows sit on a branch of an acacia tree and watch the couple.

"When you get back, it'll all feel as if you were in a bad dream." He kisses her lips as the bus pulls in. "Have fun. And stop worrying."

The bus opens its doors, and people begin to file out. On the steps, she turns. "When I get to Ptolemaida, I'll call you. Love you." She waves and smiles.

He watches her take a seat by the window. She has her black hair in a French braid. *How beautiful she is*, he thinks and feels tender. He smiles and waves as the bus speeds away, heading to the Macedonia Central Bus Station.

Neoklis walks by acacia trees along the Ancient Market, the cold wind blowing in his face. A man tosses his half-smoked cigarette on the sidewalk, and another man in ragged clothes picks it up. Neoklis takes five cigarettes out of his pack and hands them to the fellow, who takes them with an indifferent expression.

In the café, the air is warm and smells of freshly ground coffee. Cigarette smoke hovers above people sitting at tables and on bar stools. Four teenage girls, three brunettes and one blond, are on a red leather sofa near the window with their eyes glued to their cell phones. One of them says something, and they all laugh.

What would I not give to be as carefree as you girls, Neoklis thinks. He orders a coffee and a biscuit and sits at a table by the same window. From here he can see a slice of the Ancient Market and part of Aristotelous Square.

He unwraps the cinnamon biscuit the waitress sits on the table with his coffee and dips it in. After sipping his cappuccino, he lights a cigarette. Neoklis is here to meet with a friend from the old days. They talked on the phone that morning, and his friend said that he knew someone who could help him out. That was all he said. Now Neoklis can't wait to hear the rest of it. *Maybe it's about a good job*, he thinks.

The coffee perks him up and wipes the tiredness from his eyes. Glancing at his watch, he realizes his friend is fifteen minutes late. As he thumbs through the sports section of the newspaper, his cell phone rings.

His friend tells him that he can't make it. "An idiot smashed my rear bumper. I'm waiting for the traffic police. Goddamn!"

"Bummer," Neoklis says, and on a napkin, he writes down the name, telephone number, and address his friend gives him.

"Tell him I sent you. Tell him we're good friends."

"How will the man help me?"

"The guy's a moneylender."

"You mean a shylock, right?"

"Yeah, but he's different."

"Different?"

"You sound surprised."

"Of course I am."

"You haven't got any other choice, have you? I went to him as well. He's a decent man."

Decent my ass, Neoklis thinks and makes a face.

His friend tells him that he charges less interest than other moneylenders. He tells him that his nickname is Pope.

"The pope?" Neoklis raises an eyebrow.

"No, just Pope. Look, the traffic police are here. Gotta go. Talk soon."

Pope's office is near the seafront, where the city's lawyer and accountant offices are located. Neoklis smokes and thinks, drinks his coffee, puts two euros on the table, and heads out.

As he walks back home, his thoughts race. He can't believe he stands on a one-way street. *Turning to a shylock for help is degrading,* he thinks.

Neoklis sees a group of Russian tourists in warm clothes and fur hats getting off a bus and crossing the street to knot around a tall tourist guide. They all begin to climb the steps of St. Dimitrios's church. The guide must be taking them to see the famous catacomb where the saint was jailed and tortured. Every stone is engraved with Roman, Byzantine, and Ottoman influences as well as those of modern Christianity.

Neoklis turns his eyes to the old church. *If you're for real, man, help us.* But he knows that miracles happen only in the movies and books.

In the evening, he warms up the chicken soup his wife cooked and eats half a bowl in front of the television, watching the news. A camera cuts to a bar in Athens. The place looks like a war zone, with broken glasses, upturned tables, and chairs and blood splotches all over the place. The night before, a man had stood outside the bar crammed with young people and unleashed his Kalashnikov upon them.

A journalist says, "Fifteen youngsters were wounded, and three are in critical condition. The police are questioning witnesses and looking for leads."

"Fucking bastard," Neoklis says aloud as he picks up the ringing phone and hears Kiriaki on the other end say, "Sorry I didn't call you earlier, my love. I was busy. Are you watching the news? What the hell is going on in Athens? It's the third shooting within a month."

"I know honey." He lights a cigarette. "People are going nuts."

"Poor kids. I hope they get the bastard."

"I'm sure they will. We've got a top-notch police force."

"Have you had any luck with the money people owe you yet?"

"It's brewing, darling." He hears Kiriaki's mother calling her name.

"Got to go, my love. We're going to make cupcakes for my sister's kids."

He hears her family sending their love.

"Send them my love too," he says.

While he watches the flat-screen, his mind travels. He pictures himself living with his in-laws in that town. He sees the upsides: delicious dinners and good wine, card games with her family by the fireplace, long walks with Kiriaki along the canals, watching the ducks, and going to the woods for logs with her father. *He's a good man*, Neoklis thinks. *But he's often on a short fuse about something. When he isn't ranting about politics, he sits at the kitchen table for hours, solving crossword puzzles. He has a PhD in the sport. But if we end up moving in with them, everything will work out simply fine*, he reassures himself.

But within half an hour, he feels a knot in his stomach. *That town is shrouded in a layer of smog,* he thinks; picturing the power towers, he feels like choking. *And what about this apartment? What about our privacy? Our walks at the seafront? Our friends?* Every nook and cranny of their apartment is full of memories. A layer of melancholy spreads over him.

In the kitchen, he chugs a glass of water and looks out the dark window at the city lights. He draws in a breath and, hearing a webby squeak in his lungs, thinks of quitting "the killer sticks," as his wife calls them. But how the hell can he?

It's dark by the time Neoklis finds himself standing at a traffic light on Monasthriou Street, near the seafront. The traffic is bumper to bumper, and heavy rain pelts his umbrella. Nearby is the Ladadika quarter, a historic part of the city where, for centuries, neoclassical buildings housed shops selling olive oil, commercial warehouses, and brothels. Today, Ladadika forms a recreational spot with lots of restaurants, bars, and nightclubs.

Neoklis pictures himself dining and drinking wine at the taverns with his wife, either just the two of them or along with friends. He sees them sipping gin and tonics, laughing, kissing, and dancing. *Many moons have passed since then*, he thinks, and feels a bittersweet nostalgia as if he lived those moments in a dream.

The sound of horns brings his gaze to the middle of the road, where a man with a dense beard shuffles along, pushing a shopping trolley crammed with scraps of metal between cars inching ahead. The man wears lace-less boots, a khaki raincoat, and a red beanie under the hood. Rainwater streams over him to pour onto the asphalt.

Neoklis looks up past the edge of his umbrella at the lights in the windows of the office building rising above him. No matter how hard he tried to put the idea of going to Pope out of his mind, he realized that he doesn't have another option; thankfully, the secretary managed to work him into the schedule. Once he's inside the building, a janitor offers to help him. He rides an elevator to the top floor and step into Pope's outer office. The lights are dimmed. The blond secretary puts the phone down. "Neoklis, I suppose," she says.

He nods. She hangs his coat on a coat stand and puts his umbrella into an umbrella holder. Her perfume smells like lavender.

"Please, sit down." She motions him toward a black leather sofa that sits below a picture window. Before sitting, Neoklis gazes out the window and sees the dark sea and feels as though he is standing on the deck of a ship.

In an armchair across from him sits a tall, muscular man reading a magazine. He has short gray hair and blue eyes, and his face tells Neoklis that he's not someone to mess with. The man works for Pope.

"Mr. Angelidis will be with you shortly," the blonde says.

Neoklis shows her his cigarette.

"Yes, of course you can smoke. Would you like a coffee?"

"A cappuccino, please."

Neoklis drinks his coffee, smokes, and tries to put his thoughts in order. In a moment, the door of Pope's office opens, and a man in black steps out. As he goes to the door, he stares at Neoklis as if to say, "Man, you better walk out of here."

"Let the gentleman in," Pope says. He's wearing a gray suit and a black shirt. In the office, Neoklis smells roses and hears Frank Sinatra singing, "Strangers in the Night." The two men shake hands.

"Please, sit."

Neoklis sits on a crimson leather chair and watches Pope cross to a table where bottles and crystal glasses shine like gems under low light.

"Would you like a drink?"

"Sure."

Pope pours the Yamazaki twelve-year single malt into two crystal glasses and gives one to Neoklis. "This isn't an ordinary whisky. It's nectar. I brought it all the way from Japan."

The whisky slides down Neoklis's throat, soft like velvet. *You bastard,* he thinks, enjoying the whisky's aroma and its fruity aftertaste. He raises his thumb.

Pope gives a thin smile.

"Mr. Angelidis, thanks for seeing me at such short notice."

"Our mission is to help people in these difficult times."

Neoklis thinks the man must be a bit of a loony. He turns his attention to the wall, where a large black-and-white photo of Manhattan at night hangs. Images flash before his eyes, of when he and Kiriaki spent their honeymoon in the mother of all capitals.

"My son took that photograph. Have you ever been to New York?"

"Yes, I have."

A moment of uncomfortable silence moves between them. Then Pope pulls a gold coin out of his pocket. "Well, Mr. Neoklis?"

"I've never been in a tighter spot before."

"I understand you," Pope says, rolling the gold coin over his knuckles. "I had a word with your friend earlier today. He told me you're an honest man. And that's all I needed to hear. I like doing business with honest people."

"Thank you."

With a low pitch in his voice, Pope says, "I don't know what you've heard about us moneylenders. But you shouldn't give credit to rumors. Especially when it concerns me. Mr. Neoklis, people are envious, greedy, and, most of all, stupid. You help them, and when they get the chance, they stab you in the back. I've saved couples from breaking up. I've saved people from committing suicide. When families, friends, and banks slammed the door in their faces, I lent them a hand. I was their raft. I was their only salvation," He gives a thin smile. "Mr. Neoklis, do you understand what I mean?" Pope takes a sip from his Yamazaki and studies Neoklis through little eyes.

Neoklis feels as though his intelligence has been assaulted. *How could I lower myself so much?* he thinks but decides to play along nonetheless.

"I understand you. My friend put in a good word for you, too."

"Mr. Neoklis, I know your problems. Many people in Greece are in your shoes because of the economic crisis. The crisis has ruined their lives. But I'm here to help. I'm here to give people a second chance to stand back up on their feet. And that's what I'm about to do with you. Give you a second chance."

"Mr. Angelidis, I appreciate your concern—"

"How much money do you need?"

"Ten thousand euros," he quickly responds, surprised by the amount he's just asked for.

Pope's little eyes narrow to slits.

A moment passes.

"Have you got any property in your name?"

"Unfortunately, I haven't."

"Has your wife got any?"

"No, she hasn't got any either."

Pope asks him if he has a car or a motorbike, jewelry, or anything else of value. Neoklis tells him he has two vintage Omega De Ville wristwatches, a vintage Vespa motorbike, and some antique furniture. He tells Pope that if he sold those items, he could easily fetch over ten thousand euros.

Pope listens carefully, nods. "No, today they wouldn't fetch so much money."

While Pope speaks, Neoklis thinks of his wife and feels ashamed. *How could I be so stupid?* he thinks. An urge to get on his feet and rush out of the office comes over him.

"I'm interested in the watches and the Vespa. If the items are in pristine condition, I could lend you 2,500 euros. If you fail to pay me back on time, these items will be mine, of course. And suppose I lend you the rest of the money, how would you pay me back? There's a ten percent interest a month. Plus, five percent interest on top of that for not having anything to put up as collateral." He smirks.

Neoklis wants to grab him by the collar and sling him against the wall like an octopus. He pictures it and pauses before replying. "I didn't know the interest rate was so high."

Pope chuckles. "Mr. Neoklis, I'm a businessperson, not a bank. These days, cash is scarce. Who the hell will pay me back my money if you two lovebirds get killed or commit suicide?"

Neoklis can't stand him. He looks Pope straight in the eye and says, "Mr. Angelidis, you said you take huge risks. You said you like doing business with honest men. Well, I'm an honest man!"

Pope glances at his watch. "Neoklis, our time is up. If you want me to lend you the money, make a new appointment with my secretary and bring the items over."

"Thanks for the nectar," Neoklis says, stands, and unceremoniously heads out the door.

A few minutes later, Neoklis stands outside the entrance of the building, smoking. The sky rumbles in the distance, and lightning tears the dark veil. *Fucking leech*, he thinks.

In the dim red and blue neon lights of a bar in Ladadika, he downs a glass of whisky and orders another. He smokes, drinks, and thinks, *How the hell will I pay the landlord? I have been living in that apartment for twelve years, and I always pay on time.*

With the Ptolemaida scenario swirling in his tipsy head, he wobbles out of the bar and manages to open his umbrella. The front of his trousers gets wet, but he doesn't care. Anger runs in his veins, and frustration burns his heart.

Halfway across the street, he barely steps out of the way as a motorbike with two riders roars past, inches away.

"You idiots," he shouts and sees a small, black plastic bag fall out of one of their pockets. Neoklis dashes back into the street, and as the lights of an oncoming car fall on him, he snatches up the bag and shoves it into the pocket of his coat.

Back at the apartment, Neoklis sits at the kitchen table, drinking coffee as rain spatters the dark window. His wet trousers hang on a chair by the floor heater, steam rising. He stares at a stack of fifty-euro bills. It's four thousand euros. He runs his hands through his brown hair and sighs, trying to figure out whose money lies on the kitchen table. *Should I go to the police or keep the money?* He closes and opens his fingers.

He makes to call his wife, then stops. If he tells her about it, things will get more complicated. She will surely ask him to hand it over to the police. He hears her saying, "Are you out of your freaking mind, huh? This money isn't ours. Maybe it belongs to someone who needs it more than we do. Neoklis, we ought to do the right thing."

He scrambles into his clothes and shoves the money into the pocket of his coat. "Fuck it," he says. He switches off the floor heater, half opens the front door, and stops. He leans his forehead on the doorframe, closing his eyes. He thinks of Saint Dimitrios and sighs. "Miracles don't happen. Do they?" he whispers and bites his lower lip.

Neoklis doesn't hear the bickering between Anna and her boyfriend, Panagiotis, coming from next door. He doesn't hear the sounds of the spaghetti Western drifting from an apartment at the end of the corridor where Mr. Andonis, a widower, lives his days smoking his pipe and drinking wine. He doesn't smell the whiff of freshly baked bread and cakes coming from the apartment where Vasiliki and her husband, Nikos, live with their two lively kids. He just stands there, eyes closed. Neoklis feels as though his feet are glued to the floor. He draws in a long breath. "Goddamn it."

I Apologize to You, Sir

Dear Chief Editor,

Regarding an incident that shocked my whole being a few
days ago, I took the liberty to write this letter. I am a
widow with two daughters, twelve and fourteen years old. I
live in Athens, but I work as a Greek literature teacher at
a private school in Halkida, an hour's drive from Athens. I
also give private lessons at home to provide better living
standards for my children.

For a while now, I have been thinking about writing this
letter, but in the process, I thought not to and to let things
slide. But I cannot keep quiet. A rare rage has settled inside
me because of a horrendous incident from which I am still
trying to recover.

A few days ago, I was on an evening train heading to Athens.
I took a seat next to the window and started correcting my
students' homework. Half an hour into the journey, the train
pulled into Avlona. A young woman with dark skin complexion
and green eyes sat next to me. She greeted me in Greek, took
a history book out of her bag, and began to read.

When the train reached the SKA station, I looked out the
window and became alarmed. A group of young men with
their heads shaved, in military boots, khaki pants, and
flight jackets, were standing on the platform, frantically

gesturing and screaming at the train. Some of them were holding baseball bats.

When the train came to a full stop, the men started to pound on its windows and doors, shouting slogans and obscenities.

"They must be football fans," I heard a man say. But they seemed a far cry from football fans. They surged onto the train and scattered through the cars, howling.
Three sturdy men entered my car and stopped two rows down from where I was sitting. The shortest man stood with his legs apart, arms folded across his chest, and stared down at a seated man with dark skin while the other two stood by his side in the same fashion. In an authoritative
manner, the short man asked the dark-skinned man where he was from. With an accent, the man said he was from Nigeria. Rocking his leg, the short man asked for a residence and work permit.

Without protesting, the Nigerian man handed them to him. After the short man took a look at the documents, he scoffed and dropped them to the man's feet.

When the Nigerian man asked him who had given him the right to question him, the short man slapped him across his face, hard. This unexpected and shocking act swept through the car, and it made me feel as if I had been slapped. A few rows back, a baby began to cry. The Nigerian man sat there with his head down as the other two men laughed. I gathered myself to stand, but the girl next to me gave me a look.

The short man asked him for his wallet and called him a

monkey. *Haven't their parents and teachers taught these men anything of value?* I wondered, and fear heaved in my chest.

When the baby began to sob, the short man told the mother to shut it up. Then he opened the wallet, put a few euro bills in the pocket of his pants, and dropped it on the floor. When the Nigerian man bent down to collect it along with some colorful photographs that had fallen out of the wallet, the short man took him by his shoulder and slammed him back into the seat. Then, he wiped his hand on his trousers and made a face of disgust. "You should go back to your country," one of the other men said. "You aren't welcome here." Nobody dared to speak. We all sat frozen with fear and surprised by the men's impudence and cruelty.

Glancing from left to right, the short man sauntered to where I was sitting, and with the other two men standing right behind him expressionlessly, he asked the lady sitting next to me where she was from. She told him that she was born and raised in Greece. He smirked and told her that did not make her a native. Then, he asked for money.

When an old man stood up and told them to leave the young woman alone, the short man glared at him and told him to sit back down and shut up. It was then that I realized the train was not moving. "Someone must have called the police," I thought, and a faint relief fluttered in my chest as I glanced out the window, expecting to see the police. But I did not see anyone.

The young lady handed him a five-euro bill and told him that was how much his life was worth. Cursing, the short man grabbed hold of her elbow. The other two began to smirk, slyly. I now felt a rising tension in the car and hoped that someone would stand up to those men. The lady tried to get out of his grip, but to no avail.

I plucked up my courage, stood up, and told him to leave the girl alone. His cold eyes met mine. Then, he put his hand on my face and, pushing me down, said, "Sit down, you nothing." His partners laughed. But I felt disgusted, and a knot formed in my stomach.

By now, he had taken the lady by the hair, and as he tried to lift her up, she started to shout. I heard a door in the back slide open, and then I heard feet stomping. Two conductors holding crowbars came to our rescue. One of them shouted, "Let go of the girl, you bastard, or I swear I'll break every bone in your body."

When the short man let go of her, she pushed him and told him how low he was. Then she spat in his face, sat back down in her seat, and began to cry. The face of the short man hardened like wood.

As the conductors walked down the aisle with the crowbars, the three men began to back away. I put my arms around the young lady and held her tight. One of the other passengers in the back said that the police had arrived.

I looked out the window and saw the men scattering, jumping over fences and howling like wild beasts. In a few minutes, the train began to move, and my lungs opened again.

When we pulled into the Larisis station, I went over to the

Nigerian man and apologized to him. He smiled and thanked me. I also reported the incident to an officer at the station. I know that this letter may not make any difference whatsoever. But I wanted to express my rage, my shame, and my frustration toward the people and the politicians of this country and any other country where such inhumane and degrading actions still happen.

Sadly, we have not learned anything from all the bloody riots, the mad wars, the massacres, and the genocides. Sadly, we have not learned from all the tears we cried and the misery and the heartache we felt tearing inside. Sadly, we have learned nothing from the millions of crosses marking the long rows of dead. I do not want to sound melodramatic, but I am afraid that we will never learn.

Lately, I have come to think that maybe we are our own worst enemies. Maybe we are born with a self-destructive gene that is dormant inside us. And when that gene wakes up, it spews its poison like octopus ink and messes with our mind's vision. One day, we may manage to locate that gene and tear it out, or maybe, because of it, one day we will simply cease to exist.

That day, it was so difficult for me to stand up and try to stop these men. It was so difficult to stand up and say aloud, "Are you aware of what you are doing? Don't you know that we belong to the same family and share a common descent? Don't you know that happiness, compassion, and love are universal emotions? I am a mother and I know."

But I kept quiet instead. And I was disappointed with myself. As my heart ached, I realized how vulnerable and fragile we all are in the face of barbarism and violence. And at the end of the day, we are all to blame for such disgraceful outcomes.

Given the circumstances, I am grateful I came away
physically unharmed. I am grateful I am sitting at my desk
by the window, writing this letter to you, wondering where
the pure, noble, and unconditional love has gone.

Hopefully, this letter disturbs you as much as the horrendous
incident on the train disturbed me.

Thank you for reading.

                              Yours sincerely,
                              A mother

Yes, Why Not?

IT WAS FEBRUARY. The air in the living room was cold and smelled of alcohol and cigarettes. In an open box on the living room table was a piece of half-eaten pizza. Zachos—short for Zacharias—was awake but kept his eyes closed. His gaunt face was pale. He swallowed hard, his throat seared from all the beer and ouzo from the night before. Once more, he had fallen asleep on the sofa. As he lay there, curled up on his side, he got the feeling that something bad was going to happen to him today.

He drew in a breath, and a wave of lust flowed through his body. His dream had been so vivid and tangible that if he hadn't woken up, he could've lived in it for the rest of his life without realizing he was in a dream. Images of naked women played in his mind. It was the third time this week he'd had such a dream. A strange sense of loss and worry he couldn't identify swept over him.

Zachos opened his eyes and saw the pale afternoon light through the wooden shutters of the balcony door. He tried to remember how long it had been since he'd last gone to dinner with a woman. *Two years*, he thought, and the realization startled him. And it had been with the woman he had spent seven years with—until she moved to Chicago to work at her uncle's Greek restaurant.

"I've had enough of this shit!" she'd said at the kitchen table, drinking coffee and smoking a cigarette. "My uncle says that in a month, I could earn up to five thousand dollars just in tips. Imagine that! What the fuck am I doing wasting my youth and my beauty in this fucked-up country? You must have your head examined if you wanna stay in this chaos."

"And what about your job, huh?" Zachos said frowning

"I don't give a shit about my job. You've got no idea what I go through every fucking day working that job and getting paid as if I were a slave."

"And what about us, huh? Doesn't our love count for anything?"

She'd told him that if he wanted, he was welcome to go with her. But he didn't want to move abroad. For many years, he had been working at a fancy restaurant as a chef. He worked long hours, weekends, and holidays, but he liked his colleagues and his boss, and the paycheck was fair. He loved his girlfriend dearly, but he couldn't just drop everything and hop over the Atlantic to a place where he knew nobody. He had heard of her uncle, but he had never met him. Zachos was a man with his feet firmly planted on the ground; he hated hasty decisions and sudden changes of scenery. But to his girlfriend, he was stubborn, inflexible, and a coward.

For days he tried to talk sense into her. But she wouldn't budge an inch. She told him she would go and work hard and save up and come back to Greece with lots of money, and if their love counted for something, it was high time to put it to the test. She promised to Skype him a few times a week. "It'll be as if I were here in the room," she said. "And after a while, you'll come over as well."

During the first few months, things seemed to be working out just fine. They talked on Skype for a few hours a week about her new life in Chicago, about all the different things she had seen and the money she was making as a waitress in her uncle's restaurant. "Last month, I made four thousand dollars in tips. Four thousand! And you just keep on living your miserable life in Thessaloniki so as not to lose those good-for-nothing friends of yours and the cage you live in. Zachos, America is another planet. Paradise, baby, paradise. And lots of money. You better come over soon. I miss you, baby."

In the beginning, sex over Skype was awkward and bizarre, but it was better than nothing. The long and the short of it: a few months down the road, their Skype meetings began to thin out. One day, he received an email saying she had started dating another man. "I'm happy over here. I don't think I'll ever come back to Greece," she wrote and ended the email with the words "You should've come with me, but you chose to stay in that fucked-up country. Zachos, it's all your fault."

The loss knocked him off course for good. His disappointment, fused with sorrow, pushed him into the world of booze. No matter how hard his friends tried to stand by him, he wouldn't listen. Zachos withdrew to the darkest corner of his soul, where sadness and depression sang softly in his ears like the sirens in the *Odyssey* who trapped unsuspecting travelers with their charming song.

About a year ago, he'd lost his job, and a week later he drove into a ditch. He ended up in the hospital with a broken arm and leg, a ruptured spleen, and cuts and bruises. He limped out of the hospital on crutches, one of his legs inches shorter than the other. The ordeal also left him with a speech impediment—he would trip over words when he got stressed or excited—plus a lousy disability pension.

"Bitch," Zachos grunted and tried to push her out of his mind. To this day, he couldn't forgive her.

From the street below, he heard the baritone of the butcher and the scratchy voice of the fishmonger announcing how cheap and fresh their products were. He cursed at the reminder that he worked for the fishmonger on the weekend for a lousy twenty-five euros for an eight-hour shift. He had been doing that for the last year. He hated the job and hated the smell of the fish. But since the disability pension had been slashed by the government's harsh austerity measures, what could he do? As he turned these thoughts around in his head, the images of naked women came back to him and made him realize how much he missed their company and warmth. He had gone to a few ladies of the night when his girlfriend first left him, but now he could not even afford an internet connection or to have the TV set fixed.

All at once, he remembered that today a man would come to check out the spare room in his apartment. Zachos had decided to rent it out for a few months and see how the idea panned out. The man had called two days ago and said he would come over today at three. He was a builder who had gotten a job in the city. He was divorced with two grown-up children and sounded excited and impatient to have the room.

Seeing that it was a quarter to two, Zachos yanked the duvet off and got to his feet. His eyes were restless. "Goddamn you, life," he said, scooping up his clothes from the floor. He limped to the balcony door and opened the shutters, letting in a gust of wind.

He turned on the radio and, listening to the news about a dead body found in a freezer in Kalithea, a district in Athens, started to clean the apartment. He tidied up the living room, did the dishes, swept and mopped the floor, and put the rubbish out.

The flat had two bedrooms, a large living room, and a decent kitchen and was in the Vardaris district near the famous Byzantine church, the Twelve Apostles. Zachos had inherited the apartment from his parents, who had passed on years ago. They were both civil servants, and him being their only child, they managed to provide him with good training and education.

Years later, when he was in his third year studying psychology at Aristotle University, he dropped out and turned his passion for cooking into a profession.

Zachos sat by the floor heater with a satisfied expression. He drank his coffee, listened to the radio, smoked, and every few minutes, he glanced at the clock and shook his shorter leg nervously. By a quarter past three, he began to have doubts that the builder would show up. And by a quarter to four, he was pacing in the living room, cursing his bad luck, the people, and the incompetent politicians of this country. He called the man, and when he didn't pick up, Zachos kicked the floor heater. It flipped over and stopped gleaming. He lifted it clumsily and set it to work again.

The weight of his despair made his bones ache. *What have I done to deserve such a shitty life?* he thought and listened to a journalist on the radio talking about the billions of euros being deposited in Swiss banks by Greek politicians and lawyers, doctors, and businessmen. "Motherfuckers," he mumbled as it was proven to him once again that either God didn't rule the world or he didn't care about it.

Every Sunday, and well into his teenage years, his parents dressed him up and went to either the Panagia Faneromeni church up on the hill or the church of Agia Sophia in the city center. No matter how hard they tried to convince him that God was all-knowing, all-powerful, and all-good, Zachos concluded that if he existed, God was exactly the opposite.

Annoyed, he switched off the radio and the floor heater and slid into his woolen coat. It had once belonged to his grandfather, a man who fought in World War II during the conquest of Koritsa, Agioi Saranda, and Argirokastro. The heavy coat had a hole in the shoulder where his grandfather had been shot, but it didn't show. Every time Zachos wore it, his morale and confidence turned up a notch.

Outside, the sky was indifferent, and the wind had a raw edge to it. Stray cats sat on dumpsters, and a dog with matted fur rounded the corner with a bone in his mouth. Zachos crossed the street and lingered outside a bakery that smelled as sweet as a Sunday apple pie. Behind the counter, a woman talked and smiled at a customer while putting cookies in a paper bag. She was medium height, with solid hips, ample bosom, brown eyes, and dark hair. She was single, and her name was Anastasia, meaning "resurrection." Looking at her from behind the glass window, his lust grew stronger. Each time he went to buy bread, the urge to ask her out kicked in like a charging bull. But each time she asked him whether he wanted anything else, he stood there stiff as a tree trunk, questioning why on earth she would ever want to go out with him.

A few blocks down the road, Zachos walked into a coffee shop to meet with his childhood friend, Polichronis. The space was warm, and the air smelled of coffee, ouzo, and cigarette smoke. Most of the tables were occupied with men playing cards or backgammon, while others chatted or watched television. He spotted Polichronis at the far end of the room, a backgammon board already open on the table. Zachos ordered a coffee, drew up the chair, and sat. They talked about one thing and another and started the game. Half an hour later, shaking the dice in his hand, Polichronis asked Zachos, "Buddy, are you okay?" and moved a piece on the board.

"I'm all right."

"You don't look all right to me."

"I'm a bit tired." Zachos shook the dice in his palm and tossed them on the board.

"Have you seen Anastasia today?"

"No, I haven't."

"Are you sure?"

"Keep on p-p-playing."

"Why don't you tell her how you feel about her?"

Zachos wrinkled his brow.

"Do you want me to go and talk to her for you?"

A group of old men sitting at a felt table debated about the political parties in Greece, the new measures of the national insurance scheme, and the migration tragedies on the Greek islands.

"About four thousand people drowned last year," a gray-haired man said.

"Them European bastards!" another one said. "It's all their fault. They stick their noses in other people's business." A swell of approving voices rose thick in the room and then thinned out like the cigarette smoke hanging along the ceiling.

"Are we g-g-going to play backgammon or talk?"

"Look, buddy. You need a good-hearted woman by your side. You aren't getting any younger. And Anastasia is your best bet."

"How you know she's a g-g-good woman?"

"The whole neighborhood knows that. She's kind, hardworking, and, most importantly, single."

"And how are you so s-s-sure that she'd want to go out with me, huh?"

"You have a good heart and you're still a young, good-looking man. Don't give me that smile. Ask her out before some other bastard gets his dirty hands on her. You hear me, Zachos?"

"When the time's ripe, I'll a-a-ask her out."

"Time? What time?" Polichronis scoffed and reminded him how many times Zachos had talked about her. Despite Zachos's resistance, Polichronis said that if he didn't ask her out soon, he would do it for him.

"You never give up, do you?"

The two men stared at each other for a long moment.

"I'll talk to her tomorrow. I p-p-promise, okay?"

When he stepped out, the night was still young. The chilly wind, Bardaris, had cleared the city of all the smog. Now the air was crisp and fresh. Not wanting to go home, he decided to stay out. Zachos loved taking long walks at night, looking at the city's lights as well as the lighted windows of apartments, and imagining the lives of people who lived in them.

On the corner of the block was a large veggie store, lit up like a Christmas tree. Two big men in heavy coats sat by a floor heater, smoking and drinking coffee. Zachos pictured his mother handing him a shopping list when he was a boy. His favorite season of the year had been summer because of all the berries and watermelon he could eat. He still carried the exhilarating feeling of being a boy and going shopping for his mother. It seemed to him as though only yesterday he had been running down the street to the store, sometimes with his best friend, Maria, with whom he had been secretly in love and who was now married with kids.

With a feeling of bittersweet melancholy, he jaywalked across a boulevard between cars and buses and passed a kiosk and a modern gyro joint where people were sitting under heaters. He made his way past the Laikon movie theater. Today, there were two films showing: the latest James Bond and a porno. He had last come here as a teenager, back when the theater mostly played karate and crime movies. His favorite actor had been Charles Bronson, especially in *Mr. Majestic.*

Time flies, Zachos thought. *And what have I accomplished so far? One big zero.* As he brooded, he felt as if the entire world had turned its back on him.

He lingered outside a coffee shop. The wind had eased up, but the night had grown stiff and cold. Zachos felt an ache along his leg and knew that rain was imminent. But going home was out of the question. He counted his money. He had fifty-five euros and some change. He thought of going for a drink at a bar not far away, but within the span of a few breaths, he decided against it. He didn't know where to go, what to do, who to see; he just wanted to be out in the open.

He heard an airplane and pictured his ex-girlfriend. *Bitch,* he thought and found himself heading toward the main train station and the central bus terminal, where buses were grounded due to today's general strike. A couple emerged from the main entrance of the station, holding hands and smiling.

The train station was warm and completely empty. Zachos remembered the first time his parents had brought him here, to take a train to Volos, a seaside city, for their summer vacation. He remembered how excited he was that day, gazing at the sunlight as it streamed through the doors and windows of the station and feeling the energy of hundreds of people milling about. He wished he could turn the time back to that day and become a boy again.

He sat on a bench and rubbed his leg. When he thought of his ex-girlfriend, the builder, and his work at the fish shop, he cursed his luck all over again, and despair tightened its grip.

Outside, it had started to rain. He hurried across the road and dove into a food joint. The space was pleasantly warm and smelled of meat and spices. A few seated men were slurping soup and watching television. He shook the rain off his coat and sat at a table near the television. From a man with a large belly, he ordered chicken soup and a glass of white wine.

After he had eaten half of the soup, Zachos took sips from his drink, smoked, and watched the news highlights. Forty thousand people in Athens and fifteen thousand people in Thessaloniki had taken to the streets in a general strike against strict pension reforms. Buses, trains, and ferries were grounded all over the country. Hooded youths hurled Molotov cocktails at riot police in downtown Athens. Zachos was against such actions. *What good can it do*, he thought, *when people pour their repressed feelings into the streets and damage other people's property?* He paid and got out of the joint.

The rain fell harder. Despite walking under the overhangs of buildings, he was soaked. Shivering, he huddled deeper in his coat, and as he passed a bar, he heard a knock on the glass door and saw a blond woman standing behind the door, smiling at him. The neon sign read CAFÉ ROUGE. Zachos and his friends had visited such bars a couple of times, to look at the beautiful ladies who sat and drank in the company of men as long as they kept buying them drinks. In some of the bars, he remembered, there were rooms.

From the branch of a nearby acacia tree, two crows eyed Zachos.

The woman opened the door a crack and said in a husky voice, "Come on in, handsome."

He hesitated.

"Come on in." She smiled. "You'll catch your death out there." While he tried to place her foreign accent, faint Latin music reached his ears.

He studied her black stiletto heels, her short skirt, and the fishnet tights. The woman's rouged lips stood out against her blond hair and big blue eyes. The slightly loose skin about her neck and the lines near her lips and her eyes gave away her age, which matched her slender body.

"Come on in, handsome. Don't let me catch pneumonia out here."

Zachos thought of the money in his pocket and of going home but didn't budge. He was cold and his leg ached. A *drink and a chat with this lovely lady of the night will set me straight*, he thought.

A woman behind the bar counter stopped talking to her customer and spoke tersely to the blond woman in Russian, her expression impatient.

The blonde slunk toward Zachos like a cat afraid of the rain, slid her arm around his waist, and nudged him toward the bar. Her gentle touch and the sweet smell of her perfume heightened Zachos's lust. A sense of comfort and confidence blew through him and lifted the dust of his spirits.

The bar was small and warm. The lights were turned low, and tea lights burned on the tables. The air smelled of sandalwood, which made Zachos feel as if he were in some exotic locale. The woman helped him out of his coat. He put his smokes on the table and rubbed his hands.

"What's your name, handsome?"

Their eyes met. The woman's voice and accent excited him.

"Zachos," he said. "My name is Zachos." He ran his hands through his wet hair and wiped them on his trousers.

"My name is Svetlana. Nice to meet you, Zachos."

"Likewise."

"What would you like to drink?"

"Whisky and some confidence."

"You're in the right place." She smiled.

"And whatever you're drinking. Make them drinks strong."

He lit a cigarette and watched Svetlana's movements closely—the way she held the bottle with her long fingers, the way she sneaked sugary glances at him and smiled.

She took a seat next to him and crossed her legs. They raised their glasses, drank, and talked. He was jittery at first, but with the soft music, the warmth of the whisky in his chest, and her pleasant attitude, his unstable emotions began to settle.

Though Zachos knew that Svetlana was working, he felt that there was a genuine understanding between them. He could tell that much at least. But nothing was for certain when one found themselves in the company of ladies of the night. Maybe she was good company because it was a slow night and she had gotten bored. Maybe she genuinely enjoyed his companionship. He decided not to tell her the whole truth about himself.

"So, you live alone and you're a writer, huh?" She took a drag on her cigarette.

He nodded.

"Are you working on anything at the moment?"

"On a short story."

"What is it about?"

"About a man who had a tough day and goes to a bar where he meets a charming lady."

"You don't say." She tilted her head girlishly to the side and smiled.

"Do you know how the story ends?"

"No, I don't. Maybe they fall in love, decide to move away from this goddamn city, and her pimp goes after them. Maybe they make it; maybe they won't."

"You know," she said and looked at him, "I've always dreamt of being a writer. Since I was a little girl growing up in Moscow."

"And what stopped you?"

"At first, I took piano lessons. But when my mother took me to watch *Don Quixote* at the Bolshoi ballet, there and then, I knew that I wanted to become a ballet dancer."

Zachos had read about the Bolshoi ballet in a newspaper many years ago. He hadn't opened a book since he was a student, but he loved reading the papers, especially the ones that came out on Sundays. These newspapers added to the knowledge he had gathered all these years about various aspects of life and art.

"Did you ever become a ballet dancer?"

"Yes, I did ballet for many years. But unfortunately, I had to stop."

Zachos raised his eyebrows.

"You know, I had to work."

"Didn't your parents support you?"

"My father was a drunk and pulled out on us for another woman." She put a fresh cigarette in her mouth.

Zachos lit it. "Do you keep in touch with him?"

"I went to his funeral."

After a pause, Zachos raised his glass. "To all the living souls."

Svetlana mouthed the words of a song about long-lost loves that was coming over the speakers. "Μα δεν τελειώνουν οι αγάπες οι μεγάλες δεν τελειώνουν. πονάνε, υποφέρουνε, ματώνουν κι αρχίζουν πάλι απ' την αρχή."[9]*

"You have a good voice, and your Greek is fluent."

"Working in bars for over fifteen years teaches you a thing or two."

"I bet it does."

In a moment, Svetlana placed her hand on his leg. "Does this make you feel uncomfortable?"

A short, uncomfortable silence stretched between them. He lit a fresh cigarette as she stroked his leg.

"If you want, you can touch my leg as well."

He watched her face closely.

"But just my leg." She smiled.

Zachos knocked back his whisky. "Can you pour us a-a-another round?"

Svetlana asked the woman with the black hair—who was now sitting at a bar stool, engaged in conversation with a man—if she could pour the drinks. The woman made a face and moved behind the bar.

"She's always in a funny mood, but she's a good woman."

Zachos tried to pull himself together. Her hand working gently on his leg excited him so much that his manhood grew stiff. He shifted in his chair and tried to hide his embarrassment. The black-haired

---

9. * "But great loves don't end. They hurt, suffer, bleed and start all over again."

woman set the drinks on the table and said something to Svetlana in Russian.

"What did she say?"

"Nothing of importance."

They touched glasses and drank.

"Are you an only child?" Zachos said.

"No, I have two younger sisters."

"They live in Greece?"

"They did for many years, but when the crisis hit the country, my mother decided to move back to Russia. She had inherited my grandparents' apartment in Moscow."

"Don't you wanna go back?"

"My ballet years are over," she said. "Besides, I enjoy my work. I'm my own boss."

"How do you mean?"

"I don't have a pimp breathing down my neck, and this little joint belongs to the lady at the bar, who happens to be a good friend of mine. I work when I want to and talk with whomever I want to, too."

"Aren't you afraid of the crisis that has crippled this country?"

"I've got nothing to lose. All my belongings fit in a suitcase. When the shit hits the fan, I'm out of here."

"I wish I could think the same way."

"What's stopping you?"

"I don't know."

"I'm sure you will find out soon."

"Soon? I'm forty-five years old."

"You mean to say that you're forty-five years young. Besides," she continued, "you should always keep in mind that it doesn't matter how many years you've lived, but the life you've lived all those years. You shouldn't be so hard on yourself and should try not to see enemies where they don't exist."

There was silence.

"Come on, give us a smile," she said in a soft voice.

Zachos smiled, swirled the drink in his glass, and knocked it back. "Would you like to have another drink?"

He leaned over to her side and whispered, "Look, Svetlana. I'd l-l-love to have more drinks, but I don't think I h-h-have enough m-m-money." He put forty-five euros on the table.

Svetlana took thirty euros and pushed the rest toward him. "This round is on you, and the next will be on me. And put the rest in your pocket because you may need it later. In these days, fifteen euros can work miracles." She winked at him as she stood up.

They drank the third and then the fourth round of drinks, talking and laughing and listening to tango music. "Por Una Cabeza" by Pierwszy Taniec now floated from the speakers. Zachos couldn't believe that fate had finally started to smile upon him.

After she placed another round of drinks on the table, she stood in front of him and grooved to the music. "Let's dance," she said.

"I'm a lousy dancer," he said, but before he knew it, they had their arms around each other. Smelling her perfume, her shampooed hair, feeling her breath on his neck and her breasts on his chest, his manhood got stiffer.

"I believe it's time you put your money to effective use. What do you say, huh?" When she bit his earlobe gently, excitement shot through his body like a low electric current.

Back in her room, Svetlana locked the door and looked at Zachos playfully. Blue velvet curtains hung over the windows, and the air smelled of incense. Pushed against the wall was a sofa covered with red felt and black pillows. Two floor lamps burned low.

Drinks in hand, Zachos flopped down on the sofa. Svetlana lit a few candles and then stood in front of him. As he held her mesmerizing eyes, she bent over slowly and brought her face inches from his.

"Do you know you're a good-looking man?"

Her warm breath, laced with alcohol, electrified him. He ran his hands through her hair and kissed her passionately. Svetlana knelt on the carpeted floor and worked his zipper open. In a few breaths, the sweetest warmth he'd ever felt flooded to his abdomen, to his chest, and all the way up to his head, swallowing all of his pent-up emotions. He soon let out a long, drawn-out moan so powerful that he thought he would lose himself in it forever.

When he stepped out of the bar, the rain had stopped. He breathed in the wetness of the city, feeling as though he had just dropped a heavy burden from his shoulders. With an indescribable sense of well-being, he began to walk. The streets took him to the port, where on sunny days he would buy a coffee and sit on a bench in the sun and look out at the sea.

He stood on the edge of the dock, gazing at the White Tower, the landmark of the city. He checked his cell phone. There was an apologetic message from the builder saying that his car had broken down and that he would be there tomorrow at the same time.

I should have known better, Zachos thought. He turned his eyes toward a line of lights along the seafront, following them past the White Tower and down to the right where the lights stretched until they faded into the dark horizon. Somewhere among those lights was the seaside village of Peraia. When he was a boy, his parents would take him to that place on a boat, and he would spend the day swimming and playing with other kids.

It dawned on him now that even though the world was filled with ugliness, at the same time, it was beautiful and desirable. Over this past year, and maybe even before, he had been walking on dark paths. But the world had not turned its back on him; it was he who had turned his back on the world, turned his back to all this beauty.

It was his fault that he was stubborn, timid, and afraid of change. *If I had gone with my ex-girlfriend to Chicago*, he thought, *things might've turned out differently for me.* And as he stood there gazing out at sea, he realized he could have done much better even here in Greece. *My limping and the slight speech impediment have taken an unnecessary toll on me. I let things slide and took the easy way out. But it's high time I put things right.*

"I am forty-five years young," he said and smiled, faintly.

He thought of his friend Polichronis and then pictured himself going to the bakery in the morning and asking Anastasia out as he had promised. "Why not? Yes, why not?" he said louder this time, and waves of confidence and excitement swelled up in his chest.

Thessaloniki Food Bank

ON EITHER SIDE of Monastiriou Boulevard, acacia trees stand tall in full bloom. Their white flowers hang like bunches of grapes, filling the night with their strong aroma. On the corner of the street, the lights of the Food Bank are still on. Unemployed people, large families, and single mothers are qualified to shop using food stamps. Every week, they can choose goods up to the value of eighteen euros.

Today, the first of July, has been a very busy day. For both cashiers, the queues extended beyond seven meters. Save for a slight commotion at the peak of activity, things worked out just fine. People, mainly women with their kids, created a steady flow in and out of the shop, some of them holding bags, others dragging food trolleys.

Right across from the food shop, a man and a woman in faded jeans and black T-shirts slouch against a column of a building, sharing a cigarette. In the light of a lamppost, their sweaty, tanned faces shine, and their eyes are red. Further down the sidewalk stand a teenage boy and a lanky man with a knapsack, while on the other side of the road, two women chat on a bench, sitting cross-legged and smoking cigarettes. They have empty cloth bags on their laps. They are all waiting for the Food Bank to close for the day.

In one of the aisles of the Food Bank, a man in black trousers and a white shirt puts products on the shelves, muttering. He is lean and tall, and his thick, dark hair is smoothed back with pomade. His name is Dionisis. Screwing up his face, he pulls out a handkerchief from the back pocket of his trousers and wipes his face and nape. A buxom woman with wavy black hair and big brown eyes stands behind the register. Her name is Chrisa.

Dionisis looks at her and taps his index finger on his wristwatch, frowning. She hates when he does that. She ignores him and turns her eyes to the woman standing before her. The woman's teenage daughter puts the food in a cloth bag.

"Have a good weekend, you two."

"Likewise, Mrs. Chrisa," the girl says and starts for the door.

Chrisa picks up a box of chewing gum and a bar of milk chocolate.

"Lazarina!" At the entrance, Chrisa hands the goodies to her.

The girl looks at her mother. She nods yes.

"Thank you," the girl says.

Chrisa locks the large glass door and watches the two approach a car parked at the curb. A man opens the passenger door and smiles at the woman. *I wish Dionisis was like him*, she thinks.

"It's about time," Dionisis says with annoyance drawn on his face. "I'm dog tired. And we must do the register. Goddamn it."

"Stop it. You've been driving me crazy all day," Chrisa says. "Just finish stocking the shelves and put the food in the trolley. I'll do the rest."

He sighs and begins to fill the shopping trolley with the food that will expire the next day. While Chrisa does the paperwork, she lifts her eyes and, seeing his nagging expression, glares at him.

He parks the trolley next to the entrance and starts rolling a cigarette.

"Dionisis, don't smoke in here, please. How many times do I have to tell you that? If the manager finds out, we'll get in trouble."

"Fuck that son of a bitch." He lights it up and draws on it. "Woman, stop nodding your head and hurry up. I'm dying here."

"Then why don't you start putting the food in the bags?"

"Don't know which thing goes in which bag. Besides, dropping off bags of food at people's doorsteps was your idea. You're the Good Samaritan."

She opens her mouth to speak but doesn't.

The past few months have been tough on her. Dionisis has been in a constant sour mood, and she can't figure out why. She has tried to talk to him, but nothing. He is a man of few words, and he hardly ever shows his feelings. At the same time, he spends way too much time at the καφενείο, playing cards or backgammon and watching football matches, and when he gets home, his breath smells of alcohol and smoke. Chrisa hates smoking. To cap it all off, lately he's started to bicker with her teenage son. It bothers him that her son got a tattoo on his arm, that he listens to hip-hop, and that his friends spend the weekend with him at the house.

Chrisa was once happily married, but five years ago, as her husband was riding his motorbike home from work, he was hit by a bus. The pain of his death was so excruciating that she decided never to get into a relationship again. But never is a long time. After years of mourning and loneliness, she reconsidered her decision.

About two years ago, she met Dionisis at a party. Chrisa had just lost her job as an English teacher in a tutoring center. At the party, she couldn't keep her eyes off him. She thought him charming and mysterious. He wore a white linen suit and a gray T-shirt. That night, they had drinks, laughed, danced, and exchanged numbers, and after six months, he moved in with her. At the time, he worked as a security guard for a company, but a year ago he lost his job. It was then that Chrisa managed to get him hired at the Food Bank. Dionisis is divorced and has a young daughter who lives with her mother.

Seeing him exhaling smoke, she fights an urge to take the cigarette from his mouth and crush it under her shoe. She doesn't want to have another argument. *Not again*, she thinks and keeps her eyes on him. *What the hell am I doing wasting my time with him? I cook for him, wash his clothes, and clean the house, and on my bad days, I try hard to be on my best behavior. And what do I get back? He's good in bed, all right, but that's not enough. No, that's not good enough to put up with his moods.* There and then, she decides to ask him to move out of her apartment.

Dionisis smokes and stares out at cars, buses, and trucks as they roar down the road outside. From the corner of his eye, he catches sight of the couple with torn jeans crossing the road. "Fucking bums," he says through his teeth.

The couple disappears behind the corner of the Food Bank, now moving along the sidewalk and past illuminated entrances of apartment buildings. They cross the street again, to disappear in the darkness behind plane trees near a fence. Behind the fence is a field with abandoned train carriages and scattered scraps of metal and planks. At the far end stand apartment buildings with lights glowing in their windows.

Chrisa walks up to Dionisis. "Here. Hold open this bag."

She fills the bags with food from the trolley and says, "Can you please keep two bags and put the rest in the usual place?"

Dionisis places the bags by the dumpster outside and notices that more people have come for their fair share.

Chrisa activates the alarm and locks the door again.

"Look over there!" he says.

"Where?" she says and sweeps her gaze over the boulevard and a few blocks away to where a black car rolls into the gas station, smoke pouring out of its hood. The driver rushes out of the car, grabs a fire extinguisher from the trunk, and begins to spray at the flames.

"I feel sorry for him," she says.

"You feel sorry for everybody."

"What's that supposed to mean, huh?"

Annoyed, he picks up the bags and heads down the narrow sidewalk.

She hurries behind him. "I've been meaning to talk to you."

Dionisis doesn't answer. They now walk side by side, taking up the sidewalk. The windows of the apartment buildings are open, and so are their balcony doors. An old man leans on the railing of his balcony and lights a cigarette. Inside the apartment, his wife is wiping down a table with a cloth. On another balcony, four old men play cards and drink wine, serenaded by the voice of George Dalaras on the radio. A woman shouts at her children, and in the humid air drifts the smell of jasmine.

On an electrical wire, two crows watch Dionisis and Chrisa approach the corner of the block, where two stray dogs appear from behind a parked car and scamper down an alley. One of them sniffs at the rubbish strewn around a dumpster, and the other looks at the couple.

Chrisa stops.

"You okay?" Dionisis says.

"Yes, but I want to talk to you."

Without looking at her, he says, "Talk to me about what?"

His attitude deepens her irritation, reinforcing her decision to ask him to move out.

"I'll tell you about it over dinner."

By the time Chrisa and Dionisis reach the end of the sidewalk and turn the corner, the lanky man with the backpack, the teenage boy, the two women who were sitting on the bench, and four more people have gathered around the bin.

"There is plenty of food," says the lanky man. "We should share it evenly."

Dionisis waits as Chrisa goes up the stairs of an apartment building. On the fourth floor lives an old couple. Since the lady broke her hip, she can't go to the food shop. Of course, her husband could do it, but he is too proud to.

Dionisis lights another cigarette and gazes at the plane trees and the abandoned train carriages. In the dark distance, he hears a dogfight. "Fucking mongrels."

Further down the street, a car comes to a stop at a curb. Greek rebetiko music floats from its half-open window. The bearded man at the wheel leans on the horn. In a few minutes, an attractive woman in a tight black dress and stiletto shoes rushes out of a building and climbs in the car. The car roars off, leaving tire marks on the asphalt.

"Fucking idiot," Dionisis says.

"Who are you talking to?" Chrisa asks.

"Nobody."

Chrisa is happy because she just did a good deed. She returns to the sidewalk, studying Dionisis. She admires his high cheekbones, the vein on his forehead, his straight nose, and his full lips. A whiff of doubt casts a shadow on her decision, but his attitude blows it away.

"Why are you looking at me like that?"

"It's nothing."

Behind the corner of the apartment building at the end of the sidewalk, the couple with the faded jeans have their backs against the wall. The man pokes his head around the corner, and with his little red eyes, he sees Chrisa and Dionisis heading toward them. He hides again and tightens his hands around a plank.

As they near the corner of the building, an eerie feeling creeps over her. Chrisa stops.

Dionisis turns and looks at her. "What's the matter?"

"I don't know."

He sighs. "Chrisa, let's go, please," he says in an irritated tone.

As they round the corner, the man swings the plank and strikes Dionisis in his face, hard. He drops to the ground, unconscious.

Chrisa freezes, then cries out, "Dionisis!" and bends over him. Seeing blood gushing from his nose, she feels rubbery in her knees.

The woman jerks Chrisa up and pushes her against the wall, waving a blade in front of her eyes. "Bitch, if you say a word, I'll cut you open."

Chrisa sees bruises on the veins on her hands and smells the sourness of her breath.

The woman tosses Chrisa's bag over to the man. He unzips it hastily and pulls out a wallet, a wristwatch, and a mobile phone. Then, as suddenly as they attacked, the couple dashes across the narrow street, slips through an opening in a fence, and vanishes into the dark.

Chrisa turns Dionisis on his back. "Help me!" She sweeps her frightened eyes about. "Please, someone help me!"

A man runs toward her, and then another one appears from behind. Soon, a knot of people has gathered to help her.

Much later, in the reception area of the hospital, telephones ring, and voices come over speakers. Some waiting patients lean on walls, and others lie on gurneys along the corridors. Behind drawn curtains, doctors and nurses bend over patients.

Dionisis lies propped up on pillows in a bed. A drip is connected to his arm, his nose is bandaged, and his eyes are swollen and bruised. A doctor set his nose, stitched it, and put him on antibiotics and painkillers.

Chrisa sits on the bed next to him. She feels relaxed but woozy from the pill a nurse put under her tongue. She still can't believe what happened to them. It was the first time anyone has robbed her and threatened her life. She has never felt so scared. At the same time, she feels grateful that they both came away in one piece.

A young doctor pulls the curtain closed behind him. He smiles and gestures to Chrisa to stay seated. Then he studies the clipboard attached to the bed.

"Am I going to make it, Doc?" Dionisis quips.

The doctor smiles. "You sure are, but we have to keep you in until tomorrow."

"Why?"

"We need to scan your head and run a few blood tests."

"But I feel fine."

Chrisa squeezes his hand.

"Are you sure I need to put myself through this?"

"I'm afraid so."

"Fucking junkies," he says. "I can't wait to go to the canteen."

The doctor raises his eyebrows. "I don't think that would be a good idea."

"Doc, I don't go to sleep before three in the morning. And it's not even midnight yet. I'm a ticking bomb here. If I don't drink a cup of coffee and smoke a cigarette, I'll burst open."

When Chrisa notices the doctor's hesitation, and knowing Dionisis will have it his way no matter what, she says politely, "Doctor, I'll make sure my boy is safe."

"Okay. I'll have a nurse take you to a room soon. Now, if you'll excuse me."

They thank him and go to the canteen.

Outside, the air is warm. People with tired faces drink coffee, smoke, and talk in low voices. Their body language is slow, as if they have been sedated.

At the gate of the hospital, a man sits in a lighted glass cubicle. He listens to the radio, wipes his face with a hanky, and talks to a woman through an opening in the glass. People pace slowly or stand in twos and threes around the gate, smoking and talking, while others are on their phones. An ambulance drives through, siren cutting the air.

Chrisa puts two freddo cappuccinos on the table and sits. The effects of the pill are wearing off. She stirs the coffee with the straw, and when she feels Dionisis's eyes on her, she raises hers. She loves the way he's looking at her right now and wonders what is going on in his mind. It is the same way he looked at her the night she met him at the party. His gaze is enigmatic and mysterious, as if it holds an eternal secret.

"What's on your mind?" she asks.

"When I stood near the door in the shop, I spotted those junkies across the road." He clenches his jaw. "I should've guessed that something was being cooked in their fucked-up heads."

"How could you know?"

"It was the way the fucker glanced at me."

Chrisa notices an edge in his words and hopes they will not argue.

"I'm sure the police will arrest them. When I described their faces, the officer said that they knew who they were. He said they were after them."

Dionisis brushes ash from his trousers and sighs. "Those junkies better pray that the uniforms catch them soon. Because if I do, I'll bury them alive."

"Please, Dionisis, don't talk like that."

"Don't talk like that?" He points at his face. "Take a good look at me. I look and feel like shit. That son-of-a-bitch bum left his mark on me. My ancient Greek nose turned into an aubergine."

Chrisa stifles a burst of laughter.

There is silence. She touches his hand. "I'm sorry for my part in it. If we hadn't gone to deliver the bags of food—"

"None of this is your fault. These fuckers will pay for it. Chrisa, they had been watching us, for days. By now, my father's watch, the mobile phone, and our money are all turned into junk."

At his words, the calmed fear swells up in her chest. A knot forms in her stomach. From now on, she knows that she will have to look over her shoulder constantly.

"I've worked as a security guard most of my life, for Christ's sake. I was as strong as a bull. And now I haul boxes and stack food on shelves at a Food Bank. Big fucking deal." His anger is so intense that he wants to bite the edge of the table. "Because of the crisis, I lost my job, I lost my edge, I lost my fucking pride."

"Dionisis, be glad you have a job. Of all people, you should know better. Be glad you have a roof over your head and food on your table; thousands of people in Greece and abroad are homeless."

"I hate my job. I hate looking at sad-faced people coming into the shop, all drained of energy. I hate their God and I hate their hope."

"Come on, Dionisis. Don't talk like that. Hope helps people. Without hope, life would be unbearable."

"My life is unbearable. Hope is for losers." He blows smoke over the table, and it spreads between the coffee cups like a morning mist. "Why are you looking at me like that?"

"Hope isn't for losers, Dionisis. Hope is a solid raft. I wish you had a bit of hope left in you."

Dionisis leans over the table, smirking. "Baby, I don't want a raft. I want a cruise boat. When you hope, you have nothing. And I'm done hoping. Nothing counts for anything anymore. The fucking system creates junkies, thieves, racists, rapists—you name it. And then, it feeds on them like a starving lion on its prey. We always want what we don't have, right? We all could have what we want, but the system holds the line tight. People could change the situation, but instead, they bend their heads and pray to a God who never shows his fucking face. They bend their heads and then they carve their names on tombs. So I say fuck hope. Yes sir. Fuck hope. And please," he says and waves his hand at Chrisa, "please, stop looking at me with these eyes."

In all the time they have been together, she has never heard him speak in such a way. His words take her by surprise and rattle her. She opens her mouth to say something, but she feels at a loss for words.

"What's the matter, woman?"

"I'm thinking of what you just said. Give me a minute," she says in a louder voice than before.

"If I didn't have a daughter, I'd move abroad. It's the same shit as over here, but they serve it on a nicer plate."

Anger floods her chest. Even though his words about the system ring true, and even though she still loves him, she can't hold back any longer. Her decision comes back to her.

Chrisa looks him square in the face. "And what about us, huh? Don't I count for anything? Would you still go abroad if you didn't have a daughter? You're unbelievable." She shakes her head. "I've been planning to talk to you about things."

As Dionisis narrows his eyes at her, he feels pain in his nose. "What things?"

"We can talk about it when you get back home."

"If you don't tell me what's bothering you, I'm not coming back home."

"Then don't," she says angrily. "You'll do us a favor."

"Who is us, Chrisa? You and your spoiled brat?"

"You clearly don't care about us."

"Well, tell me then," he says in a sarcastic voice, "how do you care about me?"

"How?" she snaps. A few people turn their heads. Chrisa looks at them apologetically and speaks in a softer voice. "I'll tell you how. For the past few months, you haven't lifted a finger. I've been doing all the chores. At the same time, both at home and at work, I've been putting up with your fucking mood swings. We used to be good together. We used to do things. Sex isn't everything, Dionisis."

A few silent minutes squeeze between them.

"I get it, Chrisa."

She frowns. "What do you get?"

"I know you've had enough of me. You're right. I guess these past months I've gone off the deep end." He stands.

She looks at him in surprise. "Where are you going?"

"I'm following the doctor's orders." He closes the space between them as she gets to her feet and faces him. With the back of his fingers, he strokes her face as if saying, "It doesn't matter. We've had a good run." His gaze is so penetrating that she feels a pang inside.

"I'm sorry," he says.

Chrisa doesn't know how to respond.

"To make it easier on us, when I get out of here, I'll come and pick up my things. You go home now. We've said enough." He turns and moves away.

Chrisa watches him amble toward the entrance of the hospital. Images come to her. She sees him shoving his clothes in a suitcase, sees them both drinking coffee and talking at the kitchen table, sees him standing by the door, suitcase in hand.

Maybe it's for the best, she thinks. An impulse to call his name rises in her chest. She sighs, and her thoughts go to war in her head. A wind carrying traces of pine and jasmine blows in her face. Before he opens the door, she takes a few steps, raises her hand, and calls out, "Dionisis!"

This Is Not America

ON THE RING ROAD, a blue Nissan sped at eighty kilometers while the whole world was dripping wet after the rain. With the last of the light fading out on the horizon, clouds rolled back over the city of Athens. In the distance, toward Mount Parnitha, the sky roared.

Stathis, the driver, and Achilles, the passenger, listened to a woman on the radio discuss the benefits of education and virtue. Stathis wholeheartedly agreed with the woman's words about the crucial role of education in cultivating virtue and shaping the character of young people. He was impressed by the idea of teachers offering free classes to educate students about important values, such as recycling, environmental consciousness, respect, and love.

The two men were first cousins and had gone to Pelion to visit some friends in a village near the city of Volos, four hours' drive from Athens.

"Look at that!" Achilles said in a husky voice, pointing toward the other side of the road. He was a burly man with a chiseled chin and a straight nose starting high up his forehead. His hair was thick and black. He reminded Stathis of a modern Minotaur.

"Where?" Stathis said and glanced out of his window. He was thirty-five years old, with long black hair and brown eyes. He felt a bit out of tune after the ouzo and beer from last night and the hours on the road.

"Over there, look, there!" Achilles said again with an impatient look.

"Can you stop shouting in my ear?" Stathis stepped on the brakes. The needle on the speedometer dropped from eighty to fifty. He looked out his wet side window, and over the cars moving in the opposite direction with their lights on, he saw nothing of importance save for a half-built bridge and wondered what the hell his cousin was so excited about.

"Did you see them?"

"See who?

"That man and the woman."

"No, I didn't.

"Pull the car over."

"Why?"

"Just do it."

Stathis cut the wheel to the right sharply. The blue Nissan skidded to a stop a couple of inches away from a ditch, and a truck roared by, horn blasting. A warm, twitching sensation flashed in Stathis's chest.

"Goddamn horn-blowing fucking truckers," Achilles said, scowling at the truck speeding away. "Those noodleheads think they own the roads." He directed a side-glance at his cousin, who had rested his head on the steering wheel, closed his eyes, and sighed. "You okay, coz?"

Stathis glared at him. "What the hell did you want us to pull over for?" He lit a cigarette and rolled down the window. A jet of cold air carried the smell of rain and wet earth into the car.

"Didn't you see them?"

"See who?"

"A few weeks back, didn't I tell you about some people I'd heard that lived under a half-built bridge?" Achilles said enthusiastically and slapped his knee as though a fly had landed there.

Stathis pictured the two of them on the balcony of his cousin's apartment, drinking white wine and talking about the staggering number of people in Greece living without electricity and sleeping under bridges, in abandoned factories, in public places, and eating at soup kitchens run by the church.

"Yeah, I remember that day."

Achilles went on. "I just saw them. I saw smoke, too. Wouldn't it be good for your research to check out that place?"

Deep in thought, Stathis drew on his cigarette. He was a writer and was gathering material for a collection of short stories about the economic crisis in Greece. He wanted to find out how the crisis had influenced the personal and collective minds of Greek people and how they were dealing with it. Had the crisis blurred their integrity and their moral values? Had the Greeks lost heart after all the barbed wire measures imposed on them by international financial institutions? Stathis wanted to understand how far the Greeks would go to make ends meet.

"Come on, man." Achilles rubbed his hands together. "Let's go and see what's the score."

"Now?" Smoke surged out of Stathis's mouth.

"No, tomorrow." He gave his cousin a look. "Of course now!"

Stathis pictured them standing next to a mound of stones, bricks, and concrete soaked with rain, looking into the mouth under the half-built bridge. He felt weird about the image, like something bad was bound to happen to them.

"But it's growing dark and—"

Achilles banged the dashboard. "Fuck your buts. It's now or never! Aren't you going back to England in a week to begin writing your stories?"

For the past couple of years, Stathis had lived in the city of Bath with his Irish fiancée, who was a sculptor. Twice a week, he taught creative writing to master's students at the Bath Spa University, and half a year ago, he published his first novel, in America.

"What if they have knives? And guns. What if they have guns, huh?" He held Achilles's eager eyes. "You haven't thought about it, have you?"

"You worry too much. This is not America. It's an in-and-out scenario. We talk to them, gather some solid material, and off we go."

"I know this is not America, but don't you understand that homeless people are on edge?"

Achilles banged the dashboard again. "It's now or never!"

"Stop shouting and stop banging the dashboard, man. Okay? It's a fucking rental. What's with you?" he said and wondered why his cousin's mind worked that way even though he was pushing forty. *Didn't he learn his lesson when he worked as a field engineer for Konica?* Back then, he punched his boss and broke the man's jaw in two places, and now he worked at a food market, carrying crates for thirty euros a day. And many moons before, he nearly died in the hospital because someone stabbed him in his ribcage during a bar brawl.

"I just want to help," Achilles said, looking through the windshield at the wet road.

"I appreciate you, but . . ."

As Achilles turned to speak again, Stathis lifted his hand and gave him a warning scowl.

There was silence.

Stathis rubbed his temples with his fingers. *This thing could turn out to be a good story. You can't learn everything from books,* he told himself and felt curiosity rise in his chest. A breath of fresh air seemed to blow right through him, wiping away his tiredness and the soft melancholy from his eyes. He had never seen firsthand how homeless people managed to live out in the open, and now he felt the urge to talk to them, hear their thoughts, and feel how they felt, if that was possible. His cousin was right: it was now or never.

"I agree." He stared at his cousin. "But this is my show. You hear me? I'll call the shots."

Achilles nodded yes.

"I wanna hear you say it."

"All right, you call the shots."

"Can I trust you?"

"Trust me? How can you ask me such a thing? We have the same blood running in our veins. Have I ever let you down?

"Take it easy, man."

"I know I'm a bit off my head, but you can trust me." He broke into a smile.

Though Stathis wasn't convinced, he decided to take the risk. *A little adventure won't harm anyone*, he thought and got back on the road with the car fishtailing behind a bus.

The blue Nissan eased to a stop under some electrical wires where two crows were perched. The light from the lamppost reflected in a puddle of water rippling in the wind. The two cousins studied the mound rising toward the bridge, but they couldn't see inside. What they could see, though, was a beaten sign nailed on the cemented wall that read, MAD DOG, with a sketch of a dog growling.

"Mad dog my ass," Achilles scoffed. "Coz, don't sweat over it. I'll watch your back."

The crows on the wire could see straight under the bridge and all the way out to the other side. They saw a woman and a dog scurrying out of the tunnel on the other end, an old man climbing up a ladder, and an old woman crawling into a tent. The crows began to converse.

"I'm rooting for Stathis," the first crow croaked. "He's a good chap."

"Well," the second crow said, "Achilles has a good heart, too. But he's for the straitjacket."

"I couldn't agree more. He's sure for the straitjacket," the first crow said and pointed the tip of his wing to where the two men stood shrugging on their jackets and raking their eyes over the area, breaths steaming in the air. Ten meters behind the men, cars, trucks, and buses whooshed past with their headlights on.

Stathis took a few careful steps ahead and pricked his ears. He heard water dripping, smelled burned wood, and when a gust of wind rattled through the detritus under the bridge, his muscles stiffened.

Achilles glanced up at the crows. "Fucking birds," he muttered. Turning toward Stathis, he said, "Let's get in character."

The cousins stood at the mouth of the tunnel with the light of the lamppost at their backs, throwing their shadows a few meters forward to where the ground dropped. In the middle of the space, near the tent, a low fire burned. A tarpaulin hanging from the near edge of the tunnel fluttered and popped, making Stathis's eyes narrow. Through the far end of the tunnel they saw a tall wall, and behind it a dark factory with knocked-out windows.

When they heard a loud bang, nervousness swept over Stathis. He glanced at his cousin. "Maybe we should come back another time." He hoped his cousin would agree, but instead, Achilles strode forward. Stathis followed reluctantly.

Halfway through the tunnel, they stopped to look around.

"Where the fuck did they go?" Achilles said.

Their voices echoed, and their shadows moved across the walls. The sound of vehicles wafting from the road made Stathis feel like he was in a deep dream. "They might have heard us," he said. He walked past four frayed car seats positioned around the fire and touched a coffee pot sitting on a makeshift coffee table—half a door propped up on bricks. The pot was warm, and the coffee smelled good. The table also held a petroleum lamp, a half-eaten can of beef and beans, and three tin cups half filled with coffee.

The two men stared at each other. Achilles moved toward the end of the tunnel while Stathis picked up the lamp and raked its light across a line of plastic bags hanging from hooks on the wall.

At the base of the wall were cartons with food, water in plastic bottles, soft drinks, and beers. In a straw basket, Stathis saw poetry books by Andreas Embirikos, T. S. Eliot, and Federico García Lorca, along with literature by Nikos Kazantzakis, Franz Kafka, and Cormac McCarthy. He thumbed through Kafka's *Metamorphosis* and smelled it.

"Unbelievable," Stathis said and shined the light of the lamp into the opening of the tent. The space smelled of plastic and wood. When a pair of eyes stared back at him, his heart skipped a bit. "Fuck!" He tripped back, the petroleum lamp swaying in his hand.

"What's the matter?" Achilles strode toward him.

"There's someone in the tent."

"You sure?"

"Yes. I think I saw an old woman."

"Whoever you are, come out!" Achilles kept his impatient eyes on the opening of the tent where the light fell. "We don't want to hurt you."

The two men waited in vain. Stathis's heartbeat quickened. He wanted to get the hell out of there, but at the same time, he wanted to stay.

A full-grown sheepdog swung around a corner at the back end of the bridge, followed by a woman in her late twenties pulling on its leash. "You fuckers, don't move a muscle!" Her voice bounced off the walls.

The cousins turned sharply. The woman had her jeans pushed into knee-high rubber boots, was wearing a brown woolen cardigan and a thick scarf coiled around her neck, and had her blond hair tied in a loose bun.

Stathis fixed his eyes on the dog as it pulled on the frayed leash, clouds of breath forming in the air as it growled. The woman loosened the leash, and the dog rushed ahead. "If you take one more step, I'll set him free!"

The thunderous barks froze Stathis's blood.

"He'll eat you for dinner! You hear me, fuckers? For dinner! Don't you move an inch!"

Stathis brought the lamp near his face. "Lady, we came in friendship," he said, feeling weak at his knees.

"There's no excuse for trespassing on our property."

"We didn't mean to scare you," Achilleas said. "We just wanted to talk with you, that's all."

"You've got no business being here," she said in a harsh voice and squinted. "Aren't you one of them"—she pointed her index finger at Achilles—"who came to rob us a few weeks ago?"

"Yes. It was me. I came over here to rob you of your treasure," Achilles said sarcastically and grinned.

"What the fuck are you talking about?" Stathis turned his eyes to the woman. "Lady, he's kidding. Do we look like thieves to you?"

"It doesn't matter. You've trespassed, and you're going to pay for it!" She pulled on the leash as the dog kept barking.

"Pay for it?" Achilles said, jabbing his finger in the air. "You're a nutcase! This is a public space, and I do as I fucking please!" He took a step forward.

"Stay put, or I'll let the dog loose!"

"Let it loose!"

"This spot's ours now!"

"It's not yours!"

"Yes, it is!"

"This is public property!"

"Stop shouting, will you?" Stathis said, his eyes on the dog, whose mouth was now foaming.

Another gust of wind rattled the tent and flickered the flames of the fire.

The blond woman spoke in a loud voice. "It took us six months to find a good place. Whether you like it or not, this is ours now. Do you have any idea how it is to live on the streets? The police know we live here. So fuck you!"

"Fuck me? Fuck you!"

"Don't do anything stupid," Stathis said between his teeth, set the lamp down slowly, and raised his hands. "Lady, we came in friendship. We'd heard about this place, and driving past by chance, we wanted to know how you were doing."

"We're doing fine." She frowned, and suspicion clouded her eyes. "Are you spying on us? Who are you? Tell me now, or I'll let the dog loose!"

Achilles's veins stood out on his temples. "Enough already with the fucking dog!" He slid a jackknife out of his jacket. A long blade snapped out and shone in the dim light.

"What the fuck?" Stathis grabbed his cousin's elbow. "Have you lost your fucking mind! Put the blade away. Now!"

"Let your dog loose!" He squirmed out of his cousin's grip. "Let the fucker loose and I'll gut him!" He clenched his jaw, crazy eyes fixed on her.

The woman uncoiled the leash from around her hand, but Stathis noticed the hesitation in her eyes. The dog dashed forward, barking with rage, and the leash stretched and looked like it was about to snap.

Stathis tried to take the knife from his cousin, but he couldn't. He turned to the woman. "Lady, we came over to see you in good faith." He also told her that they'd brought food and pointed to where the car was parked.

"What fucking food?" Achilles frowned. His crazy eyes skipped from Stathis to the woman. "I'm not giving my food to that bitch."

Stathis balled his hand into a fist. "Shut up, man! I've had enough of you! Shut the fuck up!" The tension he felt was so strong that he thought he was going to have a stroke. He ran his hands back through his hair and drew in a breath. "Please, put the fucking jackknife away, man."

Achilles was a man hankering for danger. To him, this was like the game he played with his miniature soldiers when he was a boy. This was a movie scene, an exciting chapter from a novel, and a boost to his animal instincts. Stathis wished he were like his cousin, but he didn't know how to control the fear that made his knees weak and his hands tremble. It was fear that blocked him from doing the things he'd always wanted to do: go traveling alone, climbing, skydiving, and riding motorbikes. It was fear that kept him awake at night, thinking of death.

A deep male voice shouted above the barking, "If I were you, I'd listen to your friend."

Stathis searched for the source of the voice and couldn't believe his eyes. Three rectangular cages made of wood and wire were mounted on the roof of the underpass, hidden in the shadows. Each cage had a wooden ladder fastened with rope to its side, and from one of the cages protruded the barrel of a shotgun, aimed at Achilles.

"Throw the blade on the ground," the voice said, "or I'll shoot you where you stand!"

Achilles's eyes widened.

"Athina!" the voice said. "Quiet down the dog!"

"Okay, Father." The woman tapped the dog's head. The dog whined and then silently sat on his hind legs as though she had pressed a mute button.

"Throw the blade down, or I'll shoot you and then bury you."

Stathis felt as if his heart had been dislodged. "Throw the fucking blade down," he said, fully outraged at his cousin's behavior.

Achilles spat on the ground and wiped his mouth.

The old man climbed down a ladder. He was wearing rubber boots and a black fisherman's raincoat. He had a scar across his left eye, and white hair poked out from under a beanie. He asked Stathis to put the lamp on the table and went and stood behind it, all the while holding the shotgun on the men.

"This isn't a movie set, son."

"I'm not your son," Achilles said.

"This thing's real."

"Old man, I don't like being threatened."

"You're the one who threatens yourself, son."

Achilles straightened. "I bet you don't have bullets in your shotgun."

"There's only one way to find out, isn't there?"

"Go ahead, old man."

"Drop the jackknife."

Seeing his cousin's frightened eyes, Achilles finally dropped the knife.

"Dimitra!" the old man said. "Come on out and give us a hand."

The dog whined again.

An old woman dressed in black stood at the opening of the tent with the wind in her gray hair. As silent as a cat, she collected the jackknife and studied the men. Outside, a light drizzle fell.

With the barrel of the shotgun, he pointed at the worn-out car seats. "Move over there and sit down."

The cousins looked at each other and started for the car seats. "Keep your mouth shut," Stathis said through his teeth. "You hear me?"

Athina put a couple of logs in the fire, and save for the hiss of traffic over wet roads and the flapping of the tent in the wind, it was quiet under the bridge now.

Stathis observed the family, feeling as though he and his cousin were prisoners of war.

The old man said, "Where did you say you are from?"

"We come from Athens," Stathis said.

"Have you got IDs?"

"In the car."

The old man worked his eyes over them. "What shall we do with them?" He squinted at Athina. The dog remained next to the younger woman and kept his eyes on the men.

"Shoot them and bury them in the back." Athina jabbed her thumb over her shoulder. "Or barbecue them. I bet they taste good, especially that one." She pointed at Stathis, grinning.

"They sure will make a good stew." The old man nudged Dimitra with his elbow, said something to her, and laughed.

"Very funny," Achilles said and glanced at his cousin. He was about to continue speaking, but Stathis's stare held him in check.

In a moment, Stathis felt a slight shift in his soul. His face darkened, and his muscles tightened. The way the family looked at him made him feel insignificant, deformed, and small in stature. He drew in a breath and sat up. "If you want to shoot us, go ahead. Sir."

The face of the old man hardened. "Sit down, son."

"It's not fair holding a shotgun on us."

"Not fair?" The old man chuckled. "The whole goddamn so-called civilized world isn't fair. So, why should I be fair? I'm holding a shotgun on you because you trespassed. Don't look at me this way, son. This space here, as unreal as it may seem to you, is our home. You two birdbrains should consider yourselves lucky I didn't shoot you as soon as I saw you." He waved his shotgun. "Since we sure as hell didn't invite you, why are you here?"

"I've already told you."

"We wanna hear it one more time. Don't we?"

The women agreed.

With the light of the fire in his face, Stathis told them the truth.

Athina narrowed her eyes. "So, you're a writer."

"Yeah, I'm a writer."

The old man tucked the shotgun under his armpit and clapped his hands.

"So, Mr. Writer, can I have one of your smokes? You do smoke, don't you?"

"Yes."

"Well, then, Mr. Writer." The old man reached out his hand. "Do the honors."

Athina and the old man lit their cigarettes.

"I've always imagined that a writer's cigarettes taste different. But they don't. Listen carefully, son. Your method of research hasn't got any dignity. Did you think that by talking to us, you'd manage to feel what it's like to be homeless and then go and sit at your fancy desk and write about it?" He blew a streak of smoke toward Stathis.

"I have an ordinary desk." Anger brewed inside him.

Athina said, "Half a year ago, in the dead of the night, we woke up choking. I thought we were going to die. Someone had doused the tent with gasoline and set it on fire. We still don't know who did it." She pulled up her cardigan, revealing a red burn mark next to her navel. "Luckily, I was the only one who got burned. Anyway, within a week, we built the cages, my father got the shotgun, and I got the dog. About a month ago, a few idiots came to stir trouble, and Ares here," she said, patting the dog, "drove them away."

She told them that she had gotten her degree in American literature ten years ago. She sent out countless applications but never got appointed as a teacher. She worked different jobs to make ends meet. But they didn't last long. "I got fired, either because the companies went under or because of indecent male behavior. My last job was as a cashier in a supermarket."

The old man stepped on his cigarette. "And three months ago, a couple of cowards almost raped her, and I got the scar. I beat them with a pipe and left them there, twisted and groaning."

"Father?" Athina said and touched his shoulder.

There was silence.

"It took us a long time to find this place. Do you know how hard it is to spend almost a year drifting on the streets?" He gave Stathis a direct stare.

"No. But I can imagine."

"What? I didn't hear you, son. Speak up."

"I said I don't know what it's like to be homeless. But I can imagine."

"Imagination doesn't do justice to how it feels to be homeless, hungry, and thirsty. Imagination doesn't let you feel what it's like to be robbed of the last of your food or be kicked at in the middle of your dreamless sleep. Imagination can't tell you how it feels when you beg for money with people staring at you. It's the hardest thing I've ever lived through. Being homeless is the lowest a man can go in his life. So imagination doesn't cut it. Do you understand, son?"

"I think I do, sir."

"No, you don't understand! No, you don't know what pain is!"

Stathis felt his anger turning into a rage, but against what he wasn't sure.

Achilles said, "Old man, cut him some slack. He didn't want to come. I pushed him. We're sorry."

"No one talked to you, Mr. Minotaur."

Stathis sprang to his feet. "Old man, you are out of line!"

The dog rose as well, barking. Athina tried to calm him down.

The old man pointed the shotgun at Stathis. "Sit down!"

"Or what? What the fuck will you do?" He grabbed hold of the barrel of the gun and put it to where his heart was. The old man's eyes grew wide with surprise. The dog barked, and the old woman put her hands on her face.

"If you have the guts, old man, shoot me! Go on, shoot me, and put me out of my fucking misery!"

The old man tried to pull the shotgun out of Stathis's grip but couldn't.

Stathis growled, "A year ago, I lost my parents and my older brother. I lost my best friend. On a night like this, a drunk driver plowed into his car. My parents breathed their last on the spot, but my brother fell into a three-month comma. Just out of the blue. The driver's doing time, but my brother never woke up." He tightened the grip around the barrel until his fingers went white. "Do you understand what I'm telling you? That's fucking pain, old man! There isn't a day that goes by that I don't think of them. So go ahead and shoot me!"

Achilles tried to pull him back, but he wouldn't budge. Stathis cared nothing about himself.

The old woman said, "Please, my son. Let go of the gun. My husband is a good man. We just wanted to scare you."

"Scare us?"

"Please, my son." She touched his hand and looked at him with her kind eyes.

Bit by bit, Stathis's face softened. Staring into the old man's eyes, he pushed the barrel away from his chest, and with a trembling hand, he lit a cigarette.

Athina stroked the dog.

"Please, let's all calm down," the old woman said. "Please, sit. I'll make us fresh coffee."

A few minutes later, a car stopped a few meters from the underpass. A bearded man climbed out, picked up a few bags from the trunk, and started for the bridge. The bags he held were filled with food his wife had made: spinach and cheese pies, Greek meatballs in tomato sauce, and lentil and bean soups.

He approached the homeless family, greeted them, and set the bags down. In the light of the fire, the drizzle sparkled on his face. He regarded the men and the old woman, who was pouring coffee into cups. Athina tied the dog's leash around a rusty rod protruding from the ground nearby.

"Oh, hello there," the old man said. "We got us visitors."

The man nodded at them. He was tall and burly, like a Viking warrior.

The cousins nodded back.

"Would you care to join us?" the old man said.

"Thank you, maybe some other time," he said. "My family is waiting for me at home."

The old man rubbed his hands together above the fire.

"My wife sends her greetings."

The family thanked him. Smiling, he patted the old man on the shoulder, said good night, and took his leave, his heavy shadow following his every step.

Now they all sat with their fingers curled around metal cups, drinking coffee and smoking, staring at the fire and feeling its warmth and glancing at one another while their hearts beat in their chests and blood ran through their veins and their thoughts turned over in their heads about all the things they had lived through since they were born and all the things they would like to live through until the day they died.

"On some mornings," Athina said in a soft voice, "we find bags with food, clothes, and cigarettes. We also find euro bills. Three times a week, we go to the soup kitchens, eat, and talk with people. And twice a week, we go to the shelters and take a shower, change into clean clothes, and do some laundry."

The cousins nodded and listened carefully.

"When father becomes a pensioner in about half a year, we'll move to Ikaria Island, to a house near the sea . . ." Her voice trailed off as she looked at Stathis, who was listening to her and drawing on his smoke and thinking how kind her eyes now looked in the light of the fire.

As the night deepened the three men and two women remained seated around the crackling fire, gazing into the flickering flames, enveloped in its glow. Each person was enshrouded in their feelings and fears, in their dreams and aspirations, while the warmth of the fire caressed their bodies, hearts, and souls.

The Return

It is SUNDAY NIGHT. The headlights of the cars in the opposite lane strain Demos's eyes. He rubs his bearded face, lifts the baseball cap off his head, and runs his hand through his black hair. Then he powers down the window a crack and listens to his Jeep roar uphill and the wheels on the wet road. The wind on his face is refreshing and smells of the snow covering the hills and the mountains above him.

Demos is heading back to Thessaloniki. He spent the weekend hunting with his cousin in the Grevena mountains. Time in the mountains, hunting wild boar in the forest, is his ideal way of relaxing. It takes away the edge of his worries and gives him peace. In other words, it's his secret paradise.

If the Egnatia motorway weren't blocked, he wouldn't be driving on the uphill leading to the monastery of the Life-Giving Spring, a popular stop on the old road between the cities of Kozani and Thessaloniki, which stands 1,300 meters above sea level. He would already be close to his apartment, and soon after, he would be sitting in his living room with his girlfriend, Maria, drinking wine and telling her in detail about the hunting. He loves telling her about his adventures, and she enjoys every bit of it.

"Maria, hunting is unique. You need to have lots of patience and persistence, and sometimes frustration gets the better of you. But the pleasure you get is out of this world. You never forget all those moments, and you always search for them in your mind."

But instead, a sign reading WORKS IN PROGRESS added extra hours to his journey, and irritation nags at him. *Another two hours and I'll be home*, he thinks and sighs.

The car rounds a sharp bend, and as headlights rake along its smashed guardrail, he pictures the last day of the hunt, which started before the sun broke on the horizon. He and his cousin packed a thermos with coffee, ham-and-cheese sandwiches, and two bars of chocolate in their knapsacks, and with the two hunting dogs, they climbed into the Jeep. Both men knew the nooks and crannies of the mountains and how to single out the trails of wild boar. When they arrived, they stalked between shrubs and oak trees, trying to track down prints. After a couple of hours, they found themselves in an area hemmed in with chestnut trees, but they hadn't found game yet.

Before they headed back to the village, they decided to scope out the terrain one last time. Half an hour into their search, the dogs sniffed out deer in a zone with snowy cedar trees. Demos told his cousin he would circle the area and signal him to let the dogs loose to bring the deer out of the trees.

In less than twenty minutes, under the gray sky with the dogs barking in the distance, Demos lay in wait, rifle at the ready, the puffs of his breath thickening the air. He sighted the deer as it emerged from the trees, held his breath, and with a slight hesitation, he pulled the trigger. The rifle's blast sent a few birds fluttering up from the trees and into the gray sky. But two crows remained on a tree branch, watching the deer drop to its knees and collapse on the snowy ground.

Demos trudged through the snow toward the dead animal. It was a beautiful deer, and its horns were covered in fluff. Studying it, he felt slightly rattled for the first time in his hunting years. Though he had never hesitated to kill an animal, he stared into the eyes of the deer and felt off kilter.

Now half the deer is in the trunk of his Jeep, along with two bottles of tsipouro,[8*] a few bottles of red wine, sausages, jars of honey,

---

8. * A drink quite similar to ouzo but stronger

and goat cheese—all treats from his cousin. "Drink that nectar with your girlfriend," his cousin said and smiled.

His beloved "rattling American junk" struggles uphill. It's black, and despite its age, it has never let him down, especially up in the rough and muddy mountain roads.

He squares his broad shoulders and works his hand over his beard. His flannel shirt smells of smoke from last night's campfire.

Demos turns on the radio and hears the meek voice of a man talking about the words of Jesus from the Gospel of John: "You form opinions according to the external phenomena of my human nature. I do not judge or condemn anyone." He glances at the crucifix swaying on a chain from the rear-view mirror. He only goes to church for weddings, funerals, or baptisms. When a friend once asked him about the cross, he told him it was better to believe than not to. He had picked up that line from Isaac Newton, in an article about the scientist's belief in God.

Now Demos remembers the words the priest spoke on his wedding day. "Until death do you part, in good times and in bad." When the words "and befitting your servant and your slave" come to mind, he makes a face and turns off the radio. About a year ago, his wife left him for a banker. "I've had enough," she said to him. "I can't put up with it any longer."

A couple of times, he has imagined driving to Volos, a town on the coast of the Aegean Sea, where his son, his ex-wife, and the banker live. He imagines walking into the house and putting a bullet between the man's eyes. Demos still can't understand how she could have an affair with that man and at the same time sleep in their marriage bed.

"Marriage is a sacred thing," he once said to a friend.

"Demos," the friend lectured, "couples break up because they stop loving each other or because they get bored. It's normal and it happens frequently."

But Demos didn't agree with him. "What the fuck are you talking about, man? Have you lost your mind? We have a kid together, and she should've known better. My mother was right. I never should've married her. She's a bitch. That's what she is: an irresponsible bitch," he said, stood up, and left.

But his friend's words still sit in his stomach like an undigested piece of meat. Deep down, Demos knows the reason his wife left him; he just doesn't want to admit it. He knows he spent most weekends up in the mountains with his cousin. He knows that over the past few years, they stopped making love, hardly looked into each other's eyes, didn't talk much, and slept with their backs to each other.

The break-up was nasty. There were fights, threats, and tears. When the neighbors called the police one night, his wife took their son and left. And after a while, they moved in with the banker.

For the longest time, Demos refused to give her a divorce. "Over my dead body, you showy bitch," he said. In the lawyer's office, he hated the way that banker sat smirking in his sleek suit. Looking at them and hearing them speak was torture. Though that bastard has been good to his kid, Demos hates his existence.

The court date is set for December 18, a week from now and one day before his son's birthday, who will turn seventeen. He is the tallest guy in his class, with an athletic body and kind brown eyes, the same as his father's. He loves playing basketball but is shy around girls. "Them girls are as shy as you are," Demos told him. "You must pluck up your courage and go for it. And it's free of charge. Either you'll get a scowl or a smile." For his birthday, Demos has bought him a baseball cap and a rifle.

As the car makes a turn, he comes up behind a lorry with Bulgarian plates. Demos steps on the brakes and throws in the second gear. The Jeep bucks but picks up speed. "Goddamn it." He pulls out and over into the opposite lane, and with his headlights, he signals the driver to slow down and pull slightly over. He has the Jeep floored, now side by side with the lorry, but the car can't go any faster. "Come on, you piece of junk, come on!" The headlights of a bus from the opposite direction blind him. Demos wishes he were at the wheel of that black

Grand Cherokee Jeep with its 265 horsepower, the one he spotted two days ago in a car dealer's lot in Grevena. He took the Jeep out for a spin, and, feeling its horsepower, was as excited as a boy getting a new toy. But he couldn't afford it—at least, not yet.

The only money he has left is a wad of euro bills hidden deep in his mattress, money he managed to save up working as a painter. A few years ago, he had himself a crew of six men and a small shop. They painted shopping malls, cinemas, buildings, balustrades, you name it. He had taken over the shop from his retired father. It was a solid business with a good, clean reputation.

In the beginning, he was doing great, but after the real estate bubble burst in America and then in Europe, his business went belly up. And so did his life. He lost all his money and sold his house to pay off debts. He kept one guy on the payroll on a part-time basis. "If it was up to me, I'd put the CEO fuckers and the politicians against the wall and shoot them, one by one. But instead, those bastards manage to get away. We're trapped in a daily nightmare," he would say to his friends, again and again.

Demos pulls the Jeep back sharply behind the lorry and hears the drawn-out horn from the bus sailing past. A chill shoots through him.

Further up, he pulls over on the shoulder of the road, leans his head on the steering wheel, and concentrates on the ticking of the engine as it cools down. He stays there for a while, trying to push his pestering thoughts out of his head. And he succeeds. But as he drifts in the zone of his inner silence, the eyes of the deer come back to him.

Sighing, he climbs out of the Jeep, steps on the snow-covered ground, zips up his parka, and crunches over to the guardrail. He smells pine in the cold wind and feels the vast silence stretching all the way to the bottom of the sharp drop. In the distance, dark mountains stand tall. His agitation grows. Although he quit smoking years ago, he hankers for a cigarette now. He draws in a breath and thinks of calling his girlfriend. Though they have planned to meet later tonight, he wants to hear her voice now.

Maria is a nurse. They have been together for five months, and he is still folded up inside. He wishes he could be like a few of his friends, a bit more open about his feelings. Maria has been working double shifts at the George Genimatas hospital all week so she can take three days off in a row to be with him. When Demos thinks of her smooth skin and her smooth touch, a sense of tenderness sweeps over him. Her voice comes to him: "Everything's going to work out just fine in court. Baby, you'll see." He takes another look at the sharp drop and returns to the car.

Later, he finally passes under a bridge into Thessaloniki. The city is heavy with traffic and bright with lights. At the entrance of an empty building, people sit with bleached blankets draped over their shoulders and baseball caps pulled low over their faces. A journalist on the radio talks about unemployment in Greece. To the rumbling about overspending, salary cuts, and new laws to prevent strikes, Demos screws up his face and thinks of the so-called "legitimate" bandits in Greece and abroad, dressed in sleek suits and standing on podiums, parroting patriotic words while one and a half million of his fellow citizens are out of work.

He turns off the radio, lowers the window, and listens to the city sounds. The cold air feels good on his face. He has had enough of all the lies disguised as promises, but a slight sense of gratitude comes over him because he still has a job.

Demos rubs his stiff neck. On the dashboard, the hands of a clock show twenty to nine. He can't wait to take a hot shower. He pictures the remaining distance to his apartment; at the third traffic light, he will turn left, drive through a square with benches and pine trees, and if he is lucky, he will park in a spot under a lemon tree, just below his apartment. As he pictures himself and Maria relaxing on the couch with a glass of red wine in his hand, he smiles faintly.

A few moments later, in his side mirror, he spots two motorcycles from the DIAS squad. This unit travels in pairs of bikes, two officers to a vehicle, and they are trained to clash with protesters, navigate the city, and run checks. At the traffic light, he stops behind a line of cars and buckles up. His knapsack sits in the passenger seat. In it are his binoculars, fishing gear, matches, a flashlight, a thermos, and a knife big enough to kill a bear. "Hope for the best and prepare for the worst" is one of Demos's preferred sayings. "You've got to be sharp, and be in control at all times," he often says to his friends.

DIAS is right behind him. In the side mirror, he sees the first motorcycle flashing its headlight, but Demos acts as if he hasn't seen the signal.

The traffic light turns green, and the cars surge ahead. The DIAS squad stays on his tail. They blink the headlight again, and now Demos knows the score. He remembers the broken taillight he planned on having fixed and mumbles, "There goes my fucking luck."

One of the motorcycles flanks him, and a cop motions him to pull over. From the corner of his eye, Demos sees black boots, black kneepads, and shiny white helmets. He speeds ahead, and so do the cops. They are by his window now, and the same cop waves to him again. Sighing, he pulls over right in front of the gate of a fenced lot, where countless caravans of all shapes and sizes stand enshrouded in the dark. Some of them sit on flat wheels, others on stacks of stone slabs or blocks of wood. Behind the lot stands a billboard with torn strips of advertising paper, and beyond the factories and buildings hovers an orange light like the glow of a low-burning fire.

The motorcycles stop behind his Jeep. Drizzle falls across the beams of the headlights.

A cop walks to his door, sheriff style. The other three hang back at the rear of the Jeep. Demos peers up at the cop. He is younger than Demos, maybe in his early thirties. He has an army haircut, and his jaw is square.

"Why didn't you pull over at our signal?" His breath forms puffs in the air.

"I didn't think you were after me."

"I waved a hand at you, twice."

"I've been driving for five hours. I'm exhausted."

"Sir, may I ask where you were?"

"I was in the mountains in Grevena."

"And where are you heading to?"

"Home."

A big truck drives by, throwing up a light spray and a draft. Demos feels the Jeep move a little.

The cop puts a hand on top of the vehicle and leans in. "Do you know your taillight is broken?"

"Is that why you pulled me over?"

"Isn't that a good enough reason for you?"

Demos draws his eyebrows together. "You got to be kidding me, right?"

"Kidding you?" the cop says with a serious expression.

"I was going to fix it tomorrow morning."

"Yes, but you're still a danger to yourself and others."

"Danger? The light blinks. Just the shell of it is busted; that's all."

"The flash doesn't blink."

"It doesn't?"

"License and registration, please," the cop says with irritation in his voice.

Demos creases his brow.

The cop shifts his weight from one foot onto the other. He clears his throat and, louder this time, says, "License and registration. Please."

A lean cop approaches his partner, squinting against the drizzle.

"What's the matter?" he asks.

"Nothing's the matter." This first cop's eyes are fixed on Demos. "Everything's under control."

With a flashlight, the cop shines a beam of light over the papers, looking at the picture and then at Demos. He reads out a number on the radio.

Demos studies the man's uniform and gear. He knows that the pistol strapped in a holster is a Heckler & Koch, German-made. The cop nods to a crackling voice on the radio and hands back the papers, then asks if Demos has had anything to drink or if he has anything illegal in the car.

Demos tells him he is clean. A burly cop at the rear of the Jeep says, "Since we stopped him, let's search the car!" His voice is strict, metallic. He asks Demos to pop the trunk.

"Please, switch off the engine and step out of the car. We're going to make a search."

Demos drops his chin and sighs, wishing all this were a bad dream. A rush of frustration shooting through his veins, he steps out of the car. He knows he is in trouble. *Stay calm and just answer their questions,* he tells himself.

With his hands tucked in the pockets of his army pants, he looks at a third cop, who bends into the Jeep and shines a beam of light in corners, under the seats, at the roof, and on the dashboard.

The burly cop stands by the now open trunk, flashlight in hand.

Demos takes off his baseball cap and tilts his head back. The drizzle feels good on his warm face. He runs a hand through his hair and puts the cap back on.

Demos is a head taller than any of them. *If they were not in uniform,* he thinks, *I could knock them down.* He pictures the scenario. He headbutts the cop standing right across from him, grabs the other by the nape, slams his face against the top of the car, and hears his nose crack. Then, he kicks the third one in the balls and drives his knee in his face, hard. He ducks a punch from the fourth cop, throws a swift hook in his jaw, and sees him going down like a sack of potatoes.

Cars, buses, and trucks rattle by, tires whooshing.

"What have we here?" says the burly cop and searches for Demos's eyes with a smirk. He lifts the skinned deer by its front legs; the head hangs back, and the tongue sticks out of its mouth.

With their thumbs hooked in the loops of their pants, the other three cops bunch up and look at the dead animal as if it were a creature they once knew.

"You're a hunter, right?" the burly cop says.

"Sure."

"Do you have a hunting license?"

Demos hands it to him.

The burly cop studies the document. "Don't you know it's illegal to kill deer in Greece?"

"Yes, I know."

"And you still killed the poor animal." He narrows his small eyes in the drizzle.

"It appears so."

The cop's look hardens. "Well, I have news for you, Mr. Smarty. Since you broke the hunting law, we will confiscate your jalopy and its contents, and you will pay a six thousand euro fine and spend a night in jail. How does it sound?"

Though he is in a tight spot, there is no way on earth he will apologize or try to talk the cops into letting him off the hook. He knows what he did was against the law, and he got caught, unfortunately. Inside the pockets of his army pants, he clenches his fist and curses his luck.

As the cops begin to round things up, a lean man with a nose like a Spartan helmet's, the one who searched the inside of his car, takes a bottle of wine from the trunk and studies the label.

"Sir, where did you get the wine?"

"My cousin's a winemaker."

The men look at each other.

"You mean to say that Stefanos Raptis is your cousin?" He moves closer to Demos.

"We're first cousins. Why?"

"Stefanos is a very good friend of mine," he says with a spark in his eyes. "We were in the army together, in Evros."

"I served in Evros too. It's a tough spot."

"Tell me about it. Stefanos and I went through thick and thin. We talked on the phone a week ago." Turning the bottle of wine in his hand, he holds Demos's kind but weary eyes. "Wait here a moment, please."

Annoyance burning within, Demos watches the cops go into a huddle. They talk and nod in the drizzle.

Stefanos's friend comes back to Demos and says, "You're free to go. Don't worry about a thing. Just don't go hunting deer again."

Relief blows through Demos.

"Thanks, brother." He holds the cop's eyes. "I won't forget this one."

As Demos is closing the trunk, the husky cop says, "Not so fast."

Demos stares at the ticket the cop just handed to him. He wants to punch him in the face. It's a 350-euro fine for driving without a seat belt.

"Sons of bitches," he says as the motorcycles roar past him and blend into the traffic.

A few minutes later, Demos pushes open the glass entrance of his apartment building and steps over leaflets advertising home delivery and showing bright pictures of pizzas and gyros and meat on a spit. Then he plods up the stairs to his apartment on the first floor.

As he reaches his door, the building's power flickers off. Darkness pulls in around him. He cocks an ear forward, as he does when he is out hunting, but instead of wind moving in the trees and over boulders, the crack of dry twigs as he steps on them, and the calls of the birds, he hears a bus roaring along the road.

He peers down the stairs and sees a reflection of the emergency light. Mumbling under his breath, he goes for the light switch—then hears sounds inside his apartment. His instincts kick in. He presses his ear against the door, holds his breath, and feels his temples throb. He detects the opening of drawers and swishing sounds before it all goes quiet. He tries to remember if he locked all the windows and doors in his flat. A voice in his mind says that maybe he did. He slips out of his knapsack and parka, sets them on the floor, and takes the knife out of the bag.

Demos knows he ought to call the police, but by the time they arrive, whoever is in his apartment, sifting through his life, will have gone. He pictures the wad of money buried deep in the mattress. That money is his safety net, and without it, Demos will not be able to take his son to the mountains for his first hunting trip as his grandfather and father did for him. His anger grows larger than himself, larger than the door he stands in front of.

Knife in his strong grip, Demos feels the rush of blood in his head. He turns the key, nudges the door open, and realizes he must not have locked it when he left. He peers into the dark hallway; he sees nothing but hears mumbling. Then he slides in through the door, puts his back to the wall, slithers along its surface toward the open living room door. For a moment, he stands still and wild eyed.

Hunching his shoulders, he dashes into the living room. "I'll cut your heart out!"

Loud noises erupt from the room—sounds of screeching furniture and breaking of glass. Then, two gunshots, and it all goes quiet.

In a moment, a man in black clothes shuffles out of the apartment, screwing up his face in pain. With one hand he holds a gun, and with the other, he holds his ribs. His breathing is short and sharp, and blood trails after him as he staggers down the stairs. At the bottom, he props a hand against the wall and coughs up blood. He collapses a few meters from the glass exit, in front of Maria, who stands shell shocked at the threshold.

By the time the man in black reached for the gun, Demos had driven the blade of his knife into his liver. Unfortunately, as the burglar was tripping over his own feet on the way out the door, he shot Demos first in his shoulder and then in his gut.

Maria will call the police and the ambulance. In twenty minutes, the place will be milling with cops and paramedics. Neighbors will cluster outside Demos's apartment, and the police will question them and scribble on their notepads. Maria will be grateful she stayed at work for two extra hours because her friend asked her for a favor, and for taking almost half an hour to find a parking spot. Otherwise, she had planned to go to his place earlier and surprise him with dinner and drinks.

But right now, Demos is lying on the floor in the living room, grunting. The dining table is shoved against the wall, the chairs bunched up behind it, and broken glass from a vase is scattered on the floor, along with the purple orchids Maria put in it a few days before. Water drips from the table into a puddle on the floor. Drawers stand open, and cushions are thrown about. The curtain is torn and hangs to one side.

Face covered in sweat and flannel shirt soaked in blood, Demos continues to grunt in reaction to the burning sensation emanating from where he was shot. It feels as if salt has been put on the wounds. His breathing is slow and steady, but he has a hard time swallowing.

He coughs and, tasting blood, summons the little strength left in him to hoist himself up. But he slips on his own blood, and down he goes. He stays there, pressing on the wound and cursing. More blood dribbles out of his mouth.

He tries to stay awake, but it's hard. He feels his strength leaking out of every pore. In a few fearful breaths, he sees the beautiful eyes of the deer again, and little by little, he begins to understand how it feels to get shot, the coldness of the shuddering feeling as he tries to hold on for dear life. There and then, he begins to understand the importance of simply breathing, living, and the value of being with someone you love.

By and by, as his disappointment, his frustration, and his anger fade, he feels a relief so intense that it is as if he has no weight at all. He thinks of his son and his ex-wife, the woman he once loved. He holds their images in his mind for as long as he can. *Why was I so angry?* Now the images of the police officers surface in his mind too.

He sees them in their homes with their families, having a good time. He wishes everyone well. He wishes Maria were here. Then he slips out of consciousness.

When he opens his eyes again, he sees Maria by his side. She is on her knees, holding his hand as tears roll down her beautiful face. Demos makes to speak, but she puts a finger on his lips and strokes his face. "Try to stay calm. Everything's going to be okay."

Holding her hand, he smiles faintly.

She kisses him and tells him that help is on the way.

"You'll make it," she says in a steady and reassuring voice. "You're a big, strong man. You'll make it."

As Hard As It Gets

THE FOLLOWING STORY plays out in an apartment in the city of Athens. A few clouds move across the sky, and a half-moon hangs over the illuminated Acropolis.

A man stands in the dark, naked. He is muscular, with long black hair, a dense black beard, and sharp, high cheeks; and his eyes are glazed over. In slow motion, he runs a hand over his sweaty face.

In the dark room is a bed, a side table, a floor lamp, a reclining chair, and a built-in wardrobe where shirts and trousers droop from clothes hangers. But they are not his clothes.

Petros's penis—his "joystick," as he likes to call it—is as hard as a hammer. It's so hard that it's about to burst open. But he can't feel it, for his mind is tuned in to a different dimension.

Now, the man doesn't know where he is or who he is. He knows neither that he has been standing in this spot for over fifteen minutes nor that he is in his cousin's apartment, Thomas's, the one with the steady smile on his face who recently got married to a German woman named Helga. They both work for the same telephone company, and in an economically battered Greece, where thousands of families exist in a tight spot, the couple is doing quite well. Petros is here to "sniff out a job."

These particulars lie somewhere at the back of his head, but at this moment, the man's conscious mind is as blank as a freshly cleaned blackboard. He doesn't know whether he is a man or a woman, young or old, a dog or a cat. He just stands there, in the dark. Incidents like this, sleepwalking in the dead of the night, have happened to him before.

Once, he sleepwalked to the bathroom, took a leak, and slipped back into his bed as if nothing had happened. On another occasion, he sleepwalked to the kitchen, opened the fridge, and started to eat salami and feta cheese, and washed the food down with a glass of goat milk. Another time, he sat at the kitchen table and spoke as if there were a person sitting right across from him. Imagine waking in the dead of the night and seeing that. But the spookiest incident of all happened years ago, on a summer night at his house in the village up in the mountains.

That night, Petros put on a black suit and walked out of the house, his eyes shining in the dark like those of a wildcat. He walked the streets, crossed a square with a century-old plane tree and a church, and then a curved road took him out of the village. He did all that while everyone slept in their beds. When he woke from his sleepwalk, he found himself in the light of the full moon, standing by the grave of an old woman in the cemetery a good twenty minutes' walk from the village, near the woods.

After that night, he became afraid. Anything could have happened to him. Petros pictured knives and scissors, cliffs and gorges. And so, he began to sleep in the warehouse where his deceased parents used to store food. He turned the place into two large rooms and sleeps there in the summer because it is cool. He also covered the windows with curtains, hid all the sharp objects, and, each night, he locks doors and windows—and ties one hand to the bed with a rope.

Petros tried to cure his sleep disorder using different scientific and non-scientific methods. In the city, he saw doctors, who put him on pills that made him fuzzy and sleepy. Frustrated, he visited a palm reader, who could see the past and predict the future. She tried to hypnotize him and bring out the bad spirit, but she didn't succeed. "You're the first person I haven't been able to hypnotize," she said with traces of wonder in her voice.

He also tried to meditate. But he didn't have the patience to sit Buddha style with his eyes closed and concentrate on his breathing for a long time. Gradually, though, his sleep disorder began to wither away. Until tonight.

Petros stands still, with his joystick rock solid. He absently wipes the sweat from his forehead and lets his hand hang by his side, limp as that of a marionette. Then he walks toward the balcony door and tries to open it but can't. "Fuck," he says, and makes for the door. "Petros, you need to get out of here," he says.

A couple of hours ago, in the light of candles, Petros was sitting on a sofa in the living room of this apartment with Helga and Thomas, drinking beers because he had managed to find a job as a waiter in the infamous Plaka district. The door to the balcony was open, and a warm wind brought city sounds into the room. They sat around a low table and, during pauses in talking, glanced at the flat-screen playing a Turkish soap opera, *The Foreign Groom*—the tragic story of a Greek groom, Nikos, and his Turkish bride, Nazli.

Helga is blond with blue eyes and braces on her teeth. She wore a white T-shirt and torn jeans and sat cross-legged, smoking roll-ups and speaking Greek with a German accent. Petros listened to her talk about the coming heat wave, about food prices, and about how Thomas and herself had stopped going out to dinners or movies. Then she spoke about salary cuts, job losses, tax frauds, and other issues revolving around the current Greek reality. She said it was better to hold a part-time job and live in Greece than to have a full-time job and live in Germany.

"We're lucky to have jobs, aren't we, honey?"

Thomas nodded in agreement.

"Angela Merkel should've known better than to scorn the Greeks, and so should the German people." She took a sip from her beer and went on, "We owe Greeks our culture, and we owe them money from the Second World War as well."

These were Helga's words, verbatim. Petros didn't know what to say to that. He sank deeper in the couch with a cold Bavarian beer in his hand, listening with pleasure to Helga speak accented Greek while Thomas sat in an armchair, his hands folded on his beer belly and his legs crossed at the ankles. Under his mustache was a faded but steady smile.

Now and again, that smile gets him into trouble because when someone talks about a serious matter that calls for serious nods and expressions, Thomas's smile makes people wonder what the hell is wrong with him. On one occasion, over food and drinks, a man asked, "What the hell are you smiling at?"

"I'm not smiling."

"Do you think my story's funny?"

"That's the way my mouth is formed."

"That's the way your mouth is formed?"

"Yes, I just said that."

"Do you take me for a fool?"

"No, I don't think you're a fool," Thomas said and looked at the man with that smile on his face.

Once, at a funeral service, they asked him to step outside the church to avoid upsetting the other mourners. Since then, he has grown a thick mustache, but Petros can still see that smile. He first saw it when Thomas was a baby. His mother—Petros's favorite aunt—had just changed his diaper and let him lie in bed next to a summer window. The baby flicked his tongue back and forth in his tiny mouth and moved his chubby legs and arms, then looked at Petros and gave him that characteristic smile.

At one point last night, Thomas said, "Sweetheart, this morning I wanted to make myself a cheese-and-salami sandwich, but I didn't find anything in the fridge."

"It's not possible." She arched her well-groomed eyebrows. "Yesterday afternoon, I went shopping."

"And where did the food go?" Thomas looked perplexed.

"Honey, I'm sure I bought salami and cheese and put them in the Tupperware."

"Yes, but they were empty."

"Are you sure?"

"Of course."

Helga went to the kitchen.

Thomas glanced at his cousin. "Coz, did you by any chance eat them?"

"Eat them? No, I didn't. I don't like yellow cheese," he said convincingly and began to feel uncomfortable.

Helga sat back in her chair. "You're right." She began playing with her hair. "It's very strange."

"We may have a ghost."

"Please, honey, don't say that," Helga said as though she were scared.

A strange silence moved between them. They drank from their beer and shot glances at the muted flat-screen.

Helga turned to Petros. "See these?" she said, and with her finger, she tapped at her braces. "I put them on a few months ago. They put pressure on me, but I must endure. They'll make my teeth nice and straight." She looked at Thomas, who was giving her his full attention, and added, "Isn't that right, honey?"

Thomas put his beer on the table, cleared his throat, and spoke as if giving a speech. "We went to a good orthodontist. He's a friend of mine. He treated us perfectly, and we paid only for the cost of the material. Otherwise, we couldn't have afforded the braces. Isn't that right, sweetheart?" He looked at his wife and smiled.

The candle flames trembled in a summer breeze.

"Helga?" Thomas asked. "Would you mind showing my coz your braces again?"

"I don't mind at all." With a spark in her eyes, she clenched her teeth and rolled back her lips.

"What do you think?" Thomas asked his cousin.

Petros didn't know what to say. He has never been to a dentist. His teeth are strong from all the goat and sheep milk he drinks and the cheese he eats every single day. He is strong and heavy boned. And he didn't want to speak because he was half drunk and his best bet was to keep his mouth shut and listen. If he spoke, he might have said something stupid. And he didn't want to do that. *What would Helga think of me, huh?* But he had to say something. And since he didn't know what to say, he asked, "Is there any more beer?"

Helga sits up on the bed in the dark, her hair falling loosely and brushing against her pink silk nightgown. She has woken from a bad dream. She remembers music playing, a harp or piano, but she isn't sure. She puts a strand of hair in her mouth and smells the basil and the peppermint, plants she keeps in pots on her balcony.

She remembers that in the dream, she went into Petros's room, slithered into the bed where he was sleeping, kissed him on the mouth, pushed her tongue inside, and touched his "thing," as Helga calls men's pride and joy. To her husband she often says things like, "Honey, why don't you put that thing back in your pants. I'm not in the mood tonight," or "I'm exhausted." She has never taken his thing in her hand and showed how much she desires and loves it.

Helga feels embarrassed. She loves Thomas, dearly. She wants to have kids, three in total, and live a happy life. *Why did I have such a dream?* she thinks. *How could I crawl into Petros's bed, kiss him, and touch his thing?* And she remembers she felt good touching it. She looks down at Thomas lying in his shorts and a T-shirt, with the light coming in through the shutters and resting on his beer belly. She studies his face, sees that smile, and then her mind goes to her dream again, and to Petros. "Verdammt,"[9]* she whispers.

She kisses her husband on his brow and starts for the bathroom barefooted. As she exits, she hears a screech of furniture coming from Petros's room. She stops and listens. But the only thing she hears now is a faraway car.

9.* Damn

The first night Petros came over to their place, Helga smelled alcohol on his breath. She knew Thomas and Petros had a few beers before getting home that night. Petros had called her husband and asked if he could crash at their place. Once he landed a job, he said, he would find his own apartment. "Yes, sure," Thomas said and glanced at Helga, who sat right next to him on the couch. He then shuffled his feet into a pair of flips-flops, kissed Helga goodbye, and went off.

It was Saturday night. Two crows stood on the ledge of a window, observing Thomas and Petros as they sat at a table at a café. A brown suitcase, faded with time, sat by Petros's feet. He had traveled on a train from Thessaloniki. He said he was sorry to bother them that late at night, but he couldn't afford to go to a hotel.

"In the middle of June, the bank loan ran dry," he said in his baritone voice. "I went to the bank to ask for more money, but they gave me the finger. They said that since my coffee shop had gone belly up, they couldn't help me." He told Thomas, "Anything we do these days needs money. If they could charge us for the air we breathe, they sure would." And making a face, he said, "Bastards."

After an awkward silence, Petros added that many people had moved to the cities or abroad, and others didn't spend money on ouzo or appetizers as they used to. They went to his καφενείο and drank coffee and played cards and backgammon for hours. Some of them asked him to run a tab. When he asked them to pay the bill, they either gave him a bit of money or an excuse. "Petros, don't worry. You know me. I'm as good as gold." That's what they said. "We're as good as gold." But the end of the month came and went, and no money reached his pockets. "The tab got fatter, and I got skinnier," he said and moved his hands. "Do you understand, coz?"

With his characteristic smile hiding under his mustache and a serious expression in his eyes, Thomas said, "I understand what you mean. Of course I do. Daily life has become harder. Nowadays, people don't even have money to buy bread. Helga and I can't complain. Thank God."

Petros continued, "Tell me, coz, what was I supposed to do? Argue with my customers? Kick their asses out of my shop? Well, it doesn't work this way." He widened his eyes. "Sure, they were my customers, but they were friends as well. I didn't want to put them in a difficult position. They were going through hard times as well, and they loved hanging out at my joint." He loved it too. He could only wait and hope, but the bills caught up with him and pushed him off his shaky track.

"How long did you stay at Stelios's apartment?" Thomas asked.

"About a month. I slept on the couch and ate what he ate," he said, peeling the beer's label. "Every day, I walked the streets like a stray dog, trying to sniff out a job. But nothing, zero." He made a zero with his fingers and took a hit from the cold beer. He told Thomas what bothered him the most was having to ask his friends for money. "Look, coz, you're my last chance. If you don't help me score a job, I'm history. You hear what I'm saying to you?"

Thomas nodded.

While the two men talked at the café over beers, Helga did the dishes, made the bed for Petros in the guest room, puffed up cushions in the living room, and lit candles.

Now Helga doesn't want him to stay any longer. *He has been here for three weeks and has gotten a job in a restaurant. He could surely afford a room in a shared house now,* she thinks as she moves closer to the door of his bedroom. There is something about him she doesn't like, something dark. *In a few days, he better be on his way,* she thinks and presses her ear against the door.

She hears, "Fuck!" She swallows and blinks. She doesn't know what to do.

Then she hears, "Petros, you need to get out of here."

What the hell is he talking about? she thinks. *This is nuts.* Her heart beats faster, and her nipples stiffen under her pink silk nightgown. She makes to go, but she can't. She feels as though her feet are glued to the floor. She hears the doorknob turning, and before she has any time to draw back, the door opens.

Helga draws in a sharp breath and sees Petros standing in front of her. Sweat runs down his temples. As he stares at her with his glazed eyes, Helga hears her heart in her ears.

In a moment, her eyes skip to his hard and throbbing thing, slide past his muscular legs, and back up to his thing again. A tensed breath escapes from her slightly open mouth.

Petros and Helga don't move a muscle. They just stand at the door as her husband sleeps with that smile on his face, hands folded on his beer belly—as dreams play through people's heads, as night clouds move in the sky across the half-moon near the illuminated Acropolis, as new episodes play out in people's lives and need to be written, as the situation becomes as hard as it gets.

Helga closes and opens the fingers of her right hand. A waft of summery air drifts between them. "Verdammt," she whispers.

The first crow, now sitting on the balustrade of the couple's balcony, chuckles and says in a husky voice, "Women seem to fall for the guy."

"Tell me about it," the second crow says. "I wish I had such luck."

"Stop complaining. You're doing just fine yourself."

The second crow lets out a guttural sound.

"That could be a good story," the first crow says. "Don't you think?"

The second crow nods and says, "Can you imagine if humans could fly and see the things we see every day, huh?"

"Look, I've had enough of them humans and what they have been through. There is nothing here for us to chew. The Greeks always drag themselves out of difficult situations, since time immemorial. Let's do some birdie stuff instead."

"What's on your mind?"

"I'm getting the munchies." He rubs his belly with his wing.

"Now that you mention it, I kinda got the munchies, too."

"Would you be up for an evening snack?"

"A snack would hit the spot," the second crow says, rising into the air on his wings.

The other follows.

Flapping their wings, both crows fly off into the dark and drizzly sky.

Acknowledgments

I feel very lucky and grateful to have a list of very good and supportive people who encourage and care for me.

Many thanks to my best friend, Sofia Verginis, for re-editing the book and for all the countless hours we sat talking together about how to succeed in reaching the highest artistic outcome. Without Sofia's invaluable help, the stories would not read as well as they do now.

To Dimitris Naskos, what can I say, man? Fire and water. Even though you are a tough nut to crack, I respect you and appreciate the times we have spent together, talking for hours about so many interesting subjects. Thanks so much for lending your ear to help me with my short stories. You are an excellent artist and a good human being.

Thanks to my first cousin Stelios Patrikios, for the solid knowledge regarding hunting in Greece, guns, history, flora and fauna, as well as the interest he showed every time I needed his help.

Many thanks to my dear friend Pandelis Karagiannidis, who provided me with warmhearted hospitality at his apartment in Thessaloniki and who drove me around in the city while I conducted my research for these stories. Pandelis, thank you for your sound advice and for your good sense of humor. We had good laughs together.

My friend and editor Julian Hussley is a star in a dark sky. Thank you for being there for me all the times I needed your help, always lending me your lovely mind. You are my trooper.

Gerard Woodward, a published writer, was my professor in my creative writing program at Bath Spa University. I much appreciate your solid advice and the encouragement and confidence you have instilled in me.

Many thanks to Jeni Daniel, my dear landlady in Bath, UK. I lived in a cozy room at her sweet Gregorian house for almost a year when I was studying at Bath Spa University. Jeni, my living with you and darling Estrella was a rainbow after a storm. Thank you so much for your warm hospitality. You guys will always be in my heart.

Many thanks go to my friends Stefanos Pitias and his wife, Kristin, who put me up at their timber house in Oslo next to the woods and who never got tired of my talking about my characters in my stories. Guys, I wish I had your unyielding courage, your strength, and your perseverance. Thanks for your solid advice and for all the good laughs over the years.

Many thanks to Christos Pavlis, who rented me his wonderful apartment by the sea for next to nothing and who spent time with me over coffees, dinners, and drinks, listening to the way my stories played out. I wrote most of my stories at that lovely place of his, listening to the sound of the sea and of the wind moving through the lemon trees outside my window.

I want to thank my friend and professor of history Panagiotis Adamo, who agreed to meet with me at various cafés in the city of Thessaloniki. Using his vast knowledge, not only did he answer my questions regarding the psychosynthesis of the Greek people, but he also managed to walk me through Greek history with great passion and enthusiasm. Panagiotis, I am grateful for your invaluable help. I always enjoy listening to you talk about history over good food and wine.

I am extremely grateful to have had Hannah Woodlan, senior editor at Koehler Books, work on my stories. Her meticulous attention to detail and insightful feedback truly elevated my writing to new heights. It's safe to say that she is the best editor I have ever had the pleasure to work with. Thank you, Hannah, for your superb job and for making my stories shine.

Last but not least, I would like to acknowledge the remarkable work of my graphic designer, Christine Kettner, whose contribution to my books has undeniably been invaluable. Her ability to understand and enhance my vision has exceeded my expectations. Thank you, Christine, and I hope we will work together again.

Milton Keynes UK
Ingram Content Group UK Ltd.
UKHW042202050124
435571UK00014B/277/J